THE BEST OF JOHN RUSSELL FEARN

VOLUME TWO:
Outcasts of Eternity
And Other Stories

EDITED BY
PHILIP HARBOTTLE

THE BEST OF JOHN RUSSELL FEARN

VOLUME TWO:
Outcasts of Eternity
And Other Stories

EDITED BY
PHILIP HARBOTTLE

Cosmos Books, an imprint of Wildside Press
New Jersey . New York . California . Ohio

THE BEST OF JOHN RUSSELL FEARN
Volume 2: Outcasts of Eternity And Other Stories

Published by:

Cosmos Books, an imprint of Wildside Press
P.O. Box 45, Gillette, NJ 07933-0045
www.wildsidepress.com

For more information, contact Wildside Press.

ISBN:

1-58715-326-2

ACKNOWLEDGEMENTS

Outcasts of Eternity first published in F*antastic Adventures* in 1942

*The Devouring Tide, The Ultimate Analysi*s first published in *Thrilling Wonder* Stories in 1944

Wanderer of Time first published in *Startling Stories* in 1944

The Unbroken Chain first published in *Startling Stories* in 1946

Black Saturday first published (as "Black-out") in *Science Fantasy* in 1950

Brief Gods (as "Rim of Eternity"), *Alice, Where Art Thou?* First published in *Vargo Statten Science Fiction Magazine* in 1954

Judgment Bell first published in *Weird and Occult Library* in 1960

CONTENTS

INTRODUCTION

In 1941, as the Second World War entered its third year, full-time writers and journalists in Britain—previously in "reserved occupations"—were no longer exempt from military service.

John Russell Fearn—then the only full-time science fiction writer in Britain—took the medical test. Owing to stomach problems, he was classed as C3—unfit for active service, but he was instead obliged to undertake "essential war work" —industrial conscription. He applied for and got a job in an aircraft factory. The work was gruelling. In a letter to a friend a few months later, Fearn recalled:

"It damned near killed me; then just as I was wondering what to do, I got a letter from a cinema manager friend of mine asking if I'd like the job of chief projectionist at the local Empire Cinema Theatre. I managed to get released from war work, took the job, and am now installed as the big shot at the Empire having the time of my life surrounded by film, high resistance arcs, power packs, dimmers, shutters, and what have you... I love this work, and as the reels run - once I've seen a show through - I've ample time for writing; and the hours off are such that I get in 5,000 typed words a day as well."

Fearn's close connection with the cinema enabled him to perfect his technique of "popular writing"—a style that was easily understandable, with a deceptive simplicity. The author's meanings are instantly clear, facilitating a strong visual picture in the reader's mind. Just as a film director would introduce a change of scene or character with certain camera shots, so Fearn would smoothly develop his narrative, cutting from scene to scene and character to character as if he were a literary camera. His exceptional memory enabled him to recall filmic scenes and characters which, suitably adapted, became an aid to his writing.

Before the war, Fearn had established himself as a leading contributor to the two Ziff-Davis sf magazines edited by Ray Palmer—**Amazing Stories** and **Fantastic Adventures**. He continued to write for them during the early years of the war, under his own name and his two established pseudonyms of Thornton Ayre and Polton Cross.

The high watermark of his contributions was reached with "Outcasts of Eternity", published in the November 1942 issue of **Fantastic Adventures**. The story unfolds swiftly and relentlessly. Cinema buffs will find a pleasing resonance with several films, including in particular the 1936 Karloff and Lugosi classic, **The Invisible Ray**.

The science fictional idea behind the story was an old one—the consequences of eternal life—but Fearn approached it from a fresh angle. He tells of the fate of crew of the first manned interplanetary flight to Mars, and the criminal machinations of powerful industrialists whose commercial empires are threatened by a revolutionary new system of space travel. Despite these sf trappings, the story is really a fantasy, which was why editor Ray Palmer ran the story in **Fantastic Adventures** rather than **Amazing Stories**. That the details of the story are utterly naïve does not detract one jot from its compulsive readability in unfolding a story of genuine human tragedy. Palmer was appreciative of Fearn's technique, commending the story to his readers. "Let us know what you think of stories like this. They are Polton Cross' best work, peculiar to him only, and much like his popular "The Man From Hell" of several years ago."

Had space permitted, I would have liked to include "The Man From Hell" here also. However, that story has been reprinted in magazine form, whereas "Outcasts of Eternity" has never been reprinted until now, and so gets the nod.

Fearn might well have continued to develop this narrative style ("peculiar to him only") but events conspired to sever his connection with Palmer's magazines, and to move his career and technique in an entirely new direction.

In the summer of 1943, Fearn suddenly found himself in dispute with his American agent, whom Fearn accused of appropriating some £300 without his permission. Most of the money had been earned from the Ziff-Davis magazines, to whom Fearn directed an appeal. But "Ziff-Davis just sat on the fence," Fearn told his friend Walter Gillings. "They'd paid the money they said, so that seemed to be that—so getting nowhere with them, I transferred my affections to Standard Magazines...Leo Margulies has proved a real friend in getting me straightened out."

Margulies was the Editorial Director of **Thrilling Wonder Stories** and **Startling Stories**. Fearn had sold to them before the war, but had not contributed for some years. Margulies, on hearing of Fearn's problems, invited him to submit both short stories and novels. A string of sales resulted, and Fearn showed his gratitude by dedicating his first UK hardcover detective novel, **Black Maria, M.A.** "to Leo Margulies."

The hiatus had showed Fearn that relying on the American pulp sf magazine market was a risky business, and so he had struck out in a new direction. He decided to upgrade his writing and concentrate on novels for the British market. He succeeded in selling a string of detective novels to leading UK publishers, and he also resold his pre-war sf magazine serials as books. His first published book was coincidentally the first story he had written—**The Intelligence Gigantic** (1933). Published as a hardcover novel in 1943 by World's Work, it was historically significant as the first-ever British book to actually be labelled and marketed as "Science Fiction."

Over the next four years, whilst concentrating mainly on detective novels (and also westerns), Fearn continued to write pulp magazine sf, but only as a sideline, and exclusively for Leo Margulies. This reduction in his sf output meant that the stories were written with greater care than hitherto, and many of his 17 stories appearing in **Startling** and **Thrilling Wonder** between 1944 and 1948 were of a high standard.

Four of the best of them–two from each magazine–are reprinted here: "The Devouring Tide", "Wanderer of Time", "The Ultimate Analysis", and "The Unbroken Chain."

"The Devouring Tide" and "The Ultimate Analysis" saw Fearn revisiting some of his pre-war "thought variant" concepts, particularly his **Mathematica** stories (which were reprinted in my first volume of Fearn stories) but this time he explored them in more human terms. Magazine sf had been evolving rapidly since the pre-war days, and the "idea as hero" narratives were giving way to a much more humanised type of story. These stories are fascinating examples of sf in transition between the two trends.

"Wanderer of Time" is widely recognised as perhaps Fearn's best short story, since it has been four times anthologised, and reprinted worldwide. It was Fearn's own selection for the 1949 landmark US anthology, **My Best SF Story**, edited by Leo Margulies and Oscar J.Friend. Fearn was in fact the only British author to be selected for this collection of the best short stories as chosen by 25 leading writers.

In his introduction explaining why he had selected the story Fearn wrote:

"I regard this story as my best short insofar that it embraces so many elements, yet all of them fitting smoothly into their appointed place–the kind of discovery which gives an author a decided thrill when he comes to read his finished script....

"Each of the major developments in the story might, I suppose, have made a story in themselves–such as the after-death angle, or the world of the far future termites–but it has been my experience that if a story, and especially one so short, has the ingredients of several other stories within it, then it's got something!"

"The Unbroken Chain" is similarly remarkable for its adept handling of events that hurdle literally millions of years, all contained in the confines of a 6.000 word short story! Each of these four stories are imaginative extrapolations of the theories of the great scientist Sir James Jeans, whose speculative and philosophical books on cosmogony, most notably **The Mysterious Universe** (1930) were a constant source of inspiration to Fearn.

In 1946 there was a surprise revival of interest in magazine sf in the UK, and three new magazines were launched–**New Worlds**, edited by John Carnell, **Fantasy**, edited by Walter Gillings, and **Outlands** edited by Leslie J. Johnson. Fearn knew, and had met all three editors personally in pre-war days, and so was happy to respond to their requests for material. He had the distinction of appearing in all three of their first issues. "Black Saturday" was written for, and sold to Gillings' **Fantasy** in 1947. But the post-war paper shortages led to its early demise before the story could appear (and the same problems also quickly accounted for the other two magazines.) Fortunately, Gillings succeeded in reviving his magazine with another publisher three years later, and so "Black Saturday" finally appeared (re-titled as "Black-out") in the Winter 1950 issue of **Science Fantasy**. I have selected this story as the best of Fearn's immediate post-war British efforts, and am pleased to have the opportunity to restore the author's much more evocative original title.

But by the time this story appeared in 1950, Fearn had effectively ceased to write short stories. He was a highly successful novelist, so much so indeed that he was eventually head-hunted by UK publishers Scion Ltd, and signed to a five-year contract to write sf novels for them exclusively.

The fact that this book contains a further three short stories (and stories of exceptional merit into the bargain), published between 1954 and 1960, would therefore appear paradoxical! However, there was a perfectly logical explanation. All three stories had simply been written much earlier.

"Brief Gods" had been written by Fearn in 1947 and submitted only to Margulies. Originally entitled "Earthbound," its unusual religious theme did not find favour with Margulies. "Alice, Where Art Thou?" had been written even earlier, in 1939, when it has been originally entitled "The Machines Live On." Why this fine story was not published at the time is something of a mystery, but the most likely explanation is that its theme was such a marked departure from the conventional pulp formula, that Fearn's regular markets rejected it. Both stories were therefore part of a small cache of unsold mss that Fearn had accumulated over the years.

Fearn had been writing sf novels for Scion under the contractual pen name of "Vargo Statten" and the books had sold millions of copies and been translated world-wide. In the Autumn of 1953, Fearn's publisher decided to launch a new British sf magazine, to cash in on "Statten's" popularity. Its first issue was published in January 1954 and initially entitled **Vargo Statten Science Fiction Magazine**, but when Fearn was eventually appointed as editor from the seventh issue, he changed the name to **British Science Fiction Magazine**. Fearn was asked to supply most of the material, as part of his contract, and so he simply took the opportunity to place all of his remaining unsold magazine mss. When this inventory ran out, he cocked a snook at his rapacious publisher by reworking a number of his earlier published stories in the American magazines (under changed titles and by-lines.) The two stories reprinted here are my selections as being by far the best of the group of original Fearn stories appearing in the magazine.

Introduced to Fearn's fiction for the first time in 1969, the distinguished writer and trenchant critic Charles Platt made a remarkably perceptive assessment. In a personal letter to me he wrote: "I have never read a book by any other sf author that is so unpretentious about including really ordinary people in really ordinary backgrounds, upon whom are superimposed really strange situations and events... I found Fearn entertaining in a very charming, open, relaxed way. There is a very good atmosphere, which comes across in all his writing."

These two stories, in particular "Brief Gods", where quite ordinary people find themselves in a quite extraordinary situation, are remarkable examples of the very qualities Platt had so astutely identified. They are at the heart of what science fiction is really all about.

My final selection, "Judgment Bell", was published in the second of three issues of **Weird and Occult Library**, an obscure British paperback magazine issued by veteran publisher Gerald G. Swan, in 1960. Swan had been a one-man publishing phenomenon, issuing every conceivable type of publication, from children's comics, and annuals, through fairy stories, romances, science fiction, supernatural, crime and detective, books and magazines, and even non-fiction. At one time or another, in a long career that had begun in 1939, he had literally published anything and everything. During the difficult war years, his unusual policy of payment immediately on acceptance attracted submissions from just about every British professional writer. Fearn was no exception, and during the 1940s he had written quite a number of short stories for Swan–of all types. However, so vast was Swan's story inventory, and so swift his chopping and changing of magazines and book series, that very few of his purchased stories were published at the time of their acceptance–and some not at all! Correspondence by Fearn in my possession reveals that "Judgment Bell" had actually been sold in June, 1945.

Weird and Occult Library was part of a group of various types of genre magazines and books issued by Swan in 1960 that were, literally, his "swan song." He had decided to retire, and took a last opportunity to use up some of his vast inventory of paid-for but unpublished mss before doing so.

"Judgment Bell" is a finely wrought supernatural story that demonstrates Fearn's fantastic versatility. It is known that Fearn sold Swan further supernatural (and other) stories, some of which never appeared. These mss appear to have been irretrievably lost, which is a matter of great regret. Meanwhile we can at least be thankful that such a minor masterpiece as "Judgment Bell" was preserved. The story has never been reprinted in English, but it has previously been translated into Italian, where it was twice reprinted, including being anthologised in **Storie di fantasmi**, edited by Gianni Pilo and Sebastian Fusco, in 1995. This massive (over 1,000 pages) meticulously annotated collection presented a historical survey of the editors' choice of the best ghost stories of all time. Its featured authors included, amongst many others, Daniel Defoe, Walter Scott, Edgar Allan Poe, Sheridan Le Fanu, Charles Dickens, Bram Stoker, Robert Louis Stevenson, Wilkie Collins, Oscar Wilde, Mark Twain, Arthur Conan Doyle, M.P. Shiel, Rudyard Kipling, Algernon Blackwood, Oliver Onions, William Hope Hodgson, Lord Dunsany, Saki, H.G.Wells–and John Russell Fearn! Let the critics try and explain that one away...

There is a final, chilling irony concerning this story. Fearn never saw it in print. In the very month of its publication, he dropped down dead–in a Church. To appreciate the significance of this, you must read the story. It will surely leave you wondering, as it did me.

Fearn was only 52 when he died, forty years ago almost to the day as this is being written—the victim of a first but fatal heart attack. He was at the height of his creative powers. The old restrictive pulp markets had disappeared, and he was just beginning to explore new mediums of expression in his writing, including the stage and television. We will never know what he might have achieved.

Meanwhile, in his short life he sold more fiction that a dozen ordinary, average long-lived authors might achieve put together. Fearn never made any extravagant claims for his writing: he regarded himself as a professional journeyman, writing whatever was in demand for the markets open to him. That so much of his varied output was science fiction was simply because he loved the medium above all others. Much of his work was ephemeral, and no better than it needed to be to put food on his table, but much of it has survived—and will continue to do so. Despite the constant sustained and disparaging attacks by the literarti, Fearn's fiction has retained its popularity with successive generations of editors and readers all over the world for seven decades, and few writers can hope for a better memorial than that.

Philip Harbottle,
Wallsend,
September, 2000.

OUTCASTS OF ETERNITY

The space ship lay motionless in the long valley of sand, banked on both sides by gently sloping ocher walls. Here, eighty feet below the level of the desert surface, lurked vestiges of woefully thin Martian air.

In the control room of the spaceship were three people–Ron Dawlish, the amiable tow-haired, gray-eyed engineer who had designed this vessel and alone possessed the secret of the special fuel which drove it through the void; Nancy Dawlish, his wife–small, slender, blonde-headed, with a bright eager face testifying to the thrill she was getting out of this first manned space expedition from Earth to Mars...

And the third crew member was Clay Reynolds, Ron's lifelong friend–telecommunications expert, astronomer, Egyptologist–in fact a veritable "Admirable Crichton" of science. Right now he sat huddled over a variety of photographic plates, earnestly studying them from under drawn brows. He didn't even seem to be aware of Ron and his wife as they stood looking out of the port.

"I just wonder what it does mean?" Nancy mused, for about the twentieth time. "If we could only find out it might give us a big clue to the mystery of Martian civilizations, don't you think?"

Ron nodded slowly, gazing across the sandy valley floor. The view was the most puzzling of any they had seen on the red planet. On the valley floor sprouted queer, cactus-like vegetation, armed with numberless viciously sharp barbs. This in itself was not so very extraordinary, of course, since air was present in this spot. The extraordinary thing was that the life should be present on this one spot on Mars and yet nowhere else–for in three months of probing, photographing, and securing data, the Dawlish Expedition was quite certain this life was alone in its glory.

In itself this was remarkable enough–but perhaps even more remarkable were the unmistakable remains of onetime Martian civilization in this same spot. For across the valley from where the spaceship lay, protruding out of the yellow wall of sand, were smashed and eroded stone columns undoubtedly molded at some time by intelligent minds and hands–and since then buried through incomputable centuries by the eternally shifting sand, blown in the thin arctic wind of the dying planet.

Most fascinating of all–the thing that absorbed the attention of the three, even as it had done from the first moment–was a Martian inscription. It was hewn in the stone of an archway supported on two cracked pillars. It protruded from the waste like a forgotten signpost, or else a text or dedication of some kind.

Believing that all hieroglyphics are capable of solution, and having a sound knowledge of Egyptology and Sanskrit, Clay Reynolds had worked ceaselessly on trying to solve the inscription for nearly three weeks. First he had ventured out in a space suit and cleaned away drifted sand from the arch; then with a flame gun he had scored the marks of erosion away and laid bare the text to the weak glimmer of the Martian sun. Then he had photographed it–normally, then with infra red and ultra violet, getting every sign pin-sharp.

But, as his worried expression showed, he had given himself the devil of a task.

"Maybe it isn't anything worth bothering about at all," Nancy smiled, turning from the port and coming over to him.

"I don't like being beaten, Nan," he growled back, setting his square jaw. "Besides, I have got started. The first four words make me want to go on. They read–'To Him to Whom–' "

"Sure that's right?" Ron frowned, staring at him.

"No, I'm not sure, but it's as near as I can translate. A queer beginning, I know–but then think of some of our Earthly legal documents which begin–'To Him to Whom it May Concern.' It is possible, you see."

Ron grinned even though his gray eyes were solemn. "Be a devil if it turns out to be a quotation like 'Right is Might' or 'They Shall not Pass,' won't it?"

"Anyway," Nan said, "I don't see that we need to spend anymore time here, Clay. You can work out that idea as we travel." She glanced at Ron. "What do you think?"

"You're right. After all, the Science Institute financed and backed this expedition purely for research purposes, and we don't want to be too long over getting back. We've got everything we need–specimens, photos, samples. Locker's chock-full."

"Okay," Clay growled. "But I don't like deserting a dead Martian city without knowing all about it." He got up. "Tell you what–while you make the arrangements for departure I'll take one last look around."

"Right," Ron nodded, and motioning Nan to help him he turned to a routine check up of the firing equipment.

In a few minutes Clay heaved his heavy, powerful form into a spacesuit, strapped on camera equipment and one or two special instruments, then with a nod of his helmeted head he made for the airlock. When he had reached it he paused for a moment and switched on his audiophone.

"Not this time, Bouncer!" his voice admonished. "This is no place for Scotch terriers. Be off with you. Shoo!"

Bouncer, a long-backed, bandy legged Aberdeen, who bore the distinction of being the first dog to cross from Earth to Mars, gave Clay a disappointed glance of his red-brown eyes, then sat down disconsolately on his haunches.

"Bouncer!" Nan called, glancing round from the rocket tubes. "Bouncer, come here, boy! Come on!"

Clay grinned behind his visor, then turned to the airlock screws and twisted them. For a moment, as he tugged the lock open, Nan and Ron felt their hearts race as the air pressure dropped: then it became normal again a few moments after the lock had closed.

So intent did they become on their work, cleaning out the firing cylinders and resetting the flash points of the electrical mechanism, they hardly noticed how the time passed, nor for that matter were they concerned about it. Clay had a habit of staying away for hours at a time when he got on a hunt. Since he was well able to take care of himself that didn't matter so much.

Then at last Nan threw down a wastecloth and rubbed a grease smudge from her tip-tilted nose.

"Don't know about you, Ron," she said, "But I'm wondering if I wasn't a bit hasty in suggesting we return home. Come to think it over, I'm not so sure I want to go."

Ron stared at her in surprise. "But why not? Space is interesting, I know—fascinating if you like—but there's a limit. I can't imagine anything worse than just wandering about in the void on constant expeditions. Besides, when we get back to Earth think of the acclaim we'll get! We're the first Earthlings to travel through space to Mars, both ways, in safety! Or we will be, anyway."

Ron stopped and took a deep breath. "Don't you realize, Nan, that it means the Dawlish Space Corporation will become an established fact? And with me at the head of it because I'm the only one who knows the formula for the fuel... Wealth—power—success! Think of it! And then you stand there and say you're not so keen on returning!"

She shrugged, and he frowned at her pretty, troubled face.

"What is it, Nan?" he smiled, hugging her to him.

"Well, I know we'll get the fame and the glory; but that is simply as a matter of course. What worries me is the danger of our success. The trials of this expedition will be as nothing compared to what we'll face against the commercial moguls of Earth. Take Calver Doone for example."

"Him?" Ron looked grimly reflective. Calver Doone was head of StratAmerican Airways Corporation. The discovery of super-fast fuel and space travel by Ron had already made Doone pull sundry wires—ethical and otherwise—to learn the young inventor's secret. What he would do when he knew space travel and commerce was to become an established fact was problematical.

"Well, I'm not afraid of Doone," Ron growled at last, shrugging. "I'll have strong men behind me, just as he will. After all, one can't be unreasonable enough to expect a gigantic project like space travel to be launched on a commercial basis without certain vested interests getting jittery—and tough."

"No, I suppose not," Nan admitted, biting her lip uncertainly. "But Doone is so ruthless I feel afraid for you."

"Then don't," Ron smiled. "I'm pretty hard when I'm pushed, and Clay isn't anybody's fool— Ah, talk of the devil!" he broke off, as the airlock swung inwards momentarily and closed again. Clay came clumping in clad in his spacesuit. Slowly the air pressure went up to normal.

"Well, find anything?" Ron inquired.

"Like hell!" Clay responded, when he'd tugged off his helmet. "I'm no nearer than I was to start with, and I still don't know what the rest of those ciphers mean." He shrugged. "Well, there it is. Seems to me the best thing we can do is go back home. Everything all set?"

"I guess so," Ron nodded, moving to the control board. Then just as his hands gripped the power switches Nan gave a sudden horrified shout.

"No, no, Ron, wait a minute! There's poor Bouncer out there!"

"Bouncer!" Ron gasped, and turned to look through the port.

Sure enough there was the terrier lying on his side amidst the cactus, his ribs heaving up and down painfully as he struggled to draw in the thin air.

"The little devil!" Clay exploded. "Don't you see? He must have skipped through the airlock when I came back– Hey, Nan, where are you going?" he demanded, as he saw her twirling the airlock screws.

"Out to get him, of course," she retorted.

"But wait a minute!" Ron cried. "You can't go out just as you are! You need a–"

"Oh, I'll be all right," she said briefly. "It's only a few yards and I can hold my breath... every second counts!" And with that she slipped through the opening and closed the airlock after her.

Clay, half in and half out of his space suit, glanced at Ron. Then they both swung to the port and watched anxiously. Nan came into view almost immediately, taking the long jumps only possible in the Martian gravity. But she over-pitched her last leap and went flying a couple of yards beyond Bouncer, finally crashing into the midst of the bristly cactus.

"Ouch! I bet that stung," Ron muttered, as he watched Nan get up and massage her arm and shoulder painfully. Then she turned quickly, picked up Bouncer, and came stumbling back.

Clay swung open the airlock for her and she came staggering in, two little smears of blood under her nostrils. She reeled giddily, then Ron caught her and drew up a chair. Slowly her labored breathing became more natural and her blood-shot eyes cleared.

"Phew, that was tougher than I expected," she ejaculated. "I held my breath, only that fall into the cactus made me lose it in one grand puff." She winced suddenly. "Still got some of those cactus needles in my shoulder unless I'm mistaken."

"Soon have them out," Roil said, and reached into the cabinet for the surgical forceps. Clay, however, was already using them, pointed to half a dozen vicious needles on the bench beside the fast reviving Bouncer.

"Um, how nice," Ron said grimly.

"What about him? Be okay?"

"Sure," Clay grinned. "He's Scotch, isn't he? Bad lad," he added, as a wicked brown eye looked at him. "But I'll give him a shot of antibiotics just in case."

Within five minutes Ron had extracted four needles from Nan's shoulder. Then he administered antibiotics, bandaged her shoulder, and handed her a glass of foaming restorative.

"Thanks," she smiled. "You should have been a doctor, not an inventor."

"You feel no ill effects, Nan?" Clay asked, studying the needles under the binocular microscope.

She glanced at him in some alarm. "Why, no. Should I?"

"I don't know," he said, looking up and frowning thoughtfully. "The needles have traces of some sort of gummy substance on them. That's no reason to suspect poison, though. I'm simply remembering that we're on an alien world... Probably ordinary sap."

"It had better be!" Nan cried, getting up and coming to look at them. "I don't want to start passing out now just when we're due to collect the glory."

"We've specimens of the cactus in the locker," Ron remarked. "Why not have a look at them, Clay, and–"

"Not worth it," he interrupted. "They're at Martian temperature and pressure in that locker. Pulling them out for any length of time into these Earth-norm conditions might kill them off– In any case if there were anything wrong Bouncer would show it quickly enough and he isn't doing it," Clay finished with a grin, as the terrier got up and wagged his impudent tail.

Then Clay turned to sweep up the needles, but Nan gave him pause and instead dropped them into a small vacuum jar and clamped down the lid.

"What's the idea?" Ron asked in surprise.

"Souvenirs," she shrugged. "Some day when I'm an old woman and feel like telling yarns I'll produce these as evidence..."

Ron smiled a little, but he thought he detected a vague light of fear in Nan's blue eyes. Only her laughing mouth seemed to belie it.

"Well, what are we waiting for?" she demanded, as Ron and Clay both stood looking at her, still trying to interpret her action. "It is time we were on our way, isn't it? Let's go."

Ron nodded a silent acquiescence and settled at the switchboard, pulled over the power levers. With a blasting roar which sent tumbling sand in all directions the vessel lifted from the valley floor–climbed swiftly away from the enigma of a lost Martian civilization towards the eternal stars.

CHAPTER II

The journey back was monotonous insofar that it contained no new elements. There was none of the fascinating interest of the first trip into space. The view of the stars, the planets, the Moon and the Sun, had lost its attraction. The whole thing was boring, crossing a gulf of forty-five million miles.

So Ron, leaving the robot pilot to eat up the distance, spent most of his time classifying the specimens they had brought from Mars. Most of the period Nan helped him, or else she attended to the essential domestic part of the trip. At other times she played with Bouncer, who seemed to have quite recovered from his Martian exploit. And Nan herself had apparently quite forgotten her painful acquaintance with the cactus. Nothing untoward had presented itself, except of course a dull headache, but this she put down to space strain increasing her blood pressure.

Clay, as usual, spent every waking moment working on the Martian hieroglyphics, and little by little, as Mars waned to an orange globe and Earth increased from a green star he began to make headway, working out the root formations of the characters, their application as compared with the three words he had already solved, and so on– Until one "morning" he gave a sudden whoop.

"I've got it!" he yelled, his eyes shining triumphantly. "It checks up. So it must be right."

Ron and Nan, busy with their cataloging, looked up in breathless interest. Bouncer twisted his big head on one side

"It's a bit paradoxical," Clay went on, pondering his notebook. "Sort of silly thing to–"

"Damn that! What does it say?" Ron yelled.

"It says–'To Him to Whom Eternal Life is Given, He an Outcast Shall Become'."

"Huh?" Ron ejaculated, staring at him.

"Say it again," Nan ordered, puzzling.

So Clay repeated it and looked apologetic. "I told you it was paradoxical. Anyway I believe it's right, though I don't pretend to gather the meaning. Unless the Martians perhaps somehow found the secret of eternal life and didn't like it when they had found it. Personally, I see very few drawbacks to eternal life. Seems to me it ought to be grand to have all eternity to work in. Think of watching inventions come to full flower."

"But there's another side," Ron reflected. "I mean the tragedy of seeing those whom you love grow old and die while you remain young..." He paused and shrugged. "Well, it sounds sort of screwy to me. How eternal life could make anybody an outcast I'm damned if I can see. Seems to me that anybody with the gift of eternity should be able in time to rule the world, either wisely or ruthlessly according to temperament. What do you think, Nan?"

"I don't get it at all," she said. "Sounds like a silly sort of inscription to leave on a city archway. And it tells us nothing after all. I had hoped it might explain away the mystery of Mars' vanished civilizations or something. Too bad! Now we shall never know."

With a puzzled frown she turned back to the cataloging, then began to look around her.

"What's up?" Ron asked, watching her.

"I'm looking for my pencil–"

"Looking for it? It's in your hand!"

She stared at the pencil in her fingers blankly. "Well," she whispered, "so it is!"

"What's the matter?" Ron asked, grinning. "Forgotten where you are, or something?"

Nan did not answer him. In fact she could not. She was too utterly shocked inwardly by the realization that her first and second fingers and thumb on her right hand had lost all sense of feeling. Even now, as she wrote stiffly, the pencil was making no pressure in her grip. She tossed it down, lowered her hand to her side. It felt like something dead hanging on her wrist. She looked at it with apparent casualness, but so far as color went it was unchanged. Only the skin seemed to have a shiny touch that was definitely unusual.

"Something the matter?" Ron asked, as she stood pondering.

Nan was not a girl to be easily frightened, so she shook her head slowly— but she was remembering that this was the arm and shoulder which had had the full force of the cactus needles— Ridiculous! Absurd! Just cramp from too much writing.

"I'm getting sleepy again," she announced presently. "I think I'll turn in for a bit."

"Okay," Ron acknowledged, pondering his list.

"Uh-huh," Clay agreed, immersed in his Martian ciphers.

Nan turned and whistled Bouncer to her. He followed her along the passage. Immediately she had entered the tiny bedroom and closed the door her face settled into troubled lines. Her hand by now should have been normal but it wasn't...

"Bouncer," she whispered, "I don't feel too good. And I'm a bit scared too!"

He cocked his head and protruded his pink tongue. Struck with a sudden thought Nan turned to the dressing table. In doing so she forgot Bouncer for a moment, felt his thick front paw crunch under her foot—but his usual complaining howl failed to come forth. Instead he merely moved to one side.

Nan looked at him strangely, then squatted down and called him to her.

"Bouncer, are you dead in parts too?" she breathed, and he licked her hand in reply. She thought for a moment, then tugging a pin from her blouse she pushed the point gently into the pad of Bouncer's left foot, watching him keenly the while. He took no notice... With a deepening horror in her heart Nan drove the pin into her own numbed hand and saw it sticking firmly into the thumb surrounded by a tiny globule of blood. But reaction was totally dead. She had never even felt it.

"Bouncer," she said slowly, feeling the color drain out of her face, "something is terribly wrong with both of us! Maybe that cactus was poisoned, after all! But we're not going to tell Ron or Clay— Not yet. The effect might go off, then think what fools we'd look! 'Sides, we don't want anything to interfere with his happiness when he gets back to Earth, do we?"

Bouncer jumped to the bunk beside her as she slowly sat upon it. She cuddled him up under her arm, smiled gravely into his big, solemn looking face...

All unaware of Nan's private worries—for her queer ailment showed no signs of improvement as Earth swung nearer out of the void—Ron and Clay began to look forward eagerly to the arrival awaiting them.

They were in radio and television with Earth and they had a pretty good idea of the welcome ahead of them. In New York City, apart from the civic authorities, there were gathered the scientific representatives of every land waiting to pay due homage to the pioneers...

"Great, isn't it?" Ron breathed, as he drove slowly down at last through Earth's atmosphere. "If those television scenes we've had are any guide we're going to get the biggest ovation ever..."

"Yes, I guess we are," Nan admitted, gazing moodily down on the ever swelling, detailing landscape.

"What's wrong?" Ron demanded, clasping her dead right hand. "You've looked down in the mouth now for—ages. If it's Calver Doone still biting you just forget it. We'll take care of it. I suppose that is what's worrying you?"

Nan seized on the excuse to give a quick nod of assent. In the back of her mind she was wondering if she ought to confess how ill she felt, how curiously lifeless her whole body was fast becoming... Yet still the dim hope that she was only suffering from excessive space strain, which would soon pass away, held her back from utterance.

"To hell with Calver Doone!" Clay Reynolds snorted, as he saw Nan's nod of assent. "If he starts anything he'll get an answer—and damn quick!"

And at this precise moment Calver Doone was standing gazing through the window of his private office window on the 152nd floor of the Doone Building. In appearance he was rather different from the popular conception of a self-made financier and industrialist.

He was small, with narrow stoop-shoulders and a face as thin as an ax. In the lean, acid features and thin-lipped mouth there was something startlingly in common with a snake. It was the kind of face from which one instinctively averts the gaze.

"Look at it!" he breathed, in a voice white with anger. "Flags, bunting, ticker-tape, bands— Look well, gentlemen, for we're not gazing so much on the birth of a new age as on the death of our own!"

Four men were grouped about him, specially summoned to observe this gala occasion. There was Grant Meadows, the oil multi-millionaire—lanky, square jawed, habitually silent; Rolinac, the thick-necked, big-stomached steel king; Pascal, the immaculate, vinegary banker; and Dilson, Chief of United European Air Lines, a light eyed little man with knobbly knuckles which he incessantly massaged with his palm.

It was queer how Doone, for all his smallness, seemed to dominate the group. An observer would have felt compelled to look mainly at this little figure with the narrow back standing with hunched shoulders before the window. Sunlight set his thin gray hair into a haloed mist on his small head.

"He ought never to have succeeded!" he breathed, thumping his claw-like fist on the window frame. "According to the telecast a moment ago he's arrived back safely with several Martian specimens. His wife, and that engineer Clay Reynolds; all seem to be in good spirits... The world has acclaimed space travel.

That means that air-borne travel and commerce will be slowly superseded by the newer, faster medium."

"But there will still be a need for air traffic!" Dilson, the Air Chief, said.

"Don't be a damned fool!" Doone snarled at him. "A need, yes—but what sort of a need? This man Ron Dawlish has a super fuel, manufactured somehow from minerals. It puts gasoline right out of the picture. Hear that, Meadows?" Doone grinned malignantly at the oil man.

"He uses a new metal for his firing cylinders, and platino bases for his ship's plates. That wipes our steel out. Hear that, Rolinac? So, our three interlocked interests—airplanes, steel, and oil are wiped out by this scientist who is in truth a one-man industrial revolution. And you, Pascal, as our banker, will feel the pinch, too..."

Doone clenched his hands behind his back. "Now you see why I called you here. We're heading for being a second-rate power in world affairs: in fact I can even forsee total bankruptcy! The State itself is behind this Ron Dawlish, and so is the Science Institute. Interplanetary travel and super-fast fuels have come to stay. In a few months Dawlish's Corporation will be established and it is going to be a miracle if the Air Line shares are going to worth the paper they're written on."

There was a grim, deadly silence for a moment as each man, ruthlessly ambitious, saw his security crumbling before the winds of advancing science.

The silence was broken at last by the gradual crescendo of a band coming down Wall Street. Presently, the procession passed down the center of the street amidst the snow of ticker tape and the cheers of the packed people.

"Look at 'em!" Doone growled, glaring down on the superb automobile in which sat Clay, Ron, and Nancy, and beside them again the President himself and the white-haired chief of the Science Institute.

"Makes one wish for a bomb," the oil man muttered, rubbing his square jaw speculatively.

"Something violent, anyway," agreed Rolinac, his stomach pressing against the window ledge as he leaned to look.

Then Doone turned back irritably into the office and as a matter of course the other men turned with him. Seating himself at his desk he looked at them each in turn.

"We have got to act," he said, his venomous mouth setting. "And quickly! Violence is only to be our last resort because by its use we can get too easily involved with the law. To begin with it seems it is a job for you, Pascal."

The banker looked surprised. "Me?"

"You will get agents on the job to cajole Ron Dawlish into parting with his formula. Never mind what you offer him, but get it. If that fails then try and work a partnership with our Corporation. Whatever happens we have got to know what that formula is, even if we only get a lease on it. Promise anything until we get it. When we have it the legal elimination of Dawlish can be arranged somehow."

The four heads nodded. After thinking for a moment or two Doone looked at the steel king.

"You control most of the country's steel output, Rolinac. Ron Dawlish will need it in big quantities to build his space ship factories. You will see to it that every hindrance short of getting at loggerheads with the State is put in the way of delivery. And when delivery has to take place I'm not particular if the steel isn't of a high-class grade. Understand? You, Meadows, will slow up all oil transactions. Dawlish will need oil in big quantities. He can't use anything except oil for trucks and Deisel engines."

The oil man nodded, but he looked troubled.

"What's wrong with you?" Doone asked harshly. "Afraid you may lose on the deal, or something?"

"Not exactly that. I was just thinking that Dawlish has mighty powerful influences back of him—even the President himself. We've got to be damned careful."

"I expect you to be," Doone retorted. "It's as much in your interests as everybody else's to see that Dawlish is smashed utterly—or if not that then to see that his formula is known to us as well as to himself... As for you, Dilson, you'll launch the biggest publicity campaign ever, telling the masses that air travel is proven to be safe but that space travel is still experimental. Avoid the libel angle, but lay it on thick. Understand?"

"I get it," Dilson nodded.

"And if these efforts fail?" the steel king asked.

"Then there are other ways." Doone smiled thinly. "Forceful ways, which one way or another, will give us back the security we have got to have..."

CHAPTER III

It was not long after the speechifying and feting was over before Ron Dawlish began to feel the commercial pressures instigated by Doone—nor did he require much imagination to know the financier was back of them. But, aided as he was by Presidential and scientific support, he gradually succeeded, with Clay's help, in establishing the first of a series of spaceship factories. His actual headquarters were in New York itself. From here Ron controlled all the details, while Clay became the foreman of works.

Altogether, a couple of months after the return from Mars, Ron was feeling pretty satisfied with himself and fairly sure—so far at least—that he had beaten Calver Doone at his own game. Not that he had any illusions about Doone, however.

"Whatever he does, Nan, he'll have to put a brake on his efforts," he said one evening, as he and the girl sat at dinner in the gathering summer twilight. "We've got all people for us and precious few against us—so he'll have to watch his step!"

Nan nodded absently, but said nothing. Ron lowered his knife and fork for a moment and looked at her steadily.

"You look sort of tired, dear. Is this new place we took getting too large to handle?"

"With domestics and labor saving devices? Not a bit of it, Ron– Don't mind me. I'm still trying to get over that space trip. I think it upset my nerves a good deal."

"And I've been–and shall be–too busy to console you," Ron sighed. Then he shrugged. "So there it is! But there's a fortune to be made, and one has to put a lot of things on one side for that, eh?"

She smiled an assent, handled her knife and fork with hands that were totally dead. Instead of her queer condition improving, as she had once hoped, it had gone worse with the weeks, spreading further about her body every day. And still she had kept from worrying Ron, loaded up as he was with responsibilities. But she had made up her mind to make a move this very night if Ron went out again to catch up on work at headquarters...

Which he did, fifteen minutes later. He kissed her white cheek gently.

"Take care of yourself, sweet," he said softly. "Get to bed early and catch up on some sleep. Maybe you'll feel better then. 'By, Bouncer..."

Bouncer stirred slumbrously for a moment, then went to sleep again. Ron looked at him with a frown.

"Seems damned dopy these days... Well, I'll be back somewhere around midnight."

Nan watched him go as she stood at the window–then the moment his roadster had vanished down the drive she had Clements drive her to Dr. Andrews, the family physician since her birth twenty-five years before. In the surgery he listened with a puzzled frown as she explained her symptoms.

"And it is progressive? It gets worse?" And as she nodded his frown deepened.

"I'm getting to the limit of endurance, Dr. Andrews," she said hopelessly. "You see, I don't know if it will end in death, or what. My arms and shoulders have been dead for weeks anyway, and now it is affecting my legs and feet. Yet the puzzling part is that I can use my limbs perfectly even though they have no sensation. I'm–I'm frightened; I really am!"

Andrews led her to a chair and switched on a battery of arcs. For a long time he examined her, testing reflexes, pulse, eyesight, hearing. At the end of it he was looking more puzzled than ever.

"I just don't understand it, Mrs. Dawlish," he confessed. "In all my medical experience you are unique! You are perfectly normal despite your lack of sensation. I can only assume something or other–maybe this Martian cactus you speak of–is affecting your sensory nerves and rendering them inoperative. Certainly it isn't a circulatory trouble. Your heartbeats and blood pressure are both normal."

Nan got to her feet slowly. "I see," she said quietly. "You can't advise me, then?"

"I might if you cared to stay in my sanitarium for a week or so."

"No, no, not that. I don't want to upset my husband for one thing, and anyway I might get well again. Thanks just the same."

Andrews held her coat for her, grasped the cold hand she held out. Thoughtful, bitter indeed, she pondered her strange malady as she was driven home. Still pondering, she entered the lounge—and came to a stop. For an instant she was shocked out of her own personal worries.

In the center of the rug, stirring in a kind of horrifying blind desperation, was Bouncer. Obviously he did not hear Nan's approach, nor did he see her even though his blank, terrible eyes were fixed upon her. Fear streamed through her as she looked at him. It needed no more than a glance to see he was strangely, outrageously ill.

"Bouncer!" Nan's hands went to her lips in terror. "Oh, Bouncer, what is the matter?"

Instinct perhaps advised him of her nearness. He whimpered pitifully, lifted one paw, then the other, in a stiff sort of effort to reach her. She hesitated, uncertain what to do—then whirling round she whipped open the French window and shooed him out into the garden.

Blindly, he loped out into the moonlight. Nan watched him fixedly, stunned by the sight of strong summer grass wilting into sear dryness everywhere he wandered. In no time the lawn was streaked in a crazy patchwork of withered trails as though Death himself had walked there.

For a long time Nan could not rouse herself to grasp the situation. Her own symptoms, she knew, were identical with those of poor Bouncer, except for the fact that she, being stung much later by the Martian cactus, would naturally receive the effects with corresponding latency. But surely to God it didn't mean that she was to become a blind, desperate thing like Bouncer, stunned of all normal faculties and so diseased that everything living around instantly withered?

Dry lipped, she turned away—and it was at that very moment that her own sensations reached a climax. The moonlit grounds seemed to swirl dizzily as she was struck by a hammer blow of pain in the head. All sense of remaining feeling left her and she crashed helplessly to the carpet...

It was as though she were dead. All sight, hearing, movement, and sensation had ceased. And yet she was alive, fully aware of the fact that she had fallen and was in the grip of an iron paralysis. Then at last—she knew not how long after—there came a change. For the first tine since the deadly malady had manifested itself she was conscious of returning sensation. It flowed like a steadily swelling tide through her veins. She knew once again that she had arms and legs and nerves...

Hearing, sight, smell: they crept back upon her. She stirred a little, became aware of the fact that Bouncer was standing right alongside her, licking her face furiously.

"Bouncer!" she whispered, clutching him. "Oh, Bouncer, isn't it wonderful? We're well again—!"

She sat up, gradually got to her feet and stood thinking. Bouncer headed for the garden again and Nan's eyes followed to where he had left those trails of destruction. She hesitated, reached out towards the bowl of full-blown roses on the table.

She grasped one of them... It withered into brown petals!

Suddenly there blazed across her mind the remembrance of a Martian inscription– 'To Him to Whom Eternal Life is Given, He an Outcast Shall Become!' It was as though the truth had been yelled at her.

"Bouncer," she said slowly, as he came back to her, "you and me are alike! We don't hurt each other because we've each got the same complaint, whatever it is– We've got to go away quickly, and find out what's wrong. Ron mustn't see us–mustn't touch us..."

She turned away quickly, reached for notepaper in the bureau. She wrote a brief note, left it with the manservant before he, had the chance to contact her in any way, then she went up to her room and hastily packed some clothes. Only one other thing she included–the vacuum phial full of cactus needles which she had retained from her Martian adventure...

Ron Dawlish had completed his job of going over the plans for the next day's production schedule with Clay Reynolds, when the phone rang. Ron reached for it.

"Yeah? Dawlish speaking."

The voice from the other end was not a familiar one. Not only did Ron hear it in the receiver but Clay also through the relay speaker. His big, powerful face darkened as he listened.

"You won't know me, Dawlish, but that's beside the point. I'm just going to give you a little word of warning. You must be pretty well aware by now that certain factions are not going to allow you to exert absolute monopoly over that space fuel of yours."

"Why not call the 'certain factions' Calver Doone and done with it?" Ron snapped, looking significantly at Clay across the desk.

"Names are dangerous, Dawlish–on both sides. Up to now you have been smart enough to dodge a commercial embargo on your oil and steel supplies, and you've turned down the highest money offers for your formula. That was foolish of you, for any further obstinacy on your part is going to cost you dear."

"Listen, you–" Ron began savagely; but he was interrupted.

"You listen to me! You've a lot of power on your side; that's freely admitted, but most men start to squeal when their personal friends and relatives suffer."

"What in hell are you driving at?" Ron roared.

"I'll make it as plain as possible. Either you agree to enter into partnership with Strat-American Airways Corporation by midnight–that is in forty minutes–or things will start happening which will bring you such anguish of mind you'll be begging to surrender within a week! Forty minutes, Dawlish. I'll ring you back."

The line went dead. Ron stared bewilderedly at the receiver, then he slammed it back on its rest. Suddenly his fury exploded.

"Of all the damned, infernal impudence! Who in hell does he think he is, anyway? He can't get away with it, Clay! We'll have the authorities put the finger on Doone and Strat-American Airways before they know where they are—"

"How?" Clay demanded grimly. "We haven't an atom of proof beyond that phone call. Not a single thing we can pin on Doone personally even though we know he's back of it. But that warning was meant in earnest all right—and we've got to heed it."

"Like hell!"

Clay's big hand clutched Ron's arm across the desk.

"Listen, Ron, come to earth! We've got to think of something whereby we can gain time. Doone has agents everywhere—possibly even amongst our own staff. We can't tell—"

"Oh, don't talk like an idiot!" Ron said hotly. He sprang to his feet and paced around savagely. Presently he stowed at the window and gazed out on the lighted canyon below. "One would think you want me to comply with Doone's wishes," he muttered. "I'd never have thought it of you, Clay."

Clay got up and came over to him, swung him round.

"You know me better than that, Ron. I said we'd got to gain time. Stall. Promise anything!"

"But why the devil should I? I'm out to fight Doone, not to kowtow to him. Do you think I care what he does to me?"

"I wasn't thinking of you. I'm thinking of Nan, for one thing—even myself for another. I'm not scared of anything Doone can do, but my elimination would lose you one trusted overseer, and well you know it."

"Wait a minute," Ron said wonderingly. "Do you think for one moment that Doone would dare to drag Nan into this—"

"Dare!" Clay laughed shortly. "He'd jump at the chance! He is too snaky to wipe you out personally, and besides that wouldn't do him any good because you've got the formula he wants... That agent of his on the phone promised you plenty of anguish— That means making you comply because all those nearest and dearest to you will suffer if you don't! So—stall! Give Nan warning to leave town and hide somewhere; give me time to get on my guard— Then we'll pay Doone back in his own coin."

"I get it," Ron nodded, calming. "Sorry I blew up on you, Clay. For that matter there's nothing to stop me telling Nan right now to get away somewheres. Sooner she's on the way to safety the sooner my hands are untied."

He turned back to the phone and depressed the home number tally button.

It was the voice of Meadows, the manservant, which answered.

"Oh, hallo there, Meadows? Sorry to get you up. Ask Mrs. Dawlish to come to the phone, will you?"

"I'm sorry, sir, that's impossible. Mrs. Dawlish has left—on a sudden visit, I gathered."

Clay looked in surprise towards the loud speaker.

"Left? For where?" Ron asked blankly.

"I don't know, sir. She left a letter for you and instructed me to see that you got it."

"Oh," Ron said, thinking. "Well, all right. I'll see to it."

He rang off and clenched his fist. "Clay, this can only mean one thing. Somehow she must have got wind of danger and cleared off anyway."

"I suppose so," Clay nodded slowly. "But it's queer she did not ring you up here."

"Not altogether. She never disturbs me if she can help it. Yes, that's it right enough," Ron went on. "And it means that my hands are untied far quicker than I had expected. If you are ready for anything that might happen I'm going to tell this agent of Doone's to go to the devil when he rings back again."

Clay nodded a silent assent. After that he and Ron waited in comparative silcence until the stipuled forty minutes had finally expired. Right on the tick the bell rang.

"Well, Dawlish, have you decided?"

"Yes, I've decided," Ron answered bitterly. "You can tell Doone I'm not afraid of him, you, or any of the damned set-up. See?"

"You're a fool, Dawlish, as you'll very soon find out–"

Ron cut him off savagely and got to his feet.

"I'm through listening to those kind of threats," he snapped, getting into his coat. "I'd better be getting home and see what kind of a note Nan left for me– What are you going to do?"

"Stay here," Clay shrugged. "Way things are looking it seems advisable to me for one or other of us to be on duty all the time. We've a fight on our hands now, Ron. Doone will strain every nerve."

Ron nodded slowly, tightened his lips. "Okay–I'll be here by seven in the morning–and watch out for yourself."

With that he left and hurried out to his car. Inside ten minutes he was home, followed by the robed and tousled manservant into the lounge. He handed over the letter Nan had written.

"Mrs. Dawlish left no other instruction than that I hand you this, sir," he said.

"Um," Ron said moodily, tearing the flap. "Anybody call or ring up my wife during the evening?"

"Not to my knowledge, Mr. Dawlish."

"Okay. You can get back to bed."

"Thank you, sir. Good night." Ron didn't answer: he was too busy reading the letter–

"Dear Ron:

I know you'll forgive me, but I feel an urge to go away and rest up a bit. My nerves, as you know, have not been so good ever since we got back from Mars, and I feel I must rest. I'll stay at an hotel somewhere in the country: I'll have to let you know the address later on. I've taken Bouncer with me for company. Please don't mind, will you?

"Anyway, you'll have busy days ahead of you and maybe you will get along quicker if you know I'm trying to recuperate myself.

"Always yours,

"Nan."

"Queer," Ron muttered to himself, frowning. "But probably I'm worrying over nothing. Doesn't sound here as though she got any hints about Doone. Must be just coincidence..."

He thought for a moment. She had not explained why she had not used the phone. She hardly could, considering she had not wanted to argue the matter of her going. But it baffled Ron just the same.

At last he shoved the note in his pocket and stood staring at the rose bowl, plucked out the dead one and wondered why Meadows had not seen it. Odd for that one rose to be dead and the rest of them flourishing...

Then as he stood twirling it in his fingers the phone rang. In a moment his troubled face lighted up. He lifted the receiver.

"Yes, yes, that you, Nan–?" Then he stopped and gave a grunt as the voice of the night watchman came over the wire from his city headquarters.

"You'd better come over at once, Mr. Dawlish. Something awful has gone and happened. It's Mr. Reynolds, sir. He's gone and fallen down the elevator shaft and–"

"He what?" Ron shouted hoarsely, coming to life and clutching the phone tightly. "What did you say?"

"I don't rightly know what happened, Mr. Dawlish. I was in the office doing a bit of tidying up when Mr. Reynolds got a call to go over to the factory. He said he'd come right away and went for the elevator. Next thing I heard was a scream– I found the elevator was at the top floor. Somebody must have planned it."

"Did you call the police?" Ron asked dully.

"No, sir. Matter of fact I didn't know what to do. I found Mr. Reynolds lying dead so I rang you up and–"

"All right," Ron interrupted him. "I'll be right over."

CHAPTER IV

Walter Moorland, the real estate dictator of Newingham, a village "somewhere" outside of the city's boundaries, was distinctly puzzled by the woman in the veil who, accompanied by a Scotch terrier on a leash, arrived in his office the moment it was open the following morning.

"Good morning, madam!" He held out a cordial hand, tried not to look slighted when it was ignored. With eyebrow raised he tried to pierce the veil to the features beyond. All he could see was a worn face and alabaster-white complexion.

"You have a villa for sale with six acres of land—just down the main road? Or rather just off it..."

"That's right, madam. I can assure you it is—"

"I'm not interested in the sales talk, thanks. What's the price?"

Nan didn't hesitate at the steep figure Moorland gave. "Have the deed of sale drawn up immediately," Nan said. "I'll write you out a check."

She pulled off her gloves and Moorland found himself gazing fascinatedly at her hands. Dead white they were, superbly manicured, but totally bloodless. Except for their smoothness he could have said they were the hands of a corpse.

"I have not much time," Nan said, looking up momentarily from writing the check.

"Eh? Oh, I'm sorry." Moorland came to himself with a start, busied himself with the details of the deed. Within ten minutes, bar the official stamping, the negotiation was complete.

Moorland studied the check. "Is the name—Dawlish?" he asked finally.

"Nancy Dawlish," Nan acknowledged. "Heard it before?"

"Somewheres, I think..." Moorland shrugged. "Not that it matters. I'll get you the keys..."

He brought them over from a pegged board and held them out. Nan said briefly,

"Drop them on the desk, please."

Staring at her he complied, then his jaw sagged a little as he noticed something. In reaching for them Nan's costume sleeve brushed the fresh sweet peas on top of the desk. For some incredible reason they all turned black, then wilted into dryness. It was the most astounding thing Moorland had ever seen. Nan had seen it too and frowned in annoyance at herself. Then she straightened up and put the keys in her handbag. Her voice was quite composed.

"Thanks, Mr. Moorland. There is just one other thing..."

"Yes?" he whispered, staring at her in sober wonderment.

"If anybody should inquire as to my whereabouts—though I don't altogether expect it—you know nothing of me."

"Yes, yes, madam—of course. But look, can't I show you round the villa—?"

"Thank you, no. I've seen it already through the windows... Good morning."

Again Moorland found his proffered hand ignored, but as he pulled the door open for Nan, her fingers, reaching for the knob, inadvertently touched his wrist. With a terrific effort he mastered a scream, smiled her out from a deadly pale face.

When he looked at his wrist a moment later the back of it had three white spots where she had touched him—spots ice cold to the tapping of his other hand. Ice cold and without feeling. He stared after her as she went down the pathway, then his gaze swung to the dead sweet peas... Suddenly he realized he was wet with perspiration. Death had come into his little office this morning—

Within three days Nan had her villa duly furnished and fitted out, and everywhere she had been her strange manner and deliberate avoidance of contacting anybody had been noticeable. Only when at last she had settled in the place and locked the doors on the outer world did she feel safe, and for that matter able to fully analyze the strange sensation that had been governing her ever since her recovery from the initial paralysis. To Bouncer she summed things up, and with a solemn black face he sat and listened.

"Bouncer, I think we know now what the Martians meant, don't we?" she whispered, stroking his head and staring moodily out of the window onto the countryside. "Only you and I can touch each other and still live—but to other living things, human, animal, or vegetable, we're deadliest poison... We're outcasts, Bouncer. Eternal but damned!"

She smiled faintly. "Odd to think that we can live forever—and yet because of that very fact we must never touch anybody, never contact a living thing. But because we suffer from the same thing we're immune from each other..." Nan's face saddened as she thought of Ron. "Never, never must I see him again, Bouncer. That would mean his death..."

She stopped, reflecting. Once again she was swept by unfathomable emotions, those same emotions she had noticed so often lately. At first, upon her initial recovery from the paralysis, they had been unformed stirrings in her consciousness—dim, complex glimpses of a vast and overwhelming science. As she had been then, terrified at her physical condition, it had signified but little—but now she had realized the crushing fact that she and Bouncer were eternal outcasts in a world of the living she felt it was imperative to encourage these enigmatic conceptions struggling to be born.

Perhaps a heritage of some kind—a Martian heritage? As yet she did not know. The main obsession in her mind at the moment was to determine why she was eternal, and if possible find a way to neutralize the terrifying bequest. Eternality, at the price of bringing death to everything else that lived, was the cruelest, most terrible of jests. If it came to that, why did she bring death to those that lived if her heritage was eternal life?

Her thoughts moved on to the realization that she needed a laboratory. If indeed eternity was her heritage, there were many scientific occupations with which she would have to fill up her lonely life.

Turning, she picked up the telephone directory, looked up the numbers of the nearest construction companies.

For nearly two weeks after the death of Clay Reynolds, which Ron had not the least doubt had been deliberately engineered—though it was impossible for him to find the exact culprit—there was a continuous series of mysterious happenings which came close to driving Ron to distraction.

In the first space ship factory that was under construction there was constant sabotage and bad workmanship. Time and again steel girders collapsed without warning, bringing a gradually mounting death roll among the workers. This in turn precipitated unrest, and in some cases blank refusal to work at all. Desperately Ron argued with the men but got little satisfaction; nor was it a matter that he could refer to the State, for the workers had powerful labor combines on their side who fully supported their complaints.

On top of this things began to go wrong with the transports. One half of them found their gasoline tanks full of "treated" spirit. The great storage tanks were immediately examined and found to be full of doctored fuel.

Bitter, grim, Ron sent for the works manager. He had taken the place vacated by the highly efficient Clay and Ron had felt at the initial interview that he was the right man for the task–big, husky, genial, intelligent...

He looked rather puzzled as he faced the haggard Ron across the desk.

"Look here, Benson, where did you buy that latest consignment of steel?" Ron demanded.

"Why, from Rolinac's Syndicate, sir."

Ron leaped up. "What! What the devil do you mean by taking things into your own hands in this fashion? Didn't I give you implicit instructions to get all steel from Meredith's?"

Benson was silent, his square jaw firming.

"And the gasoline?" Ron barked. "That, I suppose you got from Meadows' Oil Company?"

Benson shrugged. "Only because they're both the biggest men in the business. So I thought–"

"Your job is to act, not think! You'd better come clean, Benson, and admit that you're in the employ of Calver Doone–that you are here with the express intention of trying to wreck my space ship projects. That's right, isn't it?" Ron reached out and caught the works' manager by the lapel of his overall.

"Okay, it's right." He grinned cynically. "And we're making a pretty good job of it, aren't we?"

Ron snatched his hand away. "Get out!" he blazed. "And stay out!"

Benson shrugged, then with a grim smile silently departed. For a moment or two Ron glared at the closed door bitterly, then sat down again at his desk. For several minutes he sat thinking, brows down, faced with ticklish problems. The worries connected with trying to start his space ship factories were legion–but back of his mind was a greater anxiety–the peculiar silence of Nan after her promise to send him further word.

So thick and fast had his troubles piled upon him he had hardly noticed the lapse of time. Surely she must have found an hotel by now? Two weeks! That she hadn't sent him a single word or even phoned him was the oddest thing out. More, it was alarming. Perhaps a matter for the police–

"Excuse me, Mr. Dawlish–"

"Well, what is it?" He looked up with a start as a clerk came in.

"There's a Mr. Doone to see you, sir–"

"Calver Doone!"

"Do you mind so much, Mr. Dawlish?" Doone himself came in behind the clerk, hands clasped tightly behind his back. He only unclasped them to take off his hat and gloves.

"You can get out," he said, to the hesitant clerk.

"That might apply just as well to you, Doone," Ron said, glaring at him.

Doone's response was to sit down. He leaned back in the chair with an acid smile.

"Suppose we get down to business, Mr. Dawlish? I think that there is little doubt that I have you just where I want you."

"Yeah?" Ron gave a grim smile. "Killing off Clay Reynolds and fixing a phony works' manager isn't the end of the world, Doone."

Doone was silent while he lighted a cigarette.

"I was lucky enough to find out about your phony dealing in time," Ron went on savagely. "Inside two hours I'll have my own steel company–Meredith's–back on the job, and my tanks will be emptied and filled with first-grade gasoline."

"Somehow," Doone said calmly, "I think you're going to be disappointed."

"Meaning what?"

"I realized that I left too many loopholes before, my friend. There were too many independent sources from which you could buy steel and oil, too many sources from which to get the resources for space ship building. So I decided it would be worth my while to use every influence I possess to secure controlling interests in all concerns likely to be of use to you. I confess it has been an expensive job, but well worth the investment. By tomorrow at the latest the final ratification of a giant merger will take place."

"By God, Doone, if you mean–"

"I mean, Mr. Dawlish, that you are powerless!" the financier snapped. "Though the final signature will not be given until tomorrow the merger is in force and you cannot get away from its influence! Oil, steel, and base metal industries are nominally unchanged so far as outside orders are affected–but where your contracts are concerned special attention will be given. Do I make myself clear?"

Doone leaned forward and slapped a thin hand on the desk. "You are cornered, Dawlish! You will only get the right materials and smoothly executed contracts when you cooperate with me–not until! And it isn't just me that you are fighting now but the commercial dictators of the day."

"Of which you are the supreme one," Ron breathed, clenching his fists. "Everybody knows you are pretty well the master mind that tells Wall Street what to do. Well, you're not getting that formula of mine! I'll get through if I have to drill for my own gasoline, mine my own ores, and build the factories nail by nail. I didn't brave a space ship journey to Mars just to hand the formula to you. When a Space Corporation comes into being I will be the President of it. Make no mistake!"

"This is all very futile with the commercial giants against you, Dawlish."

"Not so foolish with the President and the Science Institute backing my project. This isn't a two-cent discovery, Doone: it is the biggest thing since man learned to fly."

"I know," Doone said grimly. "Why else do you think I am spending millions to crush you? If you succeed, I collapse. I'm fighting for my life."

"If you and your commercial cronies were anything like men of vision instead of public-frisking moneymakers, I'd agree to compromise," Ron snapped. "But I'll have no truck with men who use murder and sabotage as their weapons..."

Doone reflected. "Clay Reynolds died, didn't he? That was a personal blow to you. It would be most unfortunate if the same thing were it happen—to another even dearer to you..."

Ron stared at the snakelike eyes. Nan! Of course! What an idiot he had been not to have seen it before. Gone away for her nerves indeed! Of course Doone had been behind her disappearance. No wonder she had sent no word. Somehow he had forced her to write that letter and—

"So you are responsible!" Ron blazed, leaping up. "You dirty, cheap gangster! You kidnapped my wife to force my hand!"

It said much for Doone's imperturbability that he made instant use of the obvious mistaken conclusion.

"I warned you, didn't I?" he said gravely. "Or rather I had you warned that worse blows might befall you. At the moment your wife is safe. Her continued well being depends entirely on you."

Ron beat his fist on the desk. "At least give me time to think about it!"

"But why?" Time was the last thing Doone could grant in case the mistake was discovered. "I've shown you what I can do, and what I will continue to do. Either you surrender that formula to me now, or you'll never hear of your wife again and your potential Corporation will never materialize."

Ron hesitated, then with a hopeless gesture he turned to the private safe in the wall....

CHAPTER V

In two weeks events had moved swiftly for Nan also. Though she had not understood at the time why she had such scientific powers, she certainly had had no difficulty in using them. First she had set about gratifying her longing to see the outer world by constructing a teledetector. Tuned to the electrical aura of any human being it automatically contacted any desired person the moment its detector beam was switched on.

To build the instrument, once she had ordered the components from various electrical firms, had taken her only three days. Immediately she had directed the X-ray-like beam towards Ron's headquarters in the city and finally, picking him up, had noted his aura frequency. From then on the instrument had—and would—pick him up the moment it operated...

For several days it had worried Nan to see and know of his anxieties on her account, to hear his words of harassment—but still dead silence on her part was necessary if she was to keep him away from his own destruction.

Most of her time she sat watching and listening to his shadow self on the big screen. At other times she took a bit of exercise on the land at the back with

Bouncer; or else she studied the cactus barbs that had brought her and the dog to such a strange pass...

And, with her newly conferred knowledge, she began not only to understand the nature of the barbs but the cause of her condition. When she finally withdrew a drop of blood from her finger and studied it she knew her deductions were right.

"Bouncer," she said, on the evening two weeks after they had fled from home, "I know what's wrong with us... In a world as barren as Mars and devoid of all water vapor, the only vegetation that could survive must be of the evergreen variety, its inner chemical structure breaking down the molecules in the dry sand and transforming them into a substance capable of supporting life—just the same way as an earthly plant breaks down poisonous nitrates and turns them into stimulants...

"It is possible—in fact probable—that the Martians realized that if a plant had the power of achieving eternal life on a dying planet, so might a human being—or at least a flesh and blood being. The Martians must have utilized the plant sap and then discovered, too late, its effect on the flesh and blood system..."

Nan paused and thought for a moment, then went on absently,

"You see, Bouncer, I think we may assume the Martians were flesh and blood like we of Earth, only with different anatomies. At any rate, I think their bloodstream must have corresponded with ours. See this drop of milky white on the microscope slide? It's my blood, Bouncer—and yours must look the same. The red corpuscles have been destroyed. Normally that would lead to extreme anemia, even death, and it was while this process was going on that we lost all sensation. But the poison of the Martian cactus supplied something else in place of the red corpuscles—a colorless fluid that is immensely powerful and readily assimilates into the bloodstream, finally turning the blood into a fluid incapable of deterioration. Because of that, ketabolism is absent and cellular breakdown cannot occur. The body is literally filled with the elixir of life..."

Nan stopped, and with a sad smile fondled the dog's head.

"But for the gift of eternality there is a dreadful price—one which the Martians discovered, hence their warning over that archway. You see, Nature must have a balance. Birth, maturity, and decay are the law of the physical world. Eternality is an outrage on Nature. All things live, Bouncer, because they are interdependent one on another. A living unit—an ordinary living unit—cannot exist unto itself: that is a fundamental law of science. And if living things are brought into contact with something which is possessed of full life-force—like you and me—the immense shock does not stimulate, it destroys! Just as some radiations are stimulating in small quantities and deadly in large quantities. The plants themselves had only their needles with which to transmit the deadly force, so we were not killed by it, but absorbed it.

"But we have our whole bodies radiating it. We stimulate all living things into instant death. Now we know what is meant by that Martian inscription... And my scientific knowledge? At first I suspected it was some kind of heritage.

Now I know differently. The brain, Bouncer, is fed by the bloodstream. According to the quality of that stream the brain is keen or dull. But now your brain and mine is fed with a non-deteriorating fluid, sharpening them in every respect. Normally I was a fair scientist: with this new bloodstream I am almost a genius. I am capable of learning and mastering problems that would have been beyond my capacity before. In time, Bouncer, as years go on, I may become the greatest scientist that ever lived... And why not indeed, with all eternity in which to accomplish it...?

"But we face a terrible ordeal, Bouncer," Nan sighed. "To be separated forever from living beings... What is there left throughout eternal life but to study and master the mysteries of science? Thereby we might find the way to either the blessed touch of a human being, or maybe... death."

With a fatalistic shrug she turned and switched on the teledetector. In a moment or two Ron became visible. Nan started to attention as she saw Calver Doone seated opposite to him at the desk.

"... you are responsible!" Ron shouted. "You dirty, cheap gangster! You kidnapped my wife to force my hand!"

Nan watched and listened grimly to the words exchanged. She got up with a futile cry of warning as Ron went over to his wall safe and tossed down his precious formula into the desk.

"Well, there it is, Doone," he snapped. "I'll risk anything and I'll face anything—except the chance of my wife's death or injury. You found the Achilles Heel, damn you!"

Doone picked up the formula, surveyed it, and nodded.

"You're a sensible man, Dawlish. But I won't be hard on you. I suggest a partnership—"

"Yeah, with you in control? Nothing doing! I shall found my own organization and you yours. Whoever gets the biggest space service has their own ingenuity to thank..."

"No," Nan whispered. "No, Ron, not that! You're just ruining yourself— You know you are!"

She stood helplessly for a moment, picked up the phone, then hesitated. The number could be traced. She turned, bundled on her hat and coat, and raced from the villa with Bouncer at her heels. In five minutes she had reached a call box and dialed hurriedly.

In his office Ron broke off his conversation with Doone to lift the receiver. He sat listening, Doone watching the expressions chasing across his face.

"But where are you?" Ron demanded at last. "I've been trying to trace you. Even the bank wouldn't help because your separate account is wrapped in mystery— Hey, wait a minute—!"

He broke off savagely, joggled the rest. Then suddenly flinging the phone down he reached over the desk and grabbed Doone by the collar, yanked him out of his chair. With his free hand he whipped the formula from the financier's breast pocket.

"Clever, weren't you?" he asked furiously. "That was my wife on the phone. You didn't kidnap her. I jumped to conclusions..."

"You're only a bit ahead of time that's all," Doone said dryly. "I'll get her somehow, Dawlish, I promise you—"

"My wife is safe," Ron interrupted. "Though she is absent for a reason I don't understand. You haven't got my formula and you won't ever get the chance again... Now get out!"

For a long moment Doone hesitated, then he turned and left. Once he got home he spent an hour in his library finishing off new plans of attack and the final details of his merger on the morrow. Then he retired to bed.

It was towards two in the morning when he fancied he heard a noise in his magnificent bedroom. Sharply, he sat up, reached for the bedside lamp and switched it on.

The sudden glare revealed a dead white hand reaching towards him from the shadows back of his bed. He fancied that for a moment he caught a glimpse of a veiled face and heard the sullen growling of a dog—

Then the hand gripped his wrist. Consciousness, life, all conception of things, streamed out of him in a tide...

Ron stayed at his headquarters for the rest of the night, laying plans just as Doone had done for defending himself against the attacks—which would undoubtedly be launched against him commercially. He needed a fresh and trusted foreman, contact with oil and steel companies who had escaped the full sweep of Doone's brush— These, he felt, were problems which could be best solved by appealing for State aid. In any case this was still a secondary anxiety. Nan was the real trouble. He had to find her.

He tried to trace her phone call, but since it had been on the automatic this was impossible. Regardless of the fact that it was early morning he rang up all her friends in the hope of getting a clue. All he did get were grumbles for being so inconsiderate.

Finally, when dawn had come, he gave it up for the time being. He had a shave, got into his car, then went out to breakfast. When he opened the morning paper he suddenly found the worst problem of his life lying solved before his eyes.

The headlines in themselves were enough—THREE MAGNATES DIE!

Astounded, his breakfast forgotten, he read the columns. There was a wealth of sensational detail, but the main facts which stood out were that Doone; Rolinac, the steel king; and Meadows, the oil czar, had all died during the night. Struck by the coincidence of the deaths, the police had investigated. Apparently death in each case was due to heart failure— but why had each victim a leprous white mark on his wrist? Foul play?

At any rate the police were anxious to trace a veiled woman with a Scotch terrier whom Officer 796 had followed from the oil king's residence to Newingham village outskirts, then he'd lost sight of her in the mists...

"Nan!" Ron whispered stupidly. "It must be her–with Bouncer. But what in God's name has she been up to...?"

The fact that his chief enemies had been wiped out, and before that merger could be ratified, was purely the background to the much greater riddle of Nan. Newingham village? Ron set about his breakfast hurriedly, called the waitress to him and got the whereabouts of the village from her.

Ten minutes later he was heading in his car out of the city. Now and again, as he dodged in and out of the traffic, he wondered if the big blue sedan in his rear was merely taking the same road by chance. His wonder deepened into suspicion when he swept along the quiet road leading to the open country.

All the way the car followed at a respectable distance, and to dodge it was impossible if he was to find Newingham. When at last he did arrive he pulled up outside the post office. All inquiry concerning Nan drew blank.

"But of course," the postmaster added, "you might try Moorland, the house agent..."

Ron did, and by skillful pumping learned all he needed to know, even about the wilted flowers. It brought recollections of a dead rose to his mind, and with it a profound bewilderment. Something was decidedly wrong somewheres.

Jumping into his car he drove on again. About two miles down the road, Moorland had said. Or rather just off the road itself in a side lane–And immediately that blue sedan came into view once more on Ron's rear mirror. He put on speed, but couldn't shake it off, then he forgot all about it for the moment as the house he wanted loomed into view, almost isolated in fields.

Bumping and bounding his car went speeding along a rough path. As he came nearer he could see a slim figure outside the villa, playing with a dog. Suddenly she must have seen him for she stopped and looked up–

Ron put on speed, only to find he was nearly involved in a collision as the blue sedan put on a sudden spurt and swerved right across his track. He jammed on the brakes and waited grimly. Four men, each armed with revolvers, tumbled out of the blue car and came walking towards him.

"Okay, Dawlish," the leader said, through the open side window, "the ride's over. Out you get!"

Powerless to do otherwise Ron obeyed, found the gun jabbed in his ribs.

"Time to settle accounts, feller," the triggerman explained. "Somehow you managed to get Doone, then you wiped out the oil and steel men just to make yourself safe. You had a woman do it according to the police. Our orders from Doone's agents were to see where the woman was and then get the pair of you, see? That's why we followed you... And I guess that's her, eh?"

Ron glanced up in a mixture of relief and alarm as he saw Nan and Bouncer coming slowly along the dusty lane. He stared at her. Her deathly white pallor; how strange she looked...

"Better finish this guy before he warns her," one of the men said, and brought up his gun. Before Ron had the slightest chance to utter a word, savage anguish tore into his chest. It came again, with even more excruciating force.

He dropped into the dust, groaning.

"Hey Slug, I don't like this," whispered the one who'd taken aim and fired at the girl. "She don't seem to be hurt–"

"You're not aiming straight, that's why," Slug retorted. "I got this guy didn't I?" He kicked the prostrate Ron, then steadying his own revolver he fired point blank at the oncoming girl. In fact he fired twice in quick succession, and he knew he was too good a marksman to miss... but still she came on.

"Hell!" he whispered dazedly, his throat dry; then with a sudden premonition of the supernatural he dived for the car with his fellow gangsters beside him. The girl had just reached the car door as Slug jammed his foot on the accelerator and drove hell for leather down the lane towards the roadway.

Nan stared at the settling cloud of dust, then back to where Ron was weakly beckoning her.

"Nan dearest–give me a hand!"

She came nearer and looked down upon him tensely, holding Bouncer away by his collar. Ron stared up through pain-glazed eyes.

"Nan, what is it? What have I done? Why don't you help me–?"

"Oh, Ron, I dare not! Don't you understand? I dare not touch you–nor dare Bouncer. If only I'd had the teledetector on I'd have known you were coming this way and would have left–. But I never even guessed. We're outcasts, Ron. Eternal–and deadly!"

"I don't get it," he said huskily, clutching his reddened shirt front.

The story came from her in a torrent. At the end of it Ron was deathly silent, gulping for breath at intervals. Then he essayed words again.

"Looks like the Martian–trip didn't do us–much good, eh?" He gave a ghastly smile. "You became an outcast and I got death."

"No, Ron, you can't–"

"I'm a goner, Nan," he said in a whisper. "A pity, because the path is clear now that you bumped off Doone and his cronies– Nan, you've got to take it on. You must! Build up an interstellar empire. Somehow! Despite this deadly ailment of yours ... Promise–promise me you will."

"I will, somehow," she said quietly.

He relaxed. "Good. I–I thought I could count on you. And–with eternality you can make–a grand job of it. Only one thing more– A kiss! I beg of you! I can't stand this any more..."

She hesitated, then came forward and went on her knees, her face close to his.

"Let me die with that sweet memory," he muttered.

She stooped until her lips touched his. When, a moment later, she looked down on the white, cold being in the dust she realized more clearly than ever before that the future was hers alone, to mold scientifically to her will...

THE DEVOURING TIDE

The invaders had come suddenly and caught Earth unprepared. Moving at the speed of light their approach had been invisible. They came in thousands—monstrous vessels whose occupants gave no warning and issued no ultimatum. Total annihilation of Earth's inhabitants seemed to be their sole objective.

The instant they crossed the sensitive etho-electric barrier, flung in a network from the far flung outposts of the System, the Earth alarms had sounded and men and women moved instantly to their stations to handle disruptive screens, the gigantic atomic force guns, the radio-vibration barrages. Others dispersed to control hurtling armadas by remote tele-radio.

The unknowns were clearly beings of a higher mental order than Earthlings. They used weapons that drew on the ether for supply. They hurled walls of shattering vibration down upon the defenses. In places the protective screens of the Earthlings smashed and buckled. Beneath these gaps whole cities rocked and split up amid a million thunders. Tens of thousands of gallant defenders died in the onslaught. Those who did survive surged to other points to reinforce their desperately pressed comrades.

Deep down in the bowels of the earth shining armies of robots marched to the tune of the Armament Master, robots which carried an unceasing flow of material and ammunition to the battling Earthlings on the surface. If the onslaught could only be stemmed there was a chance—a slim but still a real one—that Earth might yet survive....

In a still-quiet room, buried a mile below the carnage of the surface, Lester Carr worked silently, undisturbed. Though fully aware of the danger threatening the world, it was not to his task to deal directly with it. As First Physicist to the Governing Council he had his especial duties to perform. Right now he was bending over a series of tubes and dials, in the center of which reposed a grayish looking mass not unlike flesh.

Silently a woman entered. Lester Carr did not look at her even though he was aware of her presence.

"Catalyst Seventy-X-E," he ordered, regarding the substance on the testing plate. "Quickly, please!"

It was handed to him. He held the phial over the intake valve of his strange instrument. The stuff mingled instantly with the fleshy mass. It fumed saffron yellow, emitted a choking discharge. Carr closed a petcock and looked up with a grim smile.

"It may interest you to know, Freda, that our enemies are from a planetary system which has Morcas-Eighteen as its sun."

The girl started. "But that's a colossal distance away. As far as our present day telescopes can penetrate."

"It still remains a fact," Lester Carr said. "We know the contents of MorcasEighteen, and since the planets of a particular sun take on the qualities of the primary, or parent, there can be no mistake. This piece of flesh from one of the invaders contains elements which are only applicable to Morcas-Eighteen."

"But why should they pick on Earth for such an assault?" the girl demanded angrily. "Why not Mars, or Venus, or even some of the planets nearer to their own System? What have we done?"

"Just nothing," Carr shrugged. "The only explanation is that they chose Earth because they felt our science would not be able to master them, a fact which they were perhaps uncertain about in regard to planets near their own home. Why they should travel so far afield I can't imagine–yet."

There was silence for a moment. Then with a smile Carr suddenly relaxed. The stern scientific authority of his still young face melted into affectionate lines.

"In the stress of duty one would think us strangers," he murmured. "Forgive my bruskness, dearest."

"At such times as these, Les, I forget too that we are married, certified A category, and have a perfect son designated by the Eugenics Council as Super-X-A." The girl gave a little shrug of her white-coated shoulders. "After all, duty must come first. But seriously, how do you think we will make out?"

"We've got to survive, Freda. For nearly two centuries we have built up an ordered civilization of science and progress, and the inhuman senselessness of war–even from the void–must not be allowed to destroy it." Carr clenched a lean fist and beat it vexedly on the bench.

"What beats me is the senselessness of his particular attack. Why did they pick on us? The only explanation seems to be that they were driven from their own world. And a power that can drive out master-scientists en masse must be something serious indeed. That is a solemn thought."

He turned suddenly and switched on the visiplates connected to the pick-up stations on Earth's surface. Somberly he and the girl watched the sky thick with the hurtling hordes from Morcas-eighteen, hurling forth their battering rams of scientific destruction.

"Unless I am much mistaken," Carr said at length, a touch of exultation in his voice, "we're holding our own. That new Clark-Andrews multi-dimensional ray is our salvation. A bit longer and we may definitely turn the tide–"

He turned as the door opened again. It was the Second-in-Command of the Defense Force who entered. With him came two heavily armed guards holding between them with magnetic attractors a squirming, putty-gray being whose shape utterly defied all human standards. He seemed to be composed of one jellylike body, a protuberance for a head, in which were two vast hate-filled eyes. He moved with clumsy slowness on blocky legs.

"Perfect specimen of the enemy here, Carr," the S-in-C said briefly. "Find out what you can from him and report back to headquarters."

Carr nodded and motioned the guards aside. In thirty minutes he had the brain-frequency amplifier at work on the creature and exchange of thought waves began.

"Do you come from a planet which has what we call Morcas-Eighteen for a sun?" Carr demanded, indicating the spot on a cosmic map.

The jellyhead gave grudging acknowledgment.

"Then why have you attacked us? What are you seeking? Why such a wholesale flight into the void?"

"Why not?" vibrated the sullen inquiry. "It was done before us. Ages ago, when the Black Infinity threatened to engulf Miras, our nearest neighbor, the inhabitants of that planet also fled into space seeking safety. Wisely, they avoided our planet knowing that within a few thousand years it too would be engulfed. They came to Earth, vanquished the inhabitants, lived for awhile in comfort– Then, with their scientific resources built up again after the conquest, they moved on once more. Always traveling, always trying to escape the inevitable maw of the Black Infinity."

Carr stood puzzling for a moment. "This Miras you speak of. How far away was it from you?"

"Possibly as far as Sirius is from you – that is on the side away from Earth."

"Not far from the rim of the universe, then?"

"Just so. But that rim overtook and threatened to destroy Miras. Hence the exodus. Nor was there any warning because the Black Infinity moves faster than light and hence gives no warning of its approach. Finally it will engulf all planets, even this one."

Carr asked thoughtfully. "Just how long is it, in Earthly time, since the Miras scientists vanquished the Earth?" The creature hesitated as it assimilated Carr's thoughts, then:

"It would be about the middle of your Mesozoic Era."

Carr meditated over another question as the radiophone to the surface buzzed for attention. He listened, gave a grim smile, then switched off.

"It may interest you to know, my friend, that your invasion has failed," he announced. "The news has just come through."

All the assurance and power seemed to evaporate from the man of far-away.

"For me," came his thoughts, "there is nothing left!"

And with sudden, stupefying force his center of consciousness built up to a brief anguishing concentration. Literally he destroyed his fleshly cage with the force of his own thoughts!

Carr and his wife stood astounded by the occurrence for a moment. Then Carr sighed gloomily.

"A pity he had to do that. There was so much more I wanted to ask."

"What does it matter now?" Freda cried, her eyes dancing. "We've won. We've smashed the invasion. Don't you see what it means?"

"Yes," Carr said slowly, with unwonted grimness. "I think I do." He became suddenly alert. "We'd better hurry to headquarters and get the news first hand."

The return of peace and the chance to rebuild the damage done occupied the attention of practically every scientist—except Lester Carr. In hours of duty he had, of course, to do the work assigned him by his superiors. But for him the real work began when the city synchro-buzzers announced the time for recreation.

In his own modest laboratory, adjoining his city apartment, he spent a great deal of time weighing up the things he had heard and learned from the invader with whom he had communicated.

"There's no doubt," he said one night to Freda, who had followed his investigations with never-flagging interest, "that something real and deadly is going on, way out in the Universe—something defying our telescopes because it moves faster than light can travel. It is something so remote that it would take whole generations of spacemen ever to reach it and return with a report. Those beings of Morcas-Eighteen were not flesh and blood. Their power to annihilate by thought proved that. Possibly they were a form of crystalized thought, hence able to move at a speed far in excess of light. That's the only explanation for them attacking us so suddenly and without warning."

Freda watched him for a moment. "But what does it matter?" she insisted. "The danger is over and done with."

"I don't think it is," Carr interrupted grimly. "In these past months I've spent a lot of time studying the newly found records of Atlantis and Mu, produced by the Lang Expedition of Twenty Thirty-five. You will remember that they added to earlier findings of the Twentieth Century, wherein—even that long ago—it was postulated that some cataclysm or other wiped out Atlantis and other early civilizations. The cataclysm was not one of Nature, however, but an invasion like the one we've just defeated."

"Are you sure of that?" inquired Freda.

"There are countless evidences," Carr went on restlessly. "There are samples out of the sands and ruins themselves to prove that inhabitants of another world had been present. Most of the samples, according to my tests, coincide with the elements one would expect to find from invaders inhabiting such a world as Miras must have been. And the time coincides. Our captured friend said Earth was conquered in the mid-Mesozoic Era, which was approximately the time of the Atlantis tragedy. Obviously Atlantis was submerged by attack from space and the invaders became masters over the remainder. Then the invaders moved on, farther and farther away from—the Black Infinity."

Carr's words trailed off as he lost himself in speculation.

'This Black Infinity seems to suggest a hole in space—some overwhelming force beyond science to master," he resumed. "Miras was overtaken first. More recently a planet, infinitely nearer to Earth, was abandoned for the same reason.

It requires no imagination to see that this unknown horror will finally reach here, too."

"But what is the Black Infinity?" Freda demanded.

"We don't know for certain. But we can assume that it is vastly destructive, since whole populations flee from it. There may be other invasions yet, as successively nearer systems to Earth are overwhelmed."

Carr straightened up suddenly. "We're facing danger from two sources, Freda. Future invasions by races using Earth as a stopping place–and the menace of the Black Infinity, itself. We shall have to prepare against the one and master the other. I must try and get a scientists' convention arranged."

"Dearest, wait a moment," Freda caught his arm. He turned in surprise and her voice was serious. "How long do you think it will be before this Black Infinity reaches us?"

"How can I say when I don't know what it is? As a rough guess, estimating the distances between Miras and the Morcas-Eighteen System, I'd say perhaps two hundred years. But this unknown thing may–and probably will–increase its speed. Why?"

"Just that I'm wondering what you can do about it. What can any of us about it? We've not solved eternal life. As generation follows generation–especially if no more invasions come–the peril of the Black Infinity will no longer seem to be a real menace as it does to you right now. We know of it, but it is to posterity that we must hand down the knowledge. And unfortunately peril loses its sharpness with time."

Carr frowned. "There has got to be a way to hand it on," he muttered. He reflected, pacing agitatedly up and down. "And I'll find the way somehow," he said finally. "Now I must go."

The governing council, however, refused Lester Carr his application for a convention. He was listened to, purely out of courtesy, and his whole earnest speech was recorded–but that was all. Politely but firmly the council made clear to him that he was chasing rainbows.

At first he was bitter, disconsolate. Then new ideas took hold of him. For months he worked in secret. Then, one day, he returned home with his son from the State-creche.

Carrying him in his arms Carr motioned his wife to follow him into his laboratory. For the first time she saw the machine on which he had spent so much time and energy.

"This," he said eagerly, settling the child down, "is a special improvement on the Telepath we have at the laboratory–the one with which I communicated with that invader. You see, Freda, study has shown me that it is actually the particular qualities of a certain brain which produces genius, the ability of the brain that is to adapt itself uniquely to the incessant thoughts flowing in from space."

"Space!" Freda ejaculated, astonished.

Carr nodded. "Jeans of long ago referred to a mathematical God. He also referred to space itself being a mathematical abstraction. Later scientists in our own time have averred that space, if not pure thought itself, is certainly close to it. Therefore our brains simply become the transformers by which these inflowing thought waves are transformed into activities of greater or lesser intellectual power, according to the brain which receives them."

Freda nodded slowly, pondering.

"Those brains better suited than others become geniuses for that reason." Carr finished. "Such a brain has Richard here. Our Richard!" he went on proudly, rubbing the boy's curly hair. "By ordinary standards alone–according to his State grade-card–he would grow up into an extremely clever man. But I intend to make him a superman–one who will be able to carry the vast scientific responsibility which will one day be his!"

Freda's voice revealed anxiety for the first time.

"Les, just what are you going to do?"

"Use the device you see here. This machine of mine will stimulate Richard's brain with extra energy every time he is allowed to be with us at vacation period. Thus, even as a battery is sharp when freshly charged, so will his brain assimilate State lessons with consummate ease, as well as absorbing the new, untold thoughts from the void itself. He will realize where he fits in the great pattern of mortal evolution. I shall teach him what I wish him to know during the vacation periods, and I believe he will understand and retain all that I shall impress on him, thinking about those things until next vacation time comes round."

Carr stopped talking and placed the leather helmet of the device on the child's head, then stood back to survey it critically. Freda bit her lip anxiously, for the first time wavering in her trust of her husband's scientific skill. A thousand foolish yet forgivable thoughts welled in her mother's soul. They reached an agony of apprehension when Carr closed a switch dispassionately and listened attentively to the humming of the small engines embodied in the machine.

To Freda's intense relief Richard went on playing unconcernedly with the tool be had picked up. Carr watched him hawkishly, glanced at a gauge, then at last switched off.

"That'll do for this time," he commented, to Freda's satisfaction. "Now let's get him out of here and start in to teach him a few simple facts. This for us is our supreme experiment–indeed our sacrifice, and for it generations as yet unborn may have cause to be devoutly thankful. Come on."

Weeks passed into months–and months into years, but Lester Can never once let up in his extraordinary experiment. By carefully graduated doses, timed to match the boy's age, he instilled into the young, razor-keen brain the whole story of the invasion from Morcas-Eighteen, together with the threat of the Black Infinity. Richard Carr absorbed it all silently, then discussed it. At the age of ten he had the wits of a fully-grown, clever man.

At twenty Richard Carr was certificated as Double Grade-A, a degree of brilliance usually assigned only to those who were acknowledge masters of one or many sciences. At twenty-five he reached the sacrosanct region of Chairman to the Supreme Scientific Council. It seemed inevitable that he would finally become the elected ruler of the new generation.

Lester Carr had every reason to feel proud of his experiment, and indeed Freda too. They felt content now to stay in the background and watch full fruition—but this was denied them. A fault on the Tenth Traffic Parallel hurled the pair of them to death one summer evening. When he heard the news Richard Carr realized that he was alone in the world, the sole custodian of his father's grim warning of disaster to come.

To the surprise of everybody when it came to the Presidential nominations Richard Carr refused to stand. He pleaded important work in research and sought retirement to study out the problem wished on him by his far-seeing but much less brilliant father. Money he had aplenty from his scientific inventions.

Muriel Clegg, his one assistant, though a Grade-A student in astrophysics and mathematics, found Richard Carr an utterly complicated and rather arid being. He was emotionless, coldly precise, with a wizardry over science and its mysteries that was somehow godlike. In appearance he was handsome, and to hear him talk was to be aware of a calm, self-centered ego that was little short of exasperating. He treated the pretty brunette Muriel as a well precisioned machine, utterly blind to the admiration—slowly deepening to affection—which she had for him.

In his laboratory one evening he seemed to forget that the girl was even present and talked half to himself.

"There is only one explanation for the Black Infinity. The Universe, as we know it, began from the explosion of a gigantic primal atom, its matter rushing outwards from the central core to form the expanding universe. We, of the Universe, and all other matter in it, are the parts of the initial explosion. But outside of the Universe—and inside it, the central core from which the primal atom exploded—there is nothing. A non-space time..."

Carr stopped, meditating, and then went on. "The Universe is expanding—that is already acknowledged. But mathematics postulate that there must come a time when the inner explosion will overtake the outward expansion. That means that the inner core of non-space-time will overtake the exploded matter at colossal speed. Faster than light, therefore faster than matter itself can move. Matter itself is being engulfed by non-space-time! And this non-space-time expansion, moving with resistless, awful speed will eat through all matter until it joins the equal state of non-space-time existing outside the universe.

"Nothing," Carr finished hopelessly, "can stop it. Now we know why those scientists fled. They could no more defeat the laws of celestial mechanics than I can. Soon the others will flee the devouring tide. Betelgeuse, Sirius, Alpha Centauri. They will use Earth as a temporary haven no doubt, and vanquish us if they can. Then again they will flee as Earth itself comes into the danger line. The whole Universe must ultimately be swallowed up. It will be forced back into the state of non-space-time that existed before matter was."

Muriel Clegg stared at him, the immensity of his conception slowly filtering into her mind. At length his burning eyes sought her own.

"How did it all begin?" he whispered. "Whence came this primal atom that now threatens us with destruction because its power is less swift than the non-space-time which bore it? If it began once, it can, perhaps, begin again."

He broke off, and with characteristic suddenness said: "That will be all for now. I must see the Defense Council immediately."

Carr had little difficulty in convincing the Defense Council of coming invasion once he had outlined his theory. And sure enough it came, two months later.

As on that other distant occasion the alarm shield gave the initial warning of imminent danger. Richard Carr answered it by issuing vital instructions. Weapons, terrible indeed, devised by his brilliant mind, came into being. Then, satisfied that the invaders would get all they had asked for, he retreated to his laboratory, and took Muriel Clegg with him. Then he threw a switch that entirely enclosed the place in a shell of protective energy.

Even so the girl was somewhat fearful.

"What happens," she asked, as Carr stood brooding over a sheet of equations, "if they succeed in breaking through the barrier weapons?"

"They won't. They're not dealing with material things, but with transfigurations." Carr switched on the external screens and he and the girl stood watching fixedly as, without any sign of fire or blasting, the invading machines just vanished into thin air while trying to attack. It was an uncanny sight, as though they had been sidetracked into another dimension.

"The basic energy quanta of those ships," Carr said, "is rendered void because the mathematical postulations making them up are being canceled out. My weapons are based on the probability waves of the electron, incorporating nine dimensions."

He switched off again, pondered, and then saw the girl's eyes were upon him.

She asked a coldly logical question.

"If you've invented such a mighty barrier why surround this place with a force shield?"

"Because I'm not fool enough to expect an absolute exactitude in my mathematical barrier. I had to devise it hurriedly. It may not be an exact composite. The force shield here is to keep away all intruders. I've vital work to do."

He swung to the bench, but at the identical moment the communicator signaled sharply. He switched on. To his surprise Defense Controller Menrose's face appeared on the teleplate, and it was worried.

"Carr, they're getting through."

Carr gave an incredulous gasp. "It's impossible."

"Fact remains that they are and we've got to drop back on our normal defense weapons. God knows how we're going to hold out. You'd better figure out what's wrong, if it isn't too late."

Carr switched off, and stared perplexedly before him for a moment. Then he gave a start at a thunderous roar from outside. A titanic invading machine swept low over the city, dropped a complete salvo of incredibly destructive bombs.

Through the window Carr and the girl watched the Fifth and Sixth Traffic Parallels blow out in cascades of tumbling metal. The laboratory window shook violently in its frame.

"It means," Carr breathed, clenching this fist, "that these creatures are cleverer than I." He stared at the horde of machines pouring through the gap in the invisible screen. "They have worked out a system of counter-mathematics to destroy the barrier. That means—"

"We face destruction because of their immense intellect?" the girl asked bitterly. "That's the truth, isn't it?"

"Perhaps." Carr's lips tightened. "But this Earth is ours, and knowledge was given to me to try and save it. Somehow I am going to—at least save those worth saving. Quickly, come with me."

He pressed a button and a slide opened in the metal floor. Cold light gushed up from below. The girl followed Carr along a flight of steps to an elevator. Thence they traveled down into the bowels of the earth itself for nearly a mile. Finally they came out into an underground wilderness of science.

The girl had never been here before. She gazed round on glittering crystal-like engines, mighty coils, banks of tubes, flat platforms, vacuum globes— She swung, speechless with amazement, as Carr closed the insulated slide leading to the surface elevator.

"We're safe enough here," he said. "The force shield protects the upper laboratory, and therefore this place down here. This laboratory is essential. Its machinery is valuable."

He did not attempt to explain further there and then, however. Instead he looked at the girl with a meditative gaze.

"Muriel," he said, "in a short time the invaders will beat us. Blood and toil will be offered by our people, yes—but final destruction is inevitable except for the few. And for them only a little while until the Black Infinity comes. I begin to see that I can never save Earth. But at least I can hope to create a better world on which the survivors can start again."

The girl's expression showed that she did not understand. He went on in a dead level voice.

"Once I realized what had gone wrong out there in space—that it was the encroachment of non-space-time, I set to work to determine what created the Universe in the first place. I was led to the absolute conclusion reached by Jeans long ago—namely, it was willed into being, perhaps by a super-scientist, or just as possibly by quite an ordinary being. In a sea of non-space-time thought would produce, tangible vibrations from which matter itself would be born. A primal atom would be formed. You understand that?"

"I—I think so," the girl hesitated. "But where does it get us? How does it stop the outflowing of—"

"It doesn't. Nothing can. The Universe we know is doomed to extinction. When the inner core of non-space-time reaches the outer waste of non-space-time matter will cease to exist. But, if a Universe was created by thought back in the unimaginable past, so it can be again. By me!"

The girl was silent at that. She saw the light of intense ego burning in Carr's eyes. Already he imagined himself a god.

"I have this apparatus to finish," he concluded. "I shall complete it in time because I must. You cannot help me in its construction but you can attend to the lesser details–food, comforts, every report of the battle above our heads. I have to concentrate."

When the certainty of defeat was finally realized a call for help reached the laboring, sleepless, superhumanly active scientist. He was in the midst of the final assembly of his queer and complicated machinery when Muriel Clegg reported a weak signal from somewhere about fifty miles away, underground. She made the announcement rather uneasily, fearful of disturbing Carr's thoughts.

To her relief he nodded and hurried over to make full contact. Transmission was bad but just audible. The visiplate was out of action completely.

"Yes, yes, I know," he said curtly, after listening to the doleful recounting of events on the surface. "We're beaten–just as I expected we would be. Anytime now the victors will drive downward after us. That doesn't concern me. What does concern me is that we can leave a doomed world to them and, instead, start to make a universe of our own."

A voice squawked hysterical protests, and he paused, his face clouding as he listened.

"What kind of fools are you? I'm offering you the chance to be as gods. I am giving you the opportunity to create worlds at will–and you say such ideas usurp creation, destroy the power of the All Being who is the acknowledged artisan of the whole universe." Carr's mouth hardened. "There isn't such a being. It is a fallacy handed down through milennia. Heredity? Any man, if he be a scientific genius, can become a god. I can become a god!"

The transmitted reply became a little clearer.

"Your words are reaching us distinctly now, Carr. We are separated from you by fifty miles of solid rock. We have no tools to break our way out even if we wished. You cannot reach us, or we you–"

"I can reach you," Carr interrupted. "If I want to."

"If you want to!" echoed the voice. "'You've got to! You must devise new weapons for us and recast your mathematical barrier. The Earth is ours and we still want to defend it."

"Fools, the lot of you," Carr retorted contemptuously. "No power can save Earth now. The outflowing core of non-space-time will in any event soon annihilate it. That is what I am fighting. Oh, why are you so blind? Don't you see what I offer you? The chance to create another universe out of non-space-time. I know it can be done. If you are willing to come in on this last adventure–take over a world of your own creating within this as yet unborn universe–just say the word. I will find a way for you to get here to my machinery."

There was a long silence, presumably while the views of the people were sought. Then the voice resumed.

"No, Carr, you speak of science beyond human reach. There are certain limits beyond which a man's domination may not go."

Furiously Carr snapped off the switch and stalked back to his apparatus.

"Imbeciles," he breathed hotly, fingering his massive machine. "Clods! I give them omniscience, and they prefer to fight like moles against impossible odds. Was it for this that my father made me into a genius? That I should find a way out and have none with the wit to follow me?"

"Perhaps," Muriel Clegg said slowly, "your father did not realize that you would reach so far."

He relaxed slowly, staring at her. Savagely he caught her arm.

"Do you mean by that that you mistrust me, too?"

"No, I don't mistrust you," she answered frankly. "I know you to be the greatest scientist of this day and age. But I can still remember also that you are flesh and blood like the rest of us and not the omnipotent deity you would like to think yourself. Man cannot create universes, populate them, feed them, control them."

"Equations don't lie, woman," he screeched.

"Perhaps not, but if you execute the sum total of those equations you'll have a price to pay." The girl's voice was quiet. She faced his obvious fury without flinching. "Universes are the work of God, whom all obey and few understand. You propose to defy God, and that is something I don't dare contemplate."

Carr straightened up and released her arm abruptly.

"You're as earthbound as the rest of them. You have no sense of real science. I am doing what I know to be right. I am perpetuating the glorious cause of Earthly science elsewhere, starting a universe afresh."

"For what?" Muriel asked colorlessly. "A material universe will only evolve and then it will die, as this one is doing. It will leave everything unexplained, as this one has done. We will be blotted out before we even get a chance to understand it."

The young scientist nodded in agreement.

"That is the point," he cried, trying to infuse her with something of his own dynamic fire. "If however–I–or we–create a new universe we shall start from that point and work up. So we lay the foundation for a new and mightier upward climb."

"I cannot believe it," she said seriously. "What I have learned of physics tells me that, so long as you are material, so long as matter is in existence, you are bound to operate along false laws. You cannot start a Universe where another one left off. Cosmic cyclism insists that the chain is birth, maturity, death, and nothing–not even you–can ever alter it."

"At least I shall try." Carr breathed. "Don't you see?"

She said nothing and so he turned back to his machinery. For perhaps another two hours he labored, unmindful of the girl. Then at a sudden series of vast concussions he looked up sharply.

"The invaders," Muriel said quietly. "The last screen just went blank as they smashed surface contact. I saw them attacking the outer valves. Before long they'll be down here."

Carr hurried over to her, caught her shoulders.

"Muriel, I beg of you, come with me. I know I'm right. You have been so close to me through everything. You are the only one I feel I can trust. I have come nearer to loving you than anybody else I have ever known. I'll give you—What will I not give you, if you'll come..."

She shook her head slowly. "No. I feel that when everything is added up I'll be higher up the ladder to salvation than you."

"You blind, ignorant little fool!" he exploded. "Oh, why is it my lot to be cursed with numbskulls for associates? You choose death, like those other purblind idiots. Within an hour, the invaders will be down here to destroy you—and I offer you eternal life. In any case doom is inevitable while you stay on Earth."

For a second or two he saw the shadow of a doubt in her eyes.

"I won't let you sacrifice yourself," he cried. "I need you—even if only for the possibility of mating and starting a new race on a world as yet unborn. Science demands that you come."

She gave a little gasp of alarm as his hold on her shoulders tightened suddenly. Without giving her the chance to reply he whirled her to the footplate of his giant machine. She clung to him helplessly, speechless. He gave that grim smile—that smile of rocklike assurance—and reached out to the controlling switches.

Even as he did so the noise in the outlet valves to the surface increased into terrific clangor. Then it was gone!

Blank nothingness fell upon Carr and the girl, a blankness born of the sudden blasting and total destruction of all physical attributes. He no longer held the girl. Instead neither of them had bodies at all. Nothing was present except a sense of headlong motion as the faster-than-light postulations of his strange mathematical machine hurled them headlong through the infinite.

Within seconds, as it seemed to him, he was through the narrow limits of the woefully contracted Universe—hurtled out beyond into the formless space-time minus, where no matter was, where there was naught but the primal dark.

Since thought was no longer pinned by material encumbrances Carr realized that he was free.

He thought of Muriel Clegg and the fierce compulsion behind his wordless call brought her to him.

"Free thoughts in a free space," his thoughts cried. "Nothing to hold us. To us falls the vast honor of creating a Universe. Think! Concentrate! Interlocking thought vibrations must bring matter into being. We will create the primal atom."

Convinced of his titanic authority and power, he concentrated with all the scientific knowledge at his command. He felt too the weaker impact of the girl's mind. Before them something formed out of the grayness, fashioned by thought itself impinging on non-space time.

It grew, expanded outwardm, became the trembling primal atom of a new Universe. It exploded with bewildering impact, creating of itself mighty suns and nebulae...

The thought-entity which had been Richard Carr watched intently with omnipotent eyes—than as the matter formed into the gradual birth of an Expanding Universe a strange fear tugged his mind. Memory was slipping! He was commencing to forget!

"Muriel!" he concentrated desperately. And he wondered why he felt comforted to find that she was near. "Muriel, something is wrong. We have created a Universe. When planets have cooled—no matter how long it may be— we could have gone to one of them, created a race of mighty scientists. But I am forgetting. Why? What is wrong with my reasoning? Muriel, answer me!"

His intelligence was slipping so fast he could hardly grasp her reply.

"We have created the Beginning—not a new Beginning, as you had expected. Your thoughts and mine formed this Universe—and that was only possible in non-space time. But now normal space-time has again been created, all of its laws are operative, too. And you and I are compelled to obey them. It is the eternal law of physics, Richard. All the upward climb you and I have made - all the climb through our ancestors from the primal amoeba counts for nothing. Death would have been so much easier. We would still have stood a chance. Here we have none, for we have gone back to the core of the Beginning. Here we shall remain, all knowledge stripped from us, all to be relearned as we slowly climb again."

But her words had lost meaning for Richard Carr. Ego, masterful science, the longing to be a god, the ability to create and master a Universe—they had been grand dreams, all gone. Muriel had gone, too, whirled back into a remote primality.

Now he had no other awareness beyond that of dull waiting. Waiting for the dawn of life when he could again begin to climb!

Like an echo from a lost infinity he seemed to remember something, a text had it not been?

No Other Gods Before Me!

But the rest was blotted out in the unknown.

WANDERER OF TIME

Professor Hardwick once delivered a learned lecture to a group of earnest students.

"Time does not exist in actual fact," Professor Hardwick had said. "It is simply the term science applies to a condition of space which it does not fully comprehend. We know that there has been a Past, and can prove it; we also know that there is a Future, but we cannot prove it. Therein lies the need for the term 'Time,' in order that an insurmountable difficulty may become resolved into common understanding."

This excerpt from his paper—a pedantic observation without doubt—had prompted Blake Carson, spare-time dabbler in physics, to think further. Much further. He had heard Hardwick make that statement five years ago. Now Hardwick was dead, but every observation he had ever made, every treatise he bad written, had been absorbed to the full by the young physicist. Between the ages of twenty-five and thirty he had plowed through the deeper works of Einstein, Eddington, and Jeans to boot.

"Time," Blake Carson observed, to his little laboratory, when the five years had gone by, "definitely does not exist! It is a concept engendered by the limitations of a physical body. And a physical body, according to Eddington and Jeans, is the outward manifestation of thought itself. Change the thought and you change the body in like proportion. You believe you know the past. So adjust your mind to the situation and there is no reason why you shouldn't know the future."

Two years later he added an amendment.

"Time is a circle, in which thought itself and all its creations go in an everlasting cycle, repeating the process without end. Therefore, if we have in a remote past done the same things we are doing now, it is logical to assume that some hangover of memory may be left behind—a hangover from the past which, from the present standpoint, will be in the future, so far back is it in the time circle.

"The medium for thought is the brain. Therefore, any hangover must be in the brain. Find that, and you have the key to future time. All you will actually do will be to awake a memory of the remote past."

From this conception there sprouted in Blake Carson's laboratory a complicated mass of apparatus contrived from hard-earned savings and erected in spare time. Again and again he built and rebuilt, tested and experimented, finally got assistance from two other young men with ideas similar to his own.

They did not fully understand his theory but his enthusiasm certainly impressed them.

At last he had things exactly as he wanted them, summoned his two friends one Saturday evening and waved a hand to his apparatus.

Dick Glenbury was shock-haired, ruddy-faced, and blue-eyed—a man of impulses, honesty, and dependable concentration. Hart Cranshaw was the exact opposite—sallow-skinned, always unruffled, black-haired. A brilliant physicist, confirmed cynic, with only his great intelligence to save him from being a complete boor.

"Boys, I have it," Blake Carson declared with enthusiasm, gray eyes gleaming. "You know my theory regarding the hangover. This"—he motioned to the apparatus—"is the Probe."

"You don't mean you intend to use all this stuff on your brain to probe for the right spot, do you?" Dick Glenbury demanded.

"That is the idea, yes."

"When you've done this, what then?" Cranshaw asked, sticking to the practical side, as usual.

"Tell you better when I know something," Carson grinned. "Right now I want you to follow out instructions."

He seated himself in the chair immediately under the wilderness of odd-looking lenses, lamps, and tubes. Following directions Glenbury busied himself with the switchboard. One projector gave forth a violet ray that enveloped Blake Carson's head completely.

Opposite him, so he could see it clearly, a squared and numbered screen came into life and gave a perfect silhouette, X-ray wise, of his skull. It differed only from X-ray in that the convolutions of the brain were clearly shown more vividly than any other part.

"There," Carson gasped abruptly. "Look in Section Nine, Square Five. There's a black oval mark—a blind spot. No registration at all. That is a hangover."

He pressed a switch on the chair arm.

"Taking a photograph," he explained. Then giving the order to cut off the entire apparatus, he got to his feet. Within a few minutes the self-developing tank produced a finished print. He handed it round in obvious delight.

"So what?" Cranshaw growled, his sallow face mystified. "Now you have got a blind spot what good does it do you? All this is way outside the physics I ever learned. You still can't see the future." This last was added with some impatience.

"But I shall." Carson's voice was tense. "You notice that that blind spot is exactly where we might expect it to be? In the subconscious area. To get a clear knowledge of what the spot contains there is only one method to use."

"Yeah." Glenbury said grimly. "A surgeon should link up the blank portion with the active portion of your brain by means of a nerve. And would that be a ticklish business."

"I don't need a surgeon," Carson said. "Why a real nerve? A nerve is only a fleshly means of carrying minute electrical sensation. A small electric device can do it just as well. In other words an external mechanical nerve."

He turned aside and brought forth an object not unlike a stethoscope. At both ends were suction caps and small dry batteries. Between the caps was a length of strong cable.

"A brain gives off minute electric charges–anybody knows that," Carson resumed. "This mechanical device can accomplish the thing through the skull bone. Thereby the blind spot and normal brain area would be linked. At least that's how I figure it."

"Well, all right," Dick Glenbury said, with an uneasy glance at Hart Cranshaw. "To me it sounds like a novel way of committing suicide."

"Like suffocating in your own waste," Cranshaw agreed.

"If you weren't so fact-bound you'd see my point," Blake snorted. "Anyway, I'm going to try it."

Again he switched on his brain-reading equipment, studied the screen and the photograph for a moment, then he clamped one end of the artificial nerve device onto his skull. The other suction cup he moved indecisively about his head, positioning it by watching it on the screen. Time and again he fished round the blind spot, finally pressed the cap home.

A sensation of crawling sickness passed through him as though his body were being slowly turned inside out. His laboratory, the tense faces of Glenbury and Cranshaw misted mysteriously and were gone. Images as though reflected from disturbed water rippled through his brain.

An inchoate mass of impressions slammed suddenly into his consciousness. There were scurrying people superimposed on ragged cliffs, against which plunged foaming seas. From the cliffs there seemed to sprout the towers of an unknown, remote, incomparably beautiful city catching the light of an unseen sun. Machines–people–mists. A thundering, grinding pain...

He opened his eyes suddenly to find himself sprawled on the laboratory floor with brandy scorching his throat.

"Of all the darned, tomfool experiments," Dick Glenbury exploded. "You went out like a light after the first few minutes."

"I told you it was no use," Cranshaw snorted. "The laws of physics are against this kind of thing. Time is locked up–"

"No, Hart, it isn't." Carson stirred on the floor and rubbed his aching head. "Definitely it isn't," he insisted.

Getting to his feet he stared before him dreamily.

"I saw the future!" he whispered. "It wasn't anything clear–but it must have been the future. There was a city such as we have never imagined. Everything was cross-sectioned, like a montage. The reason for that was my own inaccuracy with the artificial nerve. Next time I'll do better."

"Next time?" Cranshaw echoed. "You're going on with this risk? It might even kill you before you're through."

"Perhaps," Carson admitted, in a quiet voice. He shrugged.

"Pioneers have often paid dearly for their discoveries. But I have a key. I'm going on, boys, until it swings wide open."

For months afterwards Blake Carson became absorbed in his experiments. He gave up his ordinary work, lived on what savings he had and went tooth and nail after his discovery.

At first he was elated by the precision and accuracy with which he could achieve results. Then as days passed both Hart Cranshaw and Dick Glenbury noticed that an odd change had come over him, for he seemed morose, afraid of letting some statement or other escape him.

"What is it, Blake?" Dick Glenbury insisted one evening, when he had arrived for the latest report on progress. "You're different. Something is on your mind. You can surely tell me, your best friend."

As Blake Carson smiled, Glenbury suddenly noticed how tired he looked.

"Which doesn't include Hart, eh?" Carson asked.

"I didn't mean that exactly. But he is a bit cold-blooded when it comes to truths. What's wrong?"

"I have discovered when I am to die," Blake Carson said soberly.

"So what? We all die sometime." Dick Glenbury stopped uneasily. There was a strange look on Blake Carson's worn face.

"Yes, we all die sometime, of course, but I shall go one month hence. On April fourteenth. And I shall die in the electric chair for first-degree murder."

Dick Glenbury stared, appalled. "What! You, a murderer? Why, it's utterly—say, that artificial nerve has gone cockeyed."

"I'm afraid not, Dick," answered Carson. "I realize now that death ends this particular phase of existence on this plane. The views of the future that I have seen refer to some other plane ways beyond this, the plane where successive deaths would ultimately carry me. With death, all association with things here is broken."

"I still don't believe murder is ahead of you," Dick Glenbury said.

"None the less I shall die as a convicted murderer," Carson went on, his voice harsh. "The man who gets me into this approaching mess and who will have the perfect alibi is—Hart Cranshaw."

"Hart? You mean he is going to commit a murder deliberately and blame you for it?"

"Without doubt. We know already that he is interested now in this invention of mine; we know too that he realizes he has a blind spot in his brain, just as everybody else has. Hart, cold-blooded and calculating, sees the value of this invention to gain power and control for himself. Stock markets, gambling speculations, history before it appears. He could even rule the world. He will steal the secret from me and rid himself of the only two men in the world who know of his villainy."

'The only two men?" repeated Glenbury. "You mean I, also, will be slain?"

"Yes." Blake Carson's voice had a far away sound.

"But this can't happen," Glenbury shouted huskily. "I'm not going to—to be murdered just to further the aims of Hart Cranshaw. Like blazes I am. You forget, Blake—forewarned is forearmed. We can defeat this." his voice became eager. "Now that we know about it, we can take steps to block him."

"No," Carson interrupted. "I've had many weeks to think this over, Dick—weeks that have nearly driven me mad as I realized the truth. The law of time is inexorable. It must happen! Don't you even yet realize that all I have seen is only an infinitely remote memory from a past time, over which moments we are passing again? All this has happened before. You will be murdered as surely as I knew you would come here tonight, and I shall die convicted of that murder."

Dick Glenbury's face had gone the color of putty. "When does it happen?"

"At exactly nine minutes after eleven tonight—here." Carson paused and gripped Glenbury's shoulders tightly. "Stars above, Dick, can't you realize how all this hurts me, how frightful it is for me to have to tell it all to you. It's only because I know you're a hundred percent that I spoke at all."

"Yes—I know." Glenbury sank weakly into a chair. For a moment or two his mind wandered. Next he found that his frozen gaze was fixed on the electric clock. It was exactly forty minutes past ten.

"At ten to eleven—in ten minutes, that is—Hart will come here," Carson resumed. "His first words will be—'Sorry I'm late, boys, but I got held up at an Extraordinary Board Meeting.' An argument will follow, then murder. Everything is clear up to the moment of my death. After that Hart is extinguished from my future. The vision of life continuing in a plane different from this one is something I have pondered pretty deeply."

Dick Glenbury did not speak, but Carson went on, musing aloud. "Suppose," Carson said, "I was to try an experiment with time? Suppose, because I possess knowledge no man has ever had so far—I were able to upset the order of the Circle. Suppose, I came back, after I have been electrocuted, to confront Hart with your murder and my wrongful execution?"

"No," Glenbury's mind was too lethargic to take things in.

"I've already told you that the body obeys the mind. Normally, at my death, I shall recreate my body in a plane removed from this one. But suppose my thoughts upon the moment of death are entirely concentrated on returning to this plane at a date one week after execution? That would be April twenty-first. I believe I might thereby return to confront Hart."

"Do you know you can do this?"

"No; but it seems logical to assume that I can. Since the future, after death, is on another plane, I cannot tell whether my plan would work or not. As I have told you, Hart ceases to be in my future time from the moment I die, unless I can change the course of Time and thereby do something unique. I guess I—"

Carson broke off as the door opened suddenly and Hart Cranshaw came in. He threw down his hat casually.

"Sorry I'm late, boys, but I got held up at an Extraordinary Board Meeting—" He broke off. "What's wrong, Dick? Feeling faint?"

Dick Glenbury did not answer. He was staring at the clock. It was exactly ten minutes to eleven.

"He's okay," Blake Carson said quietly, turning. "Just had a bit of a shock, that's all. I've been taking a look into the future, Hart, and I've discovered plenty that isn't exactly agreeable."

"Oh?" Hart Cranshaw looked thoughtful for a moment, then went on, "Matter of fact, Blake, it strikes me that I've been none too cordial towards you considering the brilliance of the thing you have achieved. I'd like to know plenty more about this invention if you'd tell me."

"Yes, so you can steal it!" Dick Glenbury shouted suddenly, leaping to his feet. "That's your intention. The future has shown that to Blake already. And you'll try and kill me in the doing. But you're not going to. By heavens, no! So Time can't be cheated, Blake? We'll see about that."

He raced for the door, but he did not reach it. Hart Cranshaw caught him by the arm and swung him back.

"What the devil are you raving about?" he snapped. "Do you mean to say I intend to murder you?"

"That is why you came here, Hart," Carson declared quietly. "Time doesn't lie, and all your bluster and pretended innocence makes not the least difference to your real intentions. You figure to do plenty with this invention of mine."

"All right, supposing I do?" Hart Cranshaw snapped, suddenly whipping an automatic from his pocket. "What are you going to do about it?"

Blake Carson shrugged. "Only what immutable law makes me do!"

"To blazes with this!" Dick Glenbury shouted suddenly. "I'm not standing here obeying immutable laws–not when my life's in danger. Hart, drop that gun!"

Hart Cranshaw only grinned frozenly. In desperation Glenbury dived for him, caught his foot in a snaking cable on the floor and collided with the physicist. Whether it was accident or design Blake Carson could not be sure at the moment, but the automatic certainly exploded.

Hart Cranshaw stood in momentary silence as Dick Glenbury slid gently to the floor and lay still. Blake Carson's eyes shifted to the clock–eleven-nine!

At length Hart Cranshaw seemed to recover himself. He held his automatic more firmly.

"Okay, Blake, you know the future, so you may as well know the rest–"

"I do," Blake Carson interrupted him. "You are going to pin this thing on me. You shot Dick deliberately."

"Not deliberately: it was an accident. It just happened to come sooner than I'd figured, that's all. With both of you out of the way what is to prevent me becoming even the master of the whole world with this gadget of yours? Nothing!" Hart Cranshaw gave a grim smile. "I planned it all out, Blake. For tonight I have a cast-iron alibi. It will be your task to prove yourself innocent of Dick Glenbury's murder."

"I won't succeed: I know that already."

Hart Cranshaw eyed him queerly. "Considering what I have done–and what I am going to do–you're taking it mighty calmly."

"Why not? Knowledge of the future makes one know what is inescapable—for both of us." Blake Carson spoke the last words significantly.

"I've checked on my future already and I know darn well I'm in for a good time," Hart Cranshaw retorted. He pondered for a moment then motioned with his gun. "I'm taking no chances on you wrecking this machinery, Blake. I'd shoot you first and alibi myself out of it afterwards, only I don't want things to get too complicated. Grab the 'phone and call the police. Confess to them what you have done."

With resigned calm Blake Carson obeyed. When he was through Hart Cranshaw nodded complacently.

"Good. Before the police arrive I'll be gone, leaving you this gun to explain away. Since I have kept my gloves on it puts me in the clear for fingerprints even though there won't be any of yours about. Just the same only you and Dick have been here together tonight. I have been elsewhere. I can prove it."

Blake Carson smiled grimly. "Then later you will pose as my sympathetic friend, will offer to look after my work while I am in custody, and save yourself by good lawyers and your cast-iron alibi. That's clever, Hart. But remember, to everything there is an appointed time!"

"Right now," Hart Cranshaw answered in his conceited assured tones, "the future looks quite rosy so far as I am concerned..."

Inevitably the law enacted every incident Blake Carson had already foreseen. Once in the hands of the police, cross-examined relentlessly, he saw all his chances of escape vanish. Carson was convicted of first-degree murder, and the Court pronounced the death sentence. The trial had proceeded in record time, as the murder was considered flagrant, and newspapers denounced Carson bitterly. To the horror of Carson's lawyer, he refused to take an appeal or resort to the usual methods of delay. Carson's attitude was fatalistic, and he could not be moved in his seeming determination to die.

In his cell Blake spent most of his time between sentence and execution brooding over the facts he had gleaned from his experiments. In the death house in prison he was certainly a model prisoner, quiet, preoccupied, just a little grim. His whole being was as a matter of fact built up into one fierce, unwavering concentration—the date of April twenty-first. Upon his mastery of elemental forces at the point of death depended his one chance of changing the law of time and confronting Hart Cranshaw with the impossible, a return from death.

Not a word of his intentions escaped him. He was unbowed on the last morning, listened to the prison chaplain's brief words of solace in stony silence, then walked the short length of dim corridor, between guards, to the fatal chamber. He sat down in the death chair with the calm of a man about to preside over a meeting.

The buckles on the straps clinked a little, disturbing him.

He hardly realized what was going on in the somber, dimly lighted place. If his mental concentration concerning April twenty-first had been strong before, now it had become fanatical. Rigid, perspiration streaming down his face with the urgency of his thoughts, he waited...

He felt it then—the thrilling, binding, racking current as it nipped his vitals, then spread and spread into an infinite snapping anguish in which the world and the universe was a brief blazing hell of dissolution...

Then things were quiet—oddly quiet...

He felt as though he were drifting in a sea without substance—floating alone. His concentration was superseded now by a dawning wonder, indeed a striving to come to grips with the weird situation in which he found himself.

He had died—his body had—he was convinced of that. But now, to break these iron bands of paralysis, that was the need!

He essayed a sudden effort and with it everything seemed to come abruptly into focus. He felt himself snap out of the void of in-between into normal—or at least mundane—surroundings. He stirred slowly. He was still alone, lying on his back on a somber, chilly plain of reddish dust. It occasioned him passing surprise that he was still dressed in the thin cotton shirt and pants of a prisoner.

A biting chill in the air went suddenly to his marrow. He shuddered as he got to his feet and looked down at himself.

"Of course. I held my clothes in thought as much as my body, so they were bound to be recreated also...

Baffled, he stared about him. Overhead the sky was violet blue and powdered with endless hosts of stars. To the right was a frowning ridge of higher ground. And everywhere, red soil. Time—an infinitely long span—had passed.

With a half cry he turned and ran breathlessly towards the ridge, scrambled up the rubbly slope quickly. At the top he paused, appalled.

A red sun, swollen to unheard-of size, was bisected by the far distant jagged horizon—a sun to whose edge the stars themselves seemed to reach. He was old now, unguessably old, his incandescent fires burned out.

"Millions of years, quintillions of years," Blake Carson whispered, sitting down with a thump on an upturned rock and staring out over the drear, somber vastness. "In heaven's name, what have I done? What have I done?"

He stared in front of him, forced himself by superhuman effort to think calmly. He had planned for one week beyond death. Instead he had landed here, at the virtual end of Earth's existence, where age was stamped on everything. It was in the scarcely moving sun which spoke of Earth's near-standstill from tidal drag. It was in the red soil, the ferrous oxide of extreme senility, the rusting of the metallic deposits in the ground itself. It was in the thin air that had turned the atmospheric heights violet-blue and made breathing a sheer agony.

And there was something else too apart from all this which Blake Carson had only just begun to realize. He could no longer see the future.

"I cheated the normal course of after-death," he mused. "I did not move to a neighboring plane there to resume a continuation of life, and neither did I move to April twenty-one as I should have done. It can only mean that at the last minute there was an unpredictable error. It is possible that the electricity from the chair upset my brain planning and shifted the focus of my thoughts so that I was hurled ahead, not one week—but to here. And with that mishap I also lost the power to visualize the future. Had I died by any other way but electricity there might not have been that mistake."

He shuddered again as a thin, ice-charged wind howled dismally out of the desolate waste and stabbed him through and through. Stung into movements, once more, he got up. Protecting his face from the brief, slashing hurricane he moved further along the ridge and gazed out over the landscape from a different vantage. And from here there was a new view. Ruins, apparently.

He began to run to keep himself warm, until the thin air flogged his lungs to bursting point. At a jog trot he moved on towards the mighty, hardly moving sun, stopped at last within the shadow of a vast, eroded hall.

It was red like everything else. Within it were the ponderous remains of dust-smothered machinery, colossi of power long disused and forgotten. He stared at them, unable to fathom their smallest meaning. His gaze traveled further—to the crumbled ruins of mighty edifices of rusting metal in the rear. Terrace upon terrace, to the violet sky. Here it seemed was a rusting monument to Man's vanished greatness, with the inexplicable and massive engines as the secret of his power...

And Man himself? Gone to other worlds? Dead in the red dust? Blake Carson shook himself fiercely at the inescapable conviction of total loneliness. Only the stars, the sun, and the wind—that awful wind, moaning now softly through the ruins, sweeping the distant corner of the horizon into a mighty cloud that blacked out the brazen glitter of the northern stars.

Blake Carson turned at last. At the far end of the ruins his eye had caught a faint gleam of reflection from the crimson sun. It shone like a diamond. Baffled, he turned and hurried towards it, found the distance was deceptive and that it was nearly two miles off. The nearer he came the more the brightness resolved itself into one of six massively thick glass domes some six feet in diameter.

In all there were eight of them dotted about a little plateau which had been scraped mainly free of rubble and stone. It resembled the floor of a crater with frowning walls of rock all round it. Mystified, Carson moved to the nearest dome and peered through.

In that moment he forgot the melancholy wind and his sense of desperate loneliness—for below was life! Teeming life! Not human life, admittedly, but at least something that moved. It took him a little while to adjust himself to the amazing thing he had discovered.

Perhaps two hundred feet below the dome, brightly lighted, was a city in miniature. It reminded him of a model city of the future he had once seen at an exposition. There were terraces, pedestrian tracks, towers, even aircraft. It was all there on an infinitely minute scale, and probably spread far under the earth out of his line of vision.

But the teeming hordes were–ants. Myriads of them. Not rushing about with the apparent aimlessness of his own time, but moving with a definable, ordered purpose. Ants in a dying world? Ants with their own city?

"Of course," he whispered, and his breath froze the glass. "Of course. The law of evolution–man to ant, and ant to bacteria. Science has always visualized that. This I could never have known about for the future I saw was not on this plane...

And Hart Cranshaw? The scheme of vengeance? It seemed a remote plan now. Down here was company–intelligent ants who, whatever they might think of him, would perhaps at least talk to him, help him...

Suddenly he beat his fists mightily on the glass, shouted hoarsely.

There was no immediate effect. He beat again, this time frenziedly, and the scurrying hordes below suddenly paused in their movement as though uncertain. Then they started to scatter madly like bits of dust blown by the wind.

"Open up!" he shouted. "Open up. I'm freezing."

He was not quite sure what happened then, but it seemed to him that he went a little mad. He had a confused, blurred notion of running to each dome in turn and battering his fists against its smooth, implacable surface.

Wind, an endless wind, had turned his blood to ice. At last he sank down on an out-jutting rock at the plateau edge, buried his head in his hands and shivered. An overpowering desire to go to sleep was upon him, but presently it passed as he became aware of new thoughts surging through his brain, mighty thoughts that were not his own.

He saw, in queer kaleidoscopic fashion, the ascent of man to supreme heights: he saw too man's gradual realization that he was upon a doomed world. He saw the thinning of the multitudes and the survival of the fittest–the slow, inexorable work of Nature as she adapted life to suit her latest need.

Like a panorama of the ages, hurdling great vistas of time, Blake Carson saw the human body change into that of the termite, of which the termite of his own time was but the progenitor, the experimental form, as it were. The termites, invested with more than human intelligence, had formed these underground cities themselves, cities replete with every scientific need and requiring but little of the dying Earth so small were they. Only underground was there safety from the dying atmosphere.

Yes, Nature had been clever in her organization and would be even cleverer when it came to the last mutation into bacteria. Indestructible, bacteria that could live in space, float to oilier worlds, to begin anew. The eternal cycle.

Carson looked up suddenly, puzzled as to why he should know all these things. At what he beheld he sprang to his feet, only to sit down again as he found his legs were numbed with cold.

There was a small army of ants quite close to him, like a black mat on the smooth red of the ground. Thought transference! That was how he had known. The truth had been forced into his mind deliberately. He realized it clearly now for there came a bombardment of mental questions, but from such a multitude of minds that they failed to make any sense.

"Shelter," he cried. "Food and warmth—that is what I want. I have come out of Time—a wanderer—and it was an accident that brought me here. You will regard me as an ancient type, therefore I am surely useful to you. If I stay out here the cold will soon kill me."

"You created your own accident, Blake Carson," came one clear wave of thought. "Had you died as the Time-law proclaimed you would have passed on to the next stage of existence, the stage apart from this one. You chose instead to try and defeat Time in order that you might enact vengeance. We, who understand Time, Space, and Life, see what your intentions were.

"You cannot have help now. It is the law of the cosmos that you must live and die by its dictates. And death such as you will experience this time will not be the normal transition from this plane to another but transition to a plane we cannot even visualize. You have forever warped the cosmic line of Time you were intended to pursue. You can never correct that warp."

Blake Carson stared, wishing he could shift his icebound limbs. He was dying even now, realized it clearly, but interest kept his mentality still alert.

"Is this hospitality?" he whispered. "Is this the scientific benevolence of an advanced age? How can you be so pitiless when you know why I sought revenge?"

"We know why, certainly, but it is trivial compared to your infinite transgression in trying to twist scientific law to your own ends. Offense against science is unforgivable, no matter what the motive. You are a throwback, Blake Carson—an outsider! Especially so to us. You never found Hart Cranshaw, the man you wanted. You never will."

Blake Carson's eyes narrowed suddenly. He noticed that as the thoughts reached him the body of ants had receded quite a distance, evidently giving up interest in him and returning to their domain. But the power of the thoughts reaching him did not diminish.

Abruptly he saw the reason for it. One termite, larger than the others, was alone on the red soil. Carson gazed at it with smoldering eyes, the innermost thoughts of the tiny thing probing his brain.

"I understand," he whispered. "Yes, I understand! Your thoughts are being bared to me. You are Hart Cranshaw. You are the Hart Cranshaw of this age. You gained your end. You stole my invention—yes, became the master of science, the lord of the Earth, just as you had planned. You found that there was a way to keep on the normal plane after each death, a way entirely successful if death did not come by electrocution. That was what shattered my plan—the electric chair.

"But you went on and on, dying and being born again with a different and yet identical body. An eternal man, mastering more and more each time!" Carson's voice had risen to a shriek. Then he calmed. "Until at last Nature changed you into an ant, made you the master of even the termite community. How little did I guess that my discovery would hand you the world. But if I have broken cosmic law, Hart Cranshaw, so have you. You have cheated your normal time action, time and again, with numberless deaths. You have stayed on this plane when you should have moved on to others. Both of us are transgressors. For you, as for me, death this time will mean the unknown."

A power that was something other than himself gave Blake Carson strength at that moment. Life surged back into his leaden limbs and he staggered to his feet.

"We have come together again, Hart, after all these quintillions of years. Remember what I said long ago? To everything there is an appointed time? Now I know why you don't want to save me."

He broke off as with sudden and fantastic speed the lone termite sped back towards the mass of his departing colleagues. Once among them, as Carson well knew, there would be no means of identification.

With this realization he forced himself into action and leaped. The movement was the last he could essay. He dropped on his face, and his hand closed round the scurrying insect. It escaped. He watched it run over the back of his hand–then frantically across his palm as he opened his fingers gently.

He had no idea how long he lay watching it–but at last it ran to the tip of his thumb. His first finger closed on his thumb suddenly–and crushed.

He found himself gazing at a black smear on thumb and finger.

He could move his hand no further. Paralysis had gripped his limbs completely. There was a deepening, crushing pain in his heart. Vision grew dim. He felt himself slipping– But with the transition to Beyond he began to realize something else. He had not cheated Time! Neither had Hart Cranshaw! They had done all this before somewhere–would do it again–endlessly, so long as Time itself should exist. Death–transition–rebirth–evolution–back again to the age of the amoeba–upwards to man–the laboratory–the electric chair...

Eternal. Immutable!

THE ULTIMATE ANALYSIS

The two scientists were arguing vehemently. Not that this was anything new. For the forty years of their academic lives from the days when they had mixed odors of test tubes together in the college laboratory, they had argued. The point of significance was that Dr. Enrod was usually proven correct. He had greater vision but less brilliance than his friend Professor Coltham.

Right now they stood in the Professor's private laboratory, an isolated low-roofed building well separated from the house. Coltham, brooding like a bird of prey over his smaller friend, jabbed an acid-stained finger at him.

"Your trouble, Enrod, is limitation!" he asserted. "You have always been the same—always ready to pull my experiments to pieces."

"For which very reason you have improved them." Enrod smiled, and remained unabashed. "Nor am I limited. My imagination, but not my inventive faculty, completely transcends yours!"

"Hmmm. Maybe."

"No doubt of it. And I'm telling you right now, Coltham, that if you go on with this latest invention of yours you are likely to stir up a scientific hornet's nest!"

"Supposing I do? Have not men stirred up hornet's nests before when finding new paths in science? Frankly, I don't think you have grasped the essentials, Enrod."

Because he was so sure of the fact, Coltham started to elucidate again.

"Several years ago Jeans worked out the space-time-matter conception in relation to mathematics. He was practically alone in his theory in those days, fifty years ago—practically alone in his belief that everything is in reality a mathematical abstraction, that the build-up of atoms, protons, neutrons, and so forth are just so many mathematical computations, sponsored perhaps by some creator who is mathematical to an infinite degree. Right?"

"I know," Enrod observed mildly. "You have told me all that."

"But you don't seem to have grasped it! I said that for twenty years I have worked on this theory of Jeans'. What is more, I have proved that he was right. Jeans himself said, and we of today admit it freely, that it is no longer possible to assess Nature from the engineering or chemical standpoint. Mathematics alone can completely analyze the Universe and its myriad forces. We can only progress with any benefit by knowing the mathematical changes in a substance that cause it to be possessed of progressive entropy. Our Universe, because of the Theory of Relativity, is finite—and yet unbounded. It is finite because geometrics limit it. It is infinite when understood through mathematics. Separate the mathematics from the geometry and then–then we shall understand the Universe for what it really is!"

Enrod shook his head. "I do not agree even now," he insisted. "To get to the root of mathematics is like–like trying to catch the east wind in a bottle. It just isn't there. It's a mental conception."

"There you have it!" Coltham boomed. "A mental conception! The intricate workings of mathematics are planted deep in our subconscious minds. Jeans said that, too. Because of this–because of our inability really to penetrate the subconscious mind–I have spent these years in devising a machine to do it for us, a machine which will analyze any known substance, organic or inorganic, down to the absolute mathematical basis."

Enrod shook his bald head impatiently. "You're still up a gum tree, Colthani! A mathematical formula can never tell us what a thing is–only how it behaves. It can only specify an object through its properties."

"If only the external mathematics of a thing–such as mass, width, depth, and so on–are analyzed, yes. But an absolute analysis can alone explain the mysteries of dimensions, the electron waves of probability, the Fitzgerald limit of light–endless things like that. If we have an exact analysis of everything that goes to make up the universe as we know it, a task which I reckon would take about ten years, we have also the key to infinity itself. The basic universe-forms needed are not numerous. Most of the things we know are off-shoots of an original formation–such as steel is a form of iron."

Enrod shrugged. "You intend to solve why things are? That it?"

Coltham pulled the cover from an instrument standing in the center of the laboratory floor. It reminded Enrod of a huge glass pear, stem downward. Inside its near-vacuum were queerly fashioned filaments, electrodes, and banks of tubes. Round the bottom edge of the globe, where its neck began, was a complete row of gray objects like the hammers of a piano. They formed a circle around the globe neck, and each one was carefully wired to lead to a matrix immediately under the strange contrivance.

"Remarkable!" Enrod said, studying it. "Only a man of your brilliance could have invented such a thing!" Then as Coltham remained proud and silent, Enrod added naively, "What is it?"

"A mathematical analyzer. It is composed of what I call metallic variants. You see those teeth round the inside of the globe neck? They all look alike, yet each one is specially prepared on its external surface to receive light or energy photons from anything placed in the matrix beneath. There are thirty metallic variants, each one capable of a different task. They analyze, in turn the mathematical outflow of whatever is in the matrix. Radiation, energy, light–all those different conditions have a mathematical sense which so far has escaped detection. Nothing on earth can be without some form of energy dissipation and, therefore, capable of analysis. Only in the absolute depths of space is it possible to find a body utterly at rest, and probably not even there.

"So, the metallic variants analyze the color, the mass, the height, the depth–everything–of whatever is in the matrix. This thirty-toned key system here"—Coltham indicated an array of tiny pipes of odd crystalline substance which looked like a baby organ—"responds to the metallic variants' vibrations and proceeds to perform the mathematical conceptions necessary to the analysis. From here the movement continues to what is really a glorified adding machine, sealed inside this massive box here. A result is finally arrived at—a one hundred percent analysis of anything. You, see?"

"Partly," Enrod mused. "How is the key system able to convert vibration into mathematics?"

"That," Coltham sighed, "is nearly as hard to explain as east wind in a bottle. I don't just know how the vibrations are converted into mathematics. I only know it is so—just as we know that an electron is somewhere within a probability wave. I know from experiment that the crystalline used in the key system is sensitive to the vibrations of the variants. Maybe it is something inherent in the alloy I have used, something to do with the mathematical basis of the metal itself. Like many scientists, I understand what the alloy does but do not know what it is. However, suppose I demonstrate?"

He threw a switch and the globe came to life. The various tubes glowed. Then as Coltham pulled a pencil out of his pocket and tossed it into the queerly fashioned matrix, clamping down the lid, the globe really jumped into activity.

He and Enrod stood watching as mystic, unexplainable ripplings of color started to play along the circle of metallic variants. Some of these saw-teeth shone vividly, others only glowed. The weird crystalline substance of the key system was shot through now with unholy light.

Dr. Enrod was convinced, as he watched, that some of the colors were not in the visible spectrum at all. He felt rather than saw them. A vague unease settled upon him. Little gusts of conception - fragments of amazing thoughts—twisted through his brain. Once he fancied he really understood the infinite calculus in its entirety for the first time. Then just as quickly the breathtaking conviction was gone.

"You feel the mathematical vibrations?" Coltham asked dryly, eyeing him.

"Is that it?" Enrod surveyed the globe intently. "Yes—I feel them."

"But they're as vague as waves of probability," Coltham sighed. "Vibrations from which the very universe was fashioned, no doubt. It is so hard to understand the functions of pure mathematics. Ah! I believe we are ready!"

He studied a dial for a moment, then shut off the power. The main mathematical machine continued working. The subsidiary calculator clicked suddenly and thrust out a sheet of stiff paper into Coltham's waiting hand. He smiled triumphantly, but Enrod blinked as he peered at it.

"Great heavens, it even analyzes the composition of the graphite and the basic constituents of the timber used for the pencil! Coltham, do you realize what this brain-child of yours is doing? It roots out elements that are not even in our Periodic Table! Look here—it says there is a mathematical percentage of Element 85. That is one of our blanks, but where does it fit into a common pencil?"

Coltham shrugged. "What did I tell you? Somewhere in the graphite–among these multitudinous other elements that go to create graphite - is Element Eighty-five. This, my doubting friend, is pure mathematical analysis! We see from this formula our common, or garden pencil, is made up of no fewer than seventy-five different elements! The graphite, timber, and paint are analyzed exactly into seventy-two elements, and the precise atomic formation and weight and mass of each is given." His eyes sparkled. "Now we see what a field is opened up. We might find it possible to go on analyzing down and down, to the end and the beginning of atomic energy itself– right into the microcosm–"

Coltham stopped, slightly astounded by the magnitude and depth of the thing he had plumbed. This was the first time he had given the machine a complete test. That it was successful there was no shadow of doubt.

"At least I am convinced now I am right," Enrod breathed. "I said before that you were playing with fire–and that was when I had only heard the theory. Since I have seen this thing in practice I–I tell you the device is dangerous! Suppose you were to put radium in the matrix, or something highly complicated such as that? Think of the vast number of interlocked equations and mathematical variants this thing would form. It might even turn into a thinking machine all on its own!"

"Absurd," Coltham smiled. "This machine of mine is simply a vastly improved version of the mechanical brains in use in various universities today for solving difficult problems too abstruse for tired human minds to grapple with. A thinking machine! Rubbish! No thinking machine can be made by man."

"But in the case I am stating it wouldn't be made by man," Enrod cried. "If mathematical vibrations are the basic form of the universe, what is to prevent a complex mass from forming their own thoughts and playing the devil with our known laws?"

"Since you put it that way, nothing," Coltham admitted. He frowned, then laughed off a momentary twinge of anxiety. "I'm a scientist, not a pessimist," he said. "Your imagination is going to trip you up one day, my friend. Here–you try the device. Anything you like."

Enrod elected to analyze his cigarette case, and he thought a few things about the man that had sold it to him for solid gold when he saw the equational formula. Thereafter he forgot his cold calculating prescience in sheer interest.

In fact both men became fascinated. They analyzed glass, chromium, sand, soil–got dizzying results that ran into almost incomprehensible equations and deep mathematics.

"We're worse than two kids," Coltham exclaimed at last. He was flushed with triumph. "But at least we've got something no scientists ever got before. Here, I figure we ought to finish off with a chunk of common iron. After all, it's the commonest element of the universe, if not the basis of the universe itself. Let's see what it's really composed of."

He tossed it into the matrix, closed the lid, and waited.

"Just what is the matrix made of?" Enrod asked, looking at it more closely.

"Tungsten alloy mainly, coated on the inside with my crystalline to facilitate the mathematical vibrations. Time's up!"

But this time there was no click from the calculator. And even when Coltham cut off the power the globe went on glowing steadily with some inner power of its own.

Coltham glanced uneasily at his friend and opened the lid of the matrix. A start shook him. Enrod gazed too, and it required all of his common sense to believe it.

The chunk of iron had vanished completely! The matrix was empty...

Fanny Reardon, star leg attraction in Maybury's Cafe chorus, was massaging a silk stocking onto her shapely limb when the door of her dressing room opened abruptly. A man with dark eyes, well dressed, and with heavily brilliantined hair, entered. He quickly locked the door behind him.

"You're a no class heel, Nick," Fanny observed pleasantly, continuing her dressing. "I know you ain't a gentleman, so I won't ask you why you didn't knock."

"Hush!"

Nick Blake came over to her and the urgency in his dark eyes made her glance at him in surprise.

"Well, what's steaming you up?" she asked. "You look as though the cops are right on your tail."

"They soon may be," he said, keeping his voice low. "I got him, Fanny–Spike Munro. He's deader than last night's kiss, and here's the turn-over." He flashed part of a bundle of notes. "Two hundred thousand!" he said eagerly. "Right out of his safe. Everything fixed, just like I told you it would be. I've planned it so that Boyd Amos will take the rap. We're getting out quick–to Florida!"

Fanny added more lipstick to her already heavily painted lips.

"And I get a hundred thousand out of it?" she asked. "You had better keep to your bargain, Nick. Now you've told me this much I could tip the cops off in double-quick time."

"Everything to be as we fixed it," Nick Blake said earnestly. "We have two hundred thousand between us and nothing to worry about–except getting married. The plane is all set to go from that field at the back of Logan's Auto Wrecking Dump. Meet me there in a half an hour. Now I've got to go. Remember–half an hour!

He gripped her plump arm in farewell, then hurried over to the door. For a moment or two, after he had slipped out, Fanny Reardon sat before the mirror with its horseshoe of globes, looking at her attractive reflection.

"One hundred thousand and Nick, a murderer, for my ball-and-chain?" she mused, "or should I take two hundred thousand and remain here to catch a better fish? And stay clear of a murder rap, too!" She fluffed her blonde hair daintily. "Mrs. Reardon's little girl wasn't born yesterday. No, sir..."

On the seventh floor of the Barlow Building, Joseph Barlow faced his Board of Directors–every one of them hand-picked and most of them having said "Yes!" to the big fellow more times than they could remember.

"Gentlemen!" Barlow got to his feet, tall and commanding. "I called you together especially to hear the result of our plans for the Grayham Dam. As all of you know–Or should know if you have kept abreast of politics–this Corporation of ours stands to receive a great impetus in building and constructional tenders if only I can become a Senator."

There was a general nodding of heads.

"I have always had to play second fiddle to 'Honest' Adam Grayham, as they call him. Were he out of the way there would be nothing to stop me." Barlow paused and cleared his throat. "To eliminate him in the usual way–by murder, if you want it plainly–would be too risky. There remains only one alternative, to discredit him. At last the chance is ours! As you are aware he has done a lot of political campaigning to get his bill passed authorizing the Grayham Dam project. Now he has managed it, and I have used my not inconsiderable influence to get the contract for it."

Barlow looked around the faces, then slammed his fist on the shiny table.

"Gentlemen, that dam will be built, but it will not, stand up to what Graybam expects. It will, as well, smash, irrevocably and utterly, his reputation! We shall not be implicated. I have things too well planned for that. Only Grayham and his faulty engineering theories will be involved. Inevitably I will become Senator Joseph Barlow in his stead. In due course, my power will increase."

The big fellow smiled at the rosy speculations racing through his mind...

In his penthouse-de-luxe, atop a towering apartment building, J. Clayton Withers stood facing another man across a broad desk. Withers himself, six feet of prosperous well-being, with the face of a prize bulldog, was immaculate as usual. But the other man, his secretary, was not so well dressed. In fact, he had only one thing in common with his boss–he was angry.

"I am not going to do it, Mr. Withers!" he declared flatly. "I've never refused to obey orders before, but this time I have a personal reason. If you corner Amalgamated Copper, as you intend, hundreds of small-time investors are going to lose every cent they've got–including my brother and several of my friends. No, I won't do it!"

J. Clayton Withers' eyes glinted in the fat encircling them.

"I cannot believe, Mason, that you are such an idiot as to prefer to go to jail just because you won't handle this negotiation in the usual way. For you will, I'll see to that!"

There was silence in the great room for a moment, the stock market tycoon grinning sardonically and Mason staring at him fixedly. At last Mason again shook his head firmly.

"No, sir, I won't do it. I am not going to encompass the ruin of innocent people. Get on with it yourself."

Withers reflected for a moment. Then, to Mason's surprise, he took an automatic from the desk drawer and leveled it.

"On second thought," he said slowly, "it will not suit my purpose to have you leave here. You can talk quite a lot before I get you clamped in jail. One word from you about Amalgamated Copper, and the game would be up. That being so I'm afraid our association has got to come to an end, rather abruptly. And, of course, I shall see to it that it is–suicide..."

Ten thousand million miles away in space a cruiser of the void moved with easy velocity. For nearly five years now it had been pursuing its leisurely trip from the vast reaches near Alpha Centauri.

Within its monstrous, radiation-proofed depths was almost an entire city, complete with every need–strange needs indeed, for the denizens of the space cruiser were as unlike Earthlings as anything imaginable.

In appearance the travelers were insectile, with massive chitinous bodies and saucer-like faceted eyes. Only the delicate way in which they handled machinery gave the clue to the high reasoning power motivating them. Of them all, Dath Rasor was the cleverest, a scientist infinitely superior to anything ever produced on Earth. What was more, Dath Rasor believed in defeating the cruel edicts of Nature if there was any possible way to do it.

Behind, he and his fellows had left a world suddenly overtaken by a poisonous gas outflow from Alpha Centauri, their sun. There had barely been time for them to get away. Now it meant another world on which to live, a conquest by force if need be.

A faraway pinprick of reflected light, third planet from a C-type dwarf star, looked promising enough through their enormously powerful telescopes. It was, obviously, a fresh and still youthful world, not very much unlike their own, and possessed, too, of an oxygen-hydrogen-nitrogen atmosphere. That was the thing. The life on it was not particularly advanced, could soon be destroyed.

Now that Dath Rasor came to inspect the little planet at this nearer distance he was clearly pleased. He spoke in his flutelike voice.

"Within a very short time, my friends, if we increase speed–possibly even before that distant world has even turned once more on its axis–we shall be within range of it. The animate life on it is very ordinary, composed apparently of hair-topped bipeds. Their greatest achievements, so far, seem to be television and air flight. They know nothing of bending space, of warping gravitation, of unlocking energy, all of which forces we can project from this cruiser. Within a few hours we can volatilize all the life there and prepare the place for our landing."

To Dath Rasor there did not seem to be anything ruthless about his plan. He regarded the life on distant Earth as a man might regard a horde of dangerous insects, as something to be stamped out in order to gain absolute security.

Dath Rasor's fellows glanced at each other with their huge eyes, nodded complacently, then looked back to the mirror. It was a lovely world, so young and promising, so worthy of the trivial expenditure of spatial energy necessary to feed the destructive projectors.

Soon, within hours perhaps, this eternal wearying journey through infinite space would be at an end...

Professor Coltham took another stiff drink poured out a second one for Enrod. Then they looked at each other over the emptied glasses.

"You went, too far." Enrod had been saying this for nearly an hour now. "I warned you, Coltham! The iron just couldn't vanish. It must have been transmuted into something else. It's–it's the law of Nature. Matter–energy. Energy–matter."

Coltham put his glass down rather unsteadily.

"I can't understand it," he muttered. "For over an hour now that machine has been working with the power off. I suppose we ought to take another look," he ventured. "Time's getting on, nearly twelve-thirty already. Come on! If we don't we'll be worrying all night. No use running away from science. Let's face it."

Resolute, thanks to the whisky, they returned to the laboratory for the third time since the iron had vanished. They stood wide-eyed and baffled. The matrix was still empty, but by now not only the globe but the entire machine was glowing weirdly. The metallic variants were flaming with inexplicable colors and vibrations, while the crystalline keys had become blurred, ethereal, in outline. It was as though part of the apparatus had veered into another dimension.

"What the devil's happened to it?" Enrod asked unsteadily–then all of a sudden he knew what had happened to it. It was as though somebody invisible started telling him, as though an omniscient being was pouring information into his dazed brain.

"It is because–" he started to say, but Coltham cut him short, clearly under the same influence. His pedantic voice boomed forth.

"Because we used basic iron! That's it! The machine did the very thing I conjectured–only I said it jestingly. It analyzed down to the edge of nothing. It analyzed the iron down and down into its final atomic, sub-atomic, sub-subatomic constituents, down into its eternally locked core. And because iron is the basic factor of the universe as we know it, the material universe anyway, the machine had there a mass of equations forming the basis of universe-stuff. I can't call it anything else."

Coltham drew a deep breath, appalled by the possibilities.

"Only one thing can come out of it–a new mathematical setup entirely! The iron has been converted into mathematics by the very mathematics which make it up, even as some elements are converted into a new element because they give off radiations which, when striking a catalyst, change them into the nature of the catalyst. A mathematical catalyst. What a discovery!"

Enrod was not impressed. Silent, doubtful, he prowled round the glowing machine. In fact he and Coltham both did. They argued the thing back and forth for over an hour...

"Coltham, you blasted fool, you've put your foot in it this time," Enrod cried, when his conclusions were complete. "In this infernal machine of yours you have spawned an equation or something which also probably existed when the universe began, out of which even the universe was possibly formed. Suppose this equation, or probability wave, or whatever it is, travels outward? Do you realize what might happen?"

"One could imagine it moving in a straight line, regardless of gravity," Coltham theorized. "In such a case it would be unlikely to hit above six or seven people. It is law that a straight line, even driven through a mass, can only hit about six individual units straight on. The rest are hit diagonally. Hence the difficulty that is experienced in hitting atoms–"

"Confound your theories, man! Don't you realize, that with the equation of iron in its makeup, this thing might attempt to wrest the mathematical setup of all iron? It could bring the world down round our ears! Everything has iron to some extent."

Enrod broke off and mopped his face. "Heavens, this is getting too much for me! This globe is alive and I'm getting out."

He swung for the door, but it was at that moment that the lambent, inexplicable fires in the globe seemed to build up into concrete form. A half material, half ethereal beam stabbed suddenly out of it, went right through the departing scientist and left a hole in him, flashed without a sound through the wall and left a perfect circle there, too.

Coltham twirled round, staring like a man face to face with Lucifer.

As for Enrod, his thoughts were suddenly beyond his control. This sudden change into a god was something he could not fathom, His brain reeled under an onslaught of crazy mathematical shufflings when the beam drove through him, a shuffling in which geometry and mathematics were interlocked. He realized he was in the grip of a mad probability, which at any second might yield to another probability and snuff him out of existence.

For a brief instant space seemed to roll out in front of his mental vision–time, space, matter and energy were there in complete mathematical unity, and he understood it! That was the odd thing. The probability changed, and with it all consciousness of his mortal entity. He winged, uncontrollably, through infinity–fell into a blank void.

Coltham, behind the machine, failed to get that ray–but he realized the danger the instant he saw Enrod fall with half his body cleanly removed. Whirling around, he snatched up the nearest chair and hurled it into the midst of the mathematical monster–and in so doing sealed his own doom.

The globe exploded and the beam vanished, though it had doubtless done plenty in its few moments of life. The mystical spawned equations seized on everything metallic around them, seized on everything that had an iron content, and that included Coltham. To his dazed eyes the walls and machinery turned pale blue under the invisible influence. He tripped and staggered, was caught up in the mad metamorphosis.

For him the mathematical probability-wave had of course a totally different position in space and time, hence his consciousness was briefly thrust into a setup different from that of Enrod. He was amidst gigantic palms and fat-boled trees, moving under a sky leaden with scudding, steamy clouds. Here and there flashed a strange bird—a pterodactyl, perhaps. He had slipped somehow into the early days of Earth!

The mathematical probability changed again as it tried to take from him the basic iron equations it needed. In consequence, Coltham's consciousness reeled in the opposite direction, the unknowably distant future.

Here, cities climbed into the skies, stood proud and herculean by the shores of an unknown sea of pure blue. There were people basking in the golden sunshine. Sand sparkled with the whiteness of salt. It was a vision of transcendent loveliness that whizzed and vanished like a lightning flash through Coltham's mind.

As it had been for Enrod, so it was for Coltham. His body was no longer with him. Even his consciousness was failing. He was the helpless tool of mathematical probability that was solely concerned with using his basic iron mathematics and discarding the rest. Somehow, the mathematics had to strike a balanced whole and so form into a complete unit, just as atoms, systems, and universes must balance.

Enrod and Coltham were gone, but the original beam from the globe, the richer for the equations it had derived, flashed on in a straight line at an angle of nearly forty-five degrees...

The devotees of Joseph Barlow never saw it coming. The big fellow had just turned toward the door in the corner of the huge boardroom when the hurtling straight-line ascension of Professor Coltham's equational beam arrived. To the industrialist's Yes-men it was the most amazing sight.

The corner of the room where Barlow was standing suddenly glowed with a magnificent display of spectrum colors. It was as though rainbows were interwoven with each other as those unfathomable transfigurations sought for the iron in their path.

Across a corner of the costly carpet, on the paneled rectangle forming the doorway and side wall loomed, in truth, the beginning and end of all mathematics—so brief, so overwhelming, it had gone before the Yes-men could grasp it. Gone indeed! The beam swept with it a great corner of the building, clean cut as though with a knife.

Barlow, stunned and incredulous, actually spun like a top in a luminescent haze. All thoughts of becoming senator, of altering the basic construction of the Grayham Dam, had gone right out of his mind. Instead he was permitted a view of himself as a mathematical integration fitting flawlessly into the pattern of the universe.

It only lasted a few seconds maybe, then he was conscious of himself again, hurtling away over New York's streets at a speed beyond comprehension. He marveled that he did not need to breathe or count his heartbeats!

Ahead of him he saw a vastly looming apartment building, then came a strange overwhelming pressure and for him the universe burst into myriad points of light...

Secretary Mason stood staring at Withers' gun as it leveled at him. He knew his life was forfeit and he was prepared to die–but instead he was treated to the most unexpected vision.

It was so incredible that he wondered, for a moment, if he were not already dead. There seemed to be no other way of accounting for this.

There were three J. Clayton Withers! Each one identical even to the clothing and the gun. Yet they were not in any way reversed as though mirrors were responsible.

Mason blinked, and at the same moment the most astounded expression settled on the tycoon's face. He caught sight of hit two images, dropped his gun–and they did likewise! There were three separate and distinct thuds on the carpet.

"What the devil!" three mouths shouted. Then J. Clayton Withers became conscious of the impossible. He was in three places simultaneously, and even more extraordinary was the fact that he was able to think, for a split second or so only, in three different brains at once, and keep each one distinct. He had been going to kill a man–he had unraveled the cosmic calculus–he could see into a future time–all at once!

Then the terrific tension gave way. He fell to the floor, utterly paralyzed, and at the same instant his twins vanished. But his body, before Mason's eyes, split into a myriad microscopic images of J. Clayton Withers and went hurtling toward the outer wall of the room. Clean through it–matter through matter! Then whatever it was had gone and the room was silent.

Mason felt life surge back to him. He gave one mighty scream and fled for the door. Tearing it open, he went down the corridor shouting with a hysteria that bordered on insanity...

Fanny Reardon arrived at Logan's Auto Dump on time to find Nick Blake impatiently awaiting her. Within ten minutes they were both in the plane, climbing rapidly over Long Island in the first lap of their trip to Florida.

"You got sense, kid," Nick Blake murmured, glancing at her as she sat beside him with her fur coat up to her chin. "We can skip to Florida until the heat's off. Don't forget that we're absolutely safe. Boyd Amos will take the rap for this lot, believe you me. Then we can celebrate right."

"Not we–me!" Fanny Reardon retorted. She turned suddenly as she spoke, her painted face grimly determined. Blake glanced down and started slightly at the sight of the automatic in her hand.

"What's the idea?" he snapped. "Don't forget that I'm flying this plane: If you try anything funny, it'll be too bad for us both!"

"You're not the only person who can pilot a plane, Nick! My main thought at the moment is that you're carrying two hundred thousand dollars, and that money can be mighty useful to me. I've had enough of you, Nick. You're a cheap, no-account murderer, and a girl's got to look to her future. If you drop in the Atlantic from twenty thousand feet up it won't improve your appearance. Any way you'll be dead by then—I'll see to that. Who's to know how you got in the sea?"

Blake laughed uneasily. "Quit clowning, can't you? You and me are too close for you to have such ideas."

He stopped as the gun stuck in his ribs.

"I want that money, Nick. Hand it out!"

Because he knew Fanny Reardon well he slowly pulled out his wallet, retaining control with his free hand.

"Serves me right for trusting a cheap dame," he sneered. "Here you—are!" He slammed up his wallet hand furiously on the last word but he missed for the simple reason that Fanny was expecting his move and had jerked her head back sharply. Her gun fired three times to make sure. Not a flicker of emotion passed over her painted features as Blake fell over the controls.

In a moment she had bundled his body onto the floor, righted the plane, then felt with her free hand through the wallet he had dropped. Her fingers ploughed gleefully through the bills.

"Another mile and I can drop him," she mused, staring through the window. "Let's see. I'm over Long Island, three thousand feet up."

She glanced about her, puzzled. There was a pale blue light outside the observation window, even inside the cabin itself. It was as though a blue searchlight had turned on somewheres.

"What is this?" she whispered, her lips suddenly dry.

As she turned in her seat she realized that for once in her hard-boiled life she was frightened. The dead body of Nick Blake was glowing, even through his clothes. Even the blood in the cabin floor flamed like phosphorous! Fanny just sat there, stunned, hardly conscious of the plane's wild lungings.

"You're a ghost!" she breathed, her eyes starting. "Mebbe there ain't such things, but you're one! Don't you dare touch me!"

Suddenly Nick Blake was no longer there. Fanny had no idea what happened to him. It seemed as though his corpse turned into a swirl of gas, and twisted like a cyclone. Then it disappeared.

She gulped, corrected the plane, stared outside. Something was wrong out there. A moment ago she had been heading over Long Island. Now there were little points of light all about her.

Stars! Stars by the million! And a beam cleaving toward them!

And even as she realized it her breath froze solid on the window. A cold such as she had never known bit through her fur coat into her very marrow. The motors went dead. Air had vanished.

Her mind, utterly untrained to science, grappled helplessly with this sudden retribution. Those stars meant nothing. Otherwise she would have known that the equational beam was streaking through the autumn night towards Pleiades, across the center of the Milky Way, slightly south of Procyon, and across the upper half of the bent rectangle of the star group Monoceros. Nor could she guess that pin-pointed in the angle of these groups, a space ship hovered.

She got to her feet, turned a slow somersault and, demoralized with terror, found herself upside down. Gravity had gone. What attraction remained was in the center of the cabin.

Air was vanishing fast. There were icicles round the airlock door where the void was sucking it out.

Fanny Reardon kicked savagely and turned right way up again. She clutched the window and stared out. There was still blueness everywhere, bathing the whole plane, coming from a source, way below behind Long Island somewhere. This was impossible, utterly ridiculous. Now that she came to look there was no Long Island—in fact, nothing recognizable at all.

Suddenly she screamed as she felt something like a white-hot shuttle hurtle back and forth through her body. At the same instant the plane vanished, its iron makeup converted. Fanny's body followed it but a brief second later. For two seconds of time the cheap, unscrupulous chorine was a goddess, able to fathom all time, space, and infinity. Then the iron in her makeup was resolved into its mathematical necessities and her entity ceased to be...

Dath Rasor looked up, with a start, from the space-mirror and sought the insectile faces of his comrades. Though they could not register much expression there was no denying their uneasiness.

"What has happened to that third world?" Rasor demanded. "Just look at it! Shattered by a V-shaped scar! Inexplicable chaos appears to be reigning. How strange! How annoying! Just when we had made all our preparations!"

He paused and turned as an alarm bell rang throughout the ship. Tue master pilot turned instantly to his instruments and gave a cry of alarm.

"Master, something has been projected from that third world! It seems to be—" the flutish voice was incredulous—"a ball of—of mathematical probabilities!"

"A what?" Dath Rasor stared. Then his tone grew sharp. "Where is it now?"

"About three million miles distant. Fortunately it is not in our direct path. We can observe it."

Immediately the scientists all turned to the scanning screens and watched in thoughtful silence as the incredibly fast ball of blue fled past them at the speed of light. Never had they seen so perfect a circle. It was flawless...

The scanning screens adjusted themselves automatically, kept the enigma in perfect focus as it fled towards the furthermost reaches of the cosmos. As it went, its speed increased even beyond that of light, seeming to show that it had no ordinary laws to govern it. The fact was doubly proved since the light waves from it were still visible, marking its course. In every way it defied understanding.

It passed through immense gravitational fields without any sign of divergence. It went through the core of the hottest stars, and only revealed that it had a sentient intelligence when it started to slow down. Nothing but intelligence could account for its stopping as there were no gravitational fields in the island emptiness where it finally elected to halt.

The Centaurian scientists looked at each other in amazement, and waited.

To gaze on the thing—about the size of Earth's moon—was to become conscious of things beyond imagination. Even to the highly sensitive minds of the superscientists it was suggestive of something supernal, of seeing the beginning and end of all space and time. Strange, puzzling thoughts passed through their minds—and faded.

Was it a world? A sun? Nothing was certain about it. It had no gravitation. It had no heat. Nor, according to the instruments, had it any light. And yet it could be seen.

Nothing of the scientists' devising, masters of the cosmos though they were, could get the slightest reaction out of the Thing. It was the greatest X in their vast experience. And to come up against the unknown in these primitive parts of the Cosmos was a severe setback to Dath Rasor.

He turned back suddenly to the instruments and went to work with grim vigor, ordering the ship to be halted so he could have absolute steadiness. He was clearly bewildered when at last his studies were at an end.

"I do not understand," he breathed. "'Out there is something that obviously started as a basic mathematical probability, has expanded outward with immense velocity and converted everything in its path into fresh mathematical balances—until now we see a complete whole, a perfect sublime unity of figures living on itself, within itself. An alien, thinking world in a universe of coarse matter and energy. It gives off energy, but absorbs none. It is the unknown quantity.

"I do not know what gave it birth. Maybe it sprang from some basic universal equation. Only centuries of evolution, even by us, would be able to explain it."

"Is it dangerous?" asked the master-navigator.

"I think not. That world is an equation—it has nothing more it needs. Basically we are all figures, but we are outside that Thing now because it has stabilized itself."

There was a long silence in the ship, then the master-navigator gravely asked another question.

"Do we continue to the third world?"

Dath Rasor shook his head.

"No! I am thinking that we may have been mistaken, that on that world there may be scientists far cleverer than we. Perhaps they created this mathematical figment to warn us to keep away. No, set the course at right angles."

Dath Rasor fell silent, looking into the scanner on that blue, distant thing. Then he closed the switch that blanked the screen. That unknown quantity was too enigmatic for material eyes even to look upon!

THE UNBROKEN CHAIN

Ugh-Wah, of the Fourth Glacial Age, did not know that the people of the future would call him a Neanderthal man. In fact he knew very little about anything except hunting, eating, sleeping, and keeping warm—until one day he suddenly began to devise more elaborate weapons for the snaring and slaying of the bigger beast which forever threatened safety. This feat gained for Ugh-Wah the reputation of being a wizard, and because of it distrust was bred among the others of his breed—a childish superstition of his powers.

Particularly when he talked in his boastful, snarling jargon of visions. He said he had seen landscapes that had upright men on them, men who went up and down in strange contrivances, who actually made use of the flaming ball that buried itself every night and was reborn every morning. To Ugh-Wali, though he barely understood what he was talking about, it was all very real—until he began to realize that he had perhaps said too much.

Distrust was all about him. Even his own mate, Gu Lak, was suspicious of him, alarmed at the strange light in his fierce, almost hidden little eyes.

Then came a day when Ugh-Wah, foraging, found himself in deadly danger. During his hunt for food he turned and shambled off, to stop abruptly and wheel round at the sound of mighty feet pounding behind him. For one short second he stood in paralyzed horror before an advancing mammoth whose tiny ruby-red eyes were sparkling with fury. Ugh-Wah wheeled and began to run across the ice-caked ground, shouting warnings at the top of his croaking voice. Behind him the mammoth screamed and trumpeted. The others of the tribe swung around at Ugh-Wah's yells and were instantly on the defensive. Then they became motionless with awe at an amazing sight.

Ugh-Wah, not ten yards in front of the mammoth, suddenly began to become transparent, even as he ran! The watchers could see the mammoth through his fading body.

In two seconds Ugh-Wah had disappeared, and at that identical moment a vast, overwhelming explosion cannonaded from the spot where he had been. The tribe fell back in screaming, disorganized terror before a blinding flash of flame and terrific concussion!

The tribe soon forgot all about Ugh-Wah, all save his mate—and she silently remembered that he had saved the lives of all in the tribe by the explosion. But how? That was where her undeveloped brain stumbled...

Clifford Delthorpe was the toughest problem the Board of Directors of Delthorpe's Bank had to contend with. Because he had inherited virtual ownership of the Bank from his father he was in effect the President of it—but what he knew about banking could have been written on his gold cuff-links. He left it all to the Directors and spent his time in and out of New York's social spots, using up the money his tight-fisted father had withheld from him. Which was why Delthorpe's Bank preferred his room to his company.

His wife Fay was just as bad—a former actress, shallow and vain, conspicuously devoid of culture. But she had the redeeming virtue of honestly admitting that she loved Cliff only for his money, a confession which did not worry him in the least. In fact nothing ever worried him—he had too much money for that. Which was the reason Fay got the shock of her dizzy life at breakfast one morning when Cliff refused to agree to her idea of a protracted, round-the-world tour.

"But why not?" she demanded, her egg-spoon in mid-air. "I thought we fixed it all up yesterday?"

Cliff looked at her thoughtfully. There was puzzled indignation on her pretty face, the prettier indeed for its morning absence of cosmetics.

"Yesterday has gone, Fay. It's what I say this morning that counts. The cruise is off. We're going to do something useful instead—build machinery!"

"What!" the girl bleated. "But—but I've ordered my outfit for the trip. Done everything! You just can't—"

"I control the money," Cliff snapped. "What I say goes! Get it through your empty head, Fay, that I'm resolved to do something with my life even if you are not. I've got work to do in the matter of straightening out humanity's problems."

Fay could not speak so she just stared blankly.

"Machinery," Cliff whispered softly, at length. "Machinery incorporating electronic power."

It was too much for Fay. She got to her feet in sudden anger.

"Look here, Cliff, I've had enough of this clowning! If you think I'm going to have a darned good holiday canceled while you drool about electrons and—and things, you're crazy! I won't—"

She broke off, her eyes widening as Cliff looked at her steadily. It was not the Cliff Delthorpe she was accustomed to knowing. That look in his gray eyes was one of mental force, shattering and omniscient, breaking down all her individual desires.

For nearly five seconds she stood in paralyzed amazement before his gaze. Then she flung herself from the room and slammed the door. Cliff relaxed a little and rubbed his dark hair in a worried manner. Going over to the sideboard he poured himself a stiff drink and meditated over his plan.

"Maybe lunacy," he mused, staring into the glass. "Grandfather Delthorpe went nuts—but figures did it for him. Maybe I've got the same complaint. Only figures that have interested me so far have been girls'."

He went to the mirror and studied himself, saw nothing unusual. At the back of his mind swirled odd little notions and visions—cities of supreme design reared against a dying sun—machinery of incredible efficiency.

Machinery! That did something to him. He went over to the writing desk and tugged pencil and paper towards him, began to draw...

In the ensuing days it was increasingly evident to Fay that something was radically wrong with Cliff. He became less and less like his normal self and went off into his curious, dictatorial–yet oddly brilliant–moods without warning.

He talked with an unquestionable accuracy about electrons, wave-packets, continuous union of mentality, time and space lines, and various other scientific matters which were utterly over Fay's head. He bought a plot of land out of town and had a concrete laboratory erected on it, to which machinery was delivered and gradually assembled.

Fay watched all this with a certain futility, tried once to get a brain specialist to see Cliff, until his deadly rage at the suggestion frightened the life out of her. From that point onwards she sought some relief from the nervous tension governing her.

She revived her ideas for a world tour and spent the time with Dick Morrison, an old flame, leaving Cliff to his own devices. Her own pleasure was far more important than this strange behavior anyhow–though she did secretly wonder what he was driving at.

Within two months Cliff had become completely absorbed by his ideas and had undergone a strange metamorphosis of character. He deserted the city apartment and normal ways of living, appointed a proxy to handle his connections with the Bank. Working alone–Bronson occasionally bringing him a fresh supply of provisions and laundry–he devised machines of various shapes and sizes, machines which bristled with tubes and coils as remarkable as they were revolutionary.

Nobody was admitted to this laboratory except Bronson, and–when she ran short of money–Fay. It was her first, and she hoped her last, visit. To her inward surprise she found Cliff in a more tractable mood than usual, a curious half and half state, but more understandable, more the man she had married. And yet there was still something mystifying about him.

Fay spoke peevishly, by way of opening. "At least I ought to have an explanation!" She gazed round on the banked machinery. "For instance, what is all this stuff for?"

"World betterment, I hope," Cliff answered. "Eventually, that is. What puzzles me is I'm not quite so sure about the whole thing as I was when I started."

"Still the same old gag," she sighed. "Why can't you be yourself and throw this junk away?"

"That's all it means to you?" he asked seriously.

"What else do you expect? World reformers are either nuts, or else a cinch for a kick in the pants."

He considered, ignoring her bitterness.

"There's a reason for all this," he muttered. "But I don't know yet what it is. I've been forced to take stock of myself recently, and I've arrived at a pretty definite conclusion. An intellectual force, somewhere, is trying to establish a contact with my mind. It may be something in the future. I've had curious visions that might apply to a time to come. Yet I'm definitely linked up with something else, and this something—far as I can tell—believes that the mental line of each individual is continuous from beginning to end of time."

Fay gazed at him, mystified.

"Don't tell me you include reincarnation among your tricks!" she burst out scornfully.

"Call it that if you like, but yours is a primitive term," Cliff answered curtly. "It would be more correct to say that a man or woman—never really dies— No, listen to me a moment! The mind, which had its first matter-manifestation in the amoeba, grows in knowledge during the course of its evolution, and during that evolution, it manifests myriads of different matter states from amoeba to future man until, at the finish that mind has so perfected itself that it doesn't need matter any longer for the purposes of expression, and so becomes pure intelligence."

"And of course, when we die, we're just playing hooky?" Fay asked cynically.

"The body dies, Fay, not the mind." Cliff's voice sounded as though he were talking to a child. "The mind lives on and expresses itself again through another matter form. That's what I mean by an unbroken chain of mentality from beginning to end. After all, many of the present day scientists are pretty convinced of the fact. Eddington, for instance, in his 'Nature of the Physical World,' refers to consciousness by saying, 'consciousness is not sharply defined, but fades in subconsciousness, and beyond that must be postulated something indefinite but yet continuous with our mental nature'."

Fay's eyes had become frankly contemptuous.

"If you aren't the world's prize sap! A multimillionaire, and you go haywire over a scientific theory! Anyhow," she went on impatiently, "it doesn't mean a thing to me, Cliff. I'm more interested in practical things, like enjoyment of money and—and a trip around the world."

She stopped and screwed up her painted brows in unaccustomed thought for a moment.

"Did you say something in the future is affecting you?" she asked slowly.

"I think so, yes."

"But how on earth can it?

"The future isn't here yet." Cliff smiled tolerantly. "It isn't here, but it exists. Past, present, and future always exist. We move along a definite course in Time—and that course is evolution. The unknown force that has every atom and every star in its appointed place has just as surely mapped out the road of Time.

"We pass along it to some ultimate stage, experiencing on the way what scientists call 'instants.' Eddington calls them 'special frames.' Just as on an ordinary train journey you'd experience different stations at different scheduled times. If you went from New York to Los Angeles, for instance, you wouldn't deny that Los Angeles would be at the end of the line, would you? That represents man's conquest over space and distance. How simple it must be to a greater power, then, to arrange the future at which we must arrive in due course."

"Heaven save us!" Fay groaned. "This gets worse! Anyway it still does not explain how the future can affect the present—can affect you."

"But it does!" Cliff insisted. "A person at the end of time has one very singular advantage—in fact two advantages. He has a profound scientific mentality for one thing, and for another he is able to recapture the vibrations of a past time. Even today we admit the possibility of being able to trap light from a past time, but we haven't the necessary mental development to work it out.

"Everything that is seen, or experienced is caused by the activity of electrons and dissipation of energy, all of which is distributed somewhere in the Universe and can, by machinery complicated and intricate enough, be recalled and refitted into place.

"If I had that power I might be able to see my past selves stretching away right down through history. Unfortunately I have only a limited brain. But wherever this force that is guiding me may be it's taught me plenty. Especially in the knowledge of how to build machinery to improve the world. I still have a lot to do."

Fay tightened her lips. Then with a helpless glance, she went out of the laboratory and into the small living room off the laboratory. She spent half an hour trying to decide what she ought to do. But the decision was taken out of her hands.

Just as she had made up her mind to leave, that living room, the laboratory, and everything attached thereto, went up in the mightiest explosion New York had known in many years...

* * *

The curiously contoured, big-pated figure moved very slightly in his chair, stretched out a lean knuckled claw of a hand and pulled a switch. A periscope screen came into life and pictured a view of the world existing outside this buried, Arctic laboratory. It was not a cheerful view, but none the less it was one to which this being, Drath Gofal, was accustomed.

Stretching away to the everlasting, brilliantly cold stars yawned ice fields, bordered to the west by a mountain range. Gofal might have imagined himself alone on the planet were it not for the fact that he knew, beyond the mountains, the last men of his race were eking out a waning existence in the slight but still noticeable warmth of a red, dying sun. Everlasting sun, even as just here there was everlasting dark.

The ceaseless struggle of tidal drag was over. Earth swung round her master with one face always towards him, wabbling only slightly on a faint libration which occasionally brought the barrier reefs of Twilight Mountains into the sunshine and melted the accumulated snow and ice to provide water for the last men.

Strange, inhospitable world! The husk of a once beautiful planet of soft winds, expansive seas, and life-giving sunshine. Only the stars seemed unchanged, and even they were misted by the presence of embryonic rings. The moon had returned to Earth, broken up.

Synthetic air, water just sufficient to maintain life by melting processes—Man might live on the sunward side for many thousands of years with such perfect science and synthetic powers at his command—save perhaps for one thing. The Ice Life.

Drath Gofal, out here in this specially constructed laboratory, erected in the first instance for quite a different purpose, was so far the only man—excepting his assistant Flan—who had seen the strange invader. Microscopic, destructive, insatiable life, spawning in the ice itself, life that in truth belonged to other barren worlds, that had been spewed on Earth in spore form when drawn by the moon's attraction in its Earthward movement Life which existed and thrived at 500 degrees below zero Centigrade—tiny organisms which digested the water content of the ice, life that would one day adapt itself to sunward-side conditions and devour everything before it unless something happened to bring sudden and extensive heat to this Arctic waste and destroy the queer, malignant bacteria in its early stages.

Drath Gofal sighed as he wrestled with the problem of defeating the invader.

"Heat or else explosive. Heat we cannot afford because we need every scrap we can manufacture both here and in the city. And explosive would certainly wreck this laboratory completely and ruin my experiments. A pity indeed that it happens to be directly overhead..."

He looked at the periscope screen again and studied the view of a star-lighted brownish area about a mile and a half in width lying immediately above this buried retreat.

"At the moment, Flan, we can do nothing," he observed. "We shall have to decide sooner or later which will have to go—this laboratory or the Ice Life." He turned and looked at Flan's face beneath its bulging head. "You followed out my orders and advised them in the city of the presence of this life?"

"Yes, Gofal—and also warned them to make no attack on it for fear of destroying us."

Like his superior, Flan was a short, big-headed being with a muscular pipe for a neck and thin arms and legs. His slightly smaller head was the sole indication of his inferior position to. Drath Gofal himself.

Drath Gofal switched the screen off at last, rose from his chair with a slight clink of metallic clothing, and walked across to the machinery jamming the main portion of the laboratory. For a time he stood musing before a sprawling mass of tubes, globes, and electrical equipment.

Presently he turned.

"I shall have to finish my work without delay," he said thoughtfully. "And you know, Flan, the more I dwell upon the ultimate possibilities of probing back along a mental lineal descent, the more I think we were wise in burying ourselves here, away from all interference, and likewise from all possible disturbances we may create in the final stages of the experiment. There may be danger." He paused gravely. "You realize that?"

"Science only gives her greatest secrets to those who are not afraid," Flan answered, unperturbed. He belonged, like Gofal, to a race schooled through ages to be absolute masters of emotion. His small but brilliant eyes surveyed the machinery.

"You have definitely proved then, Gofal, that such things as individual mental lines exist?" he asked.

"Beyond all doubt." Gofal nodded his massive bald pate. "From the dawn to the close of evolution everything is mapped out. Since it is beyond all question that simultaneity of instants exist all down an individual line, it is possible to make contact with one's past self–or more accurately the matter manifestation existing as one's past self–at any time in the past. That was why we set out to master the forces of electron waves."

"You set out," Flan corrected. "I have barely been able to follow your postulations. I realize only that your mind–my mind– every mind, has evolved from the beginning and has possessed various matter forms, which forms are changed only at the mutation named death. I understand, too, that all Time can be mentally explored. But beyond that–"

Gofal interrupted him.

"I have reason to know that at every state in the past a certain order of electron waves was in force. While it is almost impossible to discover the exact electron formations of inorganic, non-intelligent substances, it is possible by mathematics to determine the exact wave-form packets that made up any specified individual, myself for instance.

"Bear in mind, Flan, the fundamental truth that there was more organization in the world yesterday than there is today. The old-time scientists didn't know how to calculate the exact extent or disorganization in a single living being, though they did admit that any change occurring to a body, which can be treated as a single unit, can be undone. If they had known, and had built mathematical machines such as we have here, they would have been able to find the exact matter state of any unit or living person at any time in the past.

"With these machines of mine we know the exact entropy, the exact disorganization of energy, of any living object in the past. As I have said, inorganic substances do not concern us. I chose my own lineage because it is one in which I'm most interested. As you have seen, I merely placed myself in the core of these mathematical machines and allowed them to calculate, from the electronic state I now possess, exactly what organization I possessed at an earlier instant."

Gofal permitted an expression of satisfaction to spread over his face.

"To a certain extent I was successful," he went on pensively. "It is of course impossible to move physically in Time, and therefore my body remained where it is. But my mind, not being limited by any material force, returned down the lineal line, and when a particular instant of organization arose to which my mind definitely applied, I automatically became part of it. In truth, I took on a former body, and since Time is unalterable, I did exactly what I had done before at that period.

"The only difference lay in the fact that there was a mental overlap from my present knowledge. This had the effect of making me far cleverer than was normal to that past state. But as records have shown, I was clever in that past state. Therefore Time did not err.

"In my first venture I traveled back mentally to the limit of dawning Intelligence—a very early Neanderthal form. I think I was regarded as something of a wizard. I remember that my last experience there was of building extremely cunning traps for animals, despite a growing distrust among my people. Then I came back here and fixed the organization for a much more advanced age."

Gofal paused and smiled faintly at his recollections.

"I must have been a fool in the early modern period," he murmured. "I spent my time drinking strange substances that fuddled me and exchanged curious, paper sheets that gave me anything I wanted. Here, again, though, my present knowledge overlapped a little and I unwittingly changed my nature into that of a true scientist. I built machinery with which I honestly intended to better a very unhappy world. I found, though, that I was considered a lunatic. I was despised by my very small-brained wife, in spite of my vague effort to explain things and give her an underlying glimpse of my real intentions. In the end I got weary of it and came back here."

There was a pause. Flan waited attentively. Presently Gofal uttered a deep sigh.

"And yet, Flan, some of those early modern scientists had the right idea," he resumed. "I mean ideas on which our modern science is built. Many of them disbelieved in death and pointed to child prodigies in music, science, and religion as reincarnated geniuses carrying their knowledge over a mythical gulf. They pointed to so-called seers as people who knew the future, not realizing that such folk simply had a better sense of their Time-line than others. Still other people had memories of past incidents, memories of having seen certain places before. Dreams, amnesia, many things that explained the underlying truth that only our science has brought to fruition—the knowledge that real understanding begins where what was formerly called the subconscious region exists."

Gofal stopped talking and regarded his apparatus. Flan still maintained a respectful silence...

"The one thing that still remains to be mastered in mental science is memory!" Gofal said at last, clenching his fist. "I have proved that it is possible to retreat mentally and live in a former state, but that is not everything. Think, my friend, of the infinite wisdom that could be encompassed if one had the memory—the clear, vivid remembrance—of everything one had ever done! Think of the storehouse of knowledge, the multimillions of useful little things forgotten in the turmoil of progress. With a complete memory of everything I've ever done since mind began I could accomplish miracles, lay the foundation of a science that could mold the whole Universe to my desires!"

There was a certain fanatic urgency in his voice at the last words. He faced Flan's calm, inscrutable eyes.

"If you have accomplished so much, you can accomplish that," Flan told him.

"And if you can do it for yourself, you can do it for others–give our whole race a complete memory stock of knowledge. With that we can defeat—anything," he whispered. Then he frowned slightly. "Unless bringing past memory to a future state is an impossibility?'"

"Not at all," Gofal contradicted. "Mental force is outside the realm of time, space, and matter. It is a power of its own, something which cannot be described, something that is! Even to remember what one did a few moments before is proof of that. No matter how far back one remembers it creates no disturbance in the Universe. That is a plain fact. My idea, however, is to make memory crystal clear and not vague."

"But remembrance ends where the birth of an individual begins," Plan pointed out.

This observation gratified Gofal. "Exactly so, Flan, but in each matter state we have progressed somewhat. The same mind goes on with the mutation of death alone forming a blank between this physical experience and the one preceding it. That is why, if I eliminated all my matter states preceding this one and left only the mind–which is indestructible–in a state of complete disassociation, I would have a continuous record of my past in my memory now. It is only the individual presence of matter forms, each utilizing a portion of that complete memory stream, which prevents it being continuous."

"But how would you be born?" Flan demanded. "You are at variance with the law of Time, Gofal! By defeating your own physical forms in precedence to this one, you could not exist."

Gofal sighed. "My dear friend, how wrong you are! If a man is utterly blown to pieces it does not stop him being born again, does it? His mind cannot be destroyed, and even though his new body prevents him remembering what happened to his previous forms, his mind is that far advanced. His body is of no account. Indeed, it would not be there at all but for him holding its presence to be a fact mentally. If he could utterly disbelieve in it, it would not exist. Bodies only exist by the force of the mentality held over them. If then I separate the mind of all my previous entities from their matter bodies, they simply cease to be. I am not affected. Yet I shall be the possessor of an unbroken memory chain from the very dawn of intelligence."

"But the inconceivable number of preceding bodies you must have possessed!" Flan cried.

Gofal smiled. "Not so many as you think. With each succeeding body, life has lasted longer until, at our present stage with no untoward hostile influence, we live tens of thousands of years. According to the mathematical machines I have had seventeen thousand previous matter-existences, and no more. Each one ended in the mutation named death, and each one was packed with experiences that must contain valuable knowledge. Just to move back mentally and study each of these seventeen thousand existences would be impossible, for it would take all eternity and even then I would probably forget a good deal because of lack of union. But if I cut each physical attribute adrift and allow my mind full play, then I shall have the knowledge of all those existences!"

"And you can do this?"

Gofal looked at his machines thoughtfully.

"Yes, I have reason to believe I can. I have thought so from the outset of my experiments, and the presence of this Ice Life now demands that I act quickly. I've already mentioned the mastery of mind over matter and I have mentioned, too, the individual highly intelligent overlap I carry from this present state of evolution. Assuming then that the disorganization calculators are set at maximum—which is my present state—I allow them to work slowly backwards to the beginning through all my varied states. Also during this entire process, I shall hold in rigid concentration the fact that I am not held by material shackles. Thus all the matter states preceding this one will disappear. I shall indeed force them to do so by superior knowledge.

"By the time I've reached the lowest manifestation of matter, I'll have eliminated all the states of matter between that state and this present one. By that means, when I return here to take over my body again, I'll have the full knowledge of my entire mental past with no material interventions. It will be swift, Flan. Mind is incredibly rapid, infinitely faster than light. Mind takes no more time to remember an incident of a moment before than it does to remember a century. Indeed it is even possible that the two past selves I have already visited will hardly be aware of my present absence, so swiftly shall I resume contact."

"And then?" Flan asked slowly.

"Then I can do as I choose. With such knowledge I can even be rid of this body and become a pure Intellectual. In fact I believe I shall. I could do it now if I wished, but that would be of no advantage without past knowledge added to what I already possess. You, my friend, during this process, will see to it that I am kept fed, as on the other occasion."

Flan said no more, but he wished he could foresee exactly what would happen.

He felt that there was something which had not been taken into account. The machines, flawless though they were, were only mechanical, had not the human gift of foresight. Still, since Gofal saw nothing to impede him, it was not Flan's business to argue.

He watched as Gofal seated himself in the sunken chair in the heart of the mighty, incredibly intricate machines which built up past time-matter states from the basis of organization of energy.

"Remember to nourish my body at regular intervals, Flan, no matter how long I may be," Gofal instructed him. "I shall always be linked to it until I return, though I'll not be conscious of the fact."

Flan nodded silently and his tiny eyes watched as Gofal thrust in the main power switches in front of his chair.

Immediately, the same strange happenings as on that other brief journeying through mental realms became evident. Four unwavering bars of vermilion radiance poured from the whirring hearts of the profound mechanisms and bathed the motionless savant, Gofal, in steady fire.

His body became rigid—his eyes stared into vacancy.

He was temporarily a body without an active mind, a body still only visible as a body because of the conscious knowledge of its presence which Gofal still retained deep in his mentality, just as a man is still subconsciously aware of his body though he dreams.

Flan sat down and waited, his eyes glancing ever and again to the queerly fashioned clock on the wall. He tried to picture what must be happening to his master's mind—his whirlwind manifestations as he passed with unerring accuracy over his former states of matter, fitting flawlessly into position as the right states were merged by the machines. Right down through the gulf of mental time in an audacious effort to master all Time's knowledge in one mighty sweep.

Just for an instant Flan questioned if it was not tempting science too far...

True to his orders, Flan kept a steady watch over the motionless form at the machine, fed it with injections on long mechanical arms in order that he might not graze the fringe of the penetrating, mysterious rays built up by complex forces.

In the long, wearying intervals between, he studied the ever growing Ice Life, noted with alarm its tremendous increase.

"Gofal must return soon," he muttered. "If he does not we are still endangered and—"

"Gofal has returned!" a voice observed, at his elbow.

Flan swung round, found Gofal right beside him, an inscrutable smile on his wizened face. Flan shot a glance back at the machinery. He had been so lost in thought he had hardly noticed that it had ceased its activity, was rayless and silent.

"Gofal!" he cried. "You've succeeded! You've done what you expected!"

"Everything," the scientist assented calmly. "I was pre-eminently successful in my efforts. Not a single matter formation of my body remains between this one and the first crudely developed body of lowly intellect that I possessed which, for that very reason I did not trouble to destroy. I have memory as far back as I need it—a colossal storehouse of knowledge. All the myriads of undeveloped ideas, lost in individual lives, are now modeled into a composite whole. So colossal is my knowledge, Flan, I feel that this world is singularly uninviting, almost beneath the scope of my mentality."

Flan's expression changed. He noticed there was a curious, burning light in his master's eyes, a light of tremendous domination and with it a certain insufferable conceit.

"So, you wonder?" Gofal asked softly, reading Flan's mind. "You need not. You see, in detaching my mind from its previous matter bodies I absorbed something of the ego of each. That was unavoidable. In their different ways and different times they were me, and the gift of supreme memory means too a fraction of individual ego from each of those bodies. I am the only absolute, complete man which ever existed—mentally and physically.

"I can wing space, pit my knowledge against the superpowerful intelligences which dwell in the cosmos, master the deepest secrets beyond the furthest stars. In learning all that earthly existence can tell me, I have also learned that Earth is a playground for such an intelligence as I—the jumping-off place for finer glories."

For a moment Gofal paused and looked at Flan long and earnestly.

"Flan, I am leaving Earth," he stated simply. "I intend to eliminate this body of mine even as I have its predecessors—eliminate it from all concepts. It is the last body I shall have in the normal way. I want you to leave me and return to our people. If you would learn my secrets and have my knowledge, you must work for yourselves. You have seen my methods—the rest is up to you. I have fields so advanced to conquer that this is the parting of our companionship."

"But—but why must I go?" Flan asked anxiously. "If you depart, what is to stop me remaining here to study your machines? I can complete the details for my own use?"

"These machines are useless to you, Flan. They deal only in the energies relative to myself. But the records of their construction are in the city. You can learn about them from those. If you stay here you will be blown to pieces. I discovered something on this particular journey which I had not quite reckoned with before. The effect of destroying a concept of matter results in its very abrupt change into pure energy—the state from which it originally came—through the power of mentality governing it. The form of a body is definitely a mirror of the mind controlling it. A man can think himself into any physical state if he wants to. Remember the old time hypochondriacs.

"So the effect of sudden energy in place of matter produces an explosion of terrific violence. That is what will happen when I depart, what has happened in. every state in the past where I have destroyed the concept of my body. Oddly enough, I believe that on two occasions—my Neanderthal and early modern forms—my disappearance was actually of benefit to those left behind. That, however, is beside the point. Since only a body is killed and not the mind I have nothing on my conscience.

"The decision rests with you, Flan. If you are destroyed, you will live again in some other matter state. But if you live as you are, you will be able to follow out my experiments and one day, in some far realm of supreme intellect, we may meet again. Incidentally, my departure will produce sufficient destruction to smash this ice cap for a considerable distance. Energies will be released which will destroy this Ice Life menace completely. You have your choice."

Flan hesitated for a time, looked at the silent figure of the scientist who had mastered the ultimate secrets of matter and mind, had gained memory and knowledge unlimited. Quietly he turned and donned the heavy, insulated suit for wear on the surface.

"You will see me safely out of danger?" he asked.

"Of course."

They bowed to each other with the calm impartiality of their race, looked into each others' eyes for a moment, Then Flan opened the massive airlock which gave access to the ice tunnel leading to the plain above. He broke into a run as the tunnel's natural slope took him higher and higher, emerging at last through the great air-regulating vent system on the surface. No cold or thin air reached him through his suit. He turned his face towards Twilight Mountains. In his mind's eye he pictured Gofal at the periscope, watching his progress, impatiently noting the minutes passing by.

Finally Flan reached the vast pass through the range giving access to the distant city on the sunward side. Here he turned. He watched the sudden wild pounding and heaving of thousands of tons of ice, the spouting of vivid electric discharges. To his head-phones came the rumble of vast underground thunder.

He saw a huge area of water boil in the crumbled ice where the heat had melted it. And he saw something more–the utter incineration of a carpet of malignant brown Arctic Life, forever destroyed by that discharge of electric energy.

Flan's spirits rose. He imagined that supreme mind winging its way invisibly across the infinite towards the eternal stars. With a steadfast heart, the last determination of a last man to follow the only way of science, he turned towards the red-lighted city in the distance.

BLACK SATURDAY

The individual experiences of many thousands of people on that "Black Saturday", as it has since become known, have been retailed throughout the world. But there is one random experience, that of Robert Maitland and Irene Carr, which has not yet been recorded. In many ways it is typical of millions, and is therefore undistinguished. It is, however, notable in that these two ordinary people, caught in circumstances very similar to millions of others and equally mystified by them, were yet able to deduce for themselves the simple explanation of what had occurred—the explanation that eluded most of us until the scientists, with all the data they needed, presented it to the wondering world.

Think back. Recall your own bafflement, your sense of utter helplessness, your fear, and you may grant the noteworthiness of this particular experience of two people who were no better equipped than millions of their kind to realize the nature of the apparent catastrophe which had overtaken them. Yet, amid all the acclamation we have accorded the scientists, we have entirely overlooked the perseverance and good sense of those few who, like these two, refused to give way to despair until they had tried to work out the problem for themselves.

Dr. Robert Maitland lived, at that time, in a modest house in Windermere. His practice was small but full of promise: he was making a name for himself among the villagers and the rustic community of the Lake District. On the morning of July 8th he was awakened early by a telephone call. One of his patients, badly injured in a farming accident the day before, had taken a turn for the worse. In the chill of the summer dawn, Maitland listened to the high, tremulous voice of the stricken man's wife over the wire. He promised to be over right away, rubbed the sleep out of his eyes, and set about dressing hastily.

Robert Maitland was not the type that is addicted to nervous fancies. He stood five feet ten, was solidly built, and his lean, swarthy face had strength and responsibility in every line. And yet—he was seeing things. Things that, in the urgency of his dressing and with the purpose of his errand uppermost in his thoughts, did not immediately absorb his attention, yet which vaguely puzzled him.

For instance, as he brushed his thick, dark hair hurriedly before the mirror, he could have sworn that his reflection moved very slightly from side to side. A measure might have shown at least an inch of movement, as if he were swaying on his feet, though he was certain he was standing perfectly still. Then, through his bedroom window, he could see across the rolling pastureland to the distant mountains grouped about Helvellyn; and as he looked it seemed that the mountains glided slowly sideways, then drifted back into their normal position.

There were no warps in the window glass; he was sure of that. The mirror, too, was a good one. Maitland closed his eyes tightly, opened them again, and decided that he felt well enough. It must be some slight liverishness, or perhaps it was just tiredness—he wasn't as completely awake yet as he'd thought. It would soon pass...

He was, of course, unaware that millions of people all over the world were trying to account for similar manifestations at that precise moment. Nor did he realize that the world's scientists were even then busily communicating by cable and radio, seeking among themselves some clue to the peculiar phenomena they had observed.

Maitland left the house after scribbling a note to his housekeeper that he had gone on an urgent call. He hurried outside to the garage. It was getting warmer now. The Sun was struggling through the fast dispersing mists from the valleys and there was every sign that the day would be a perfect one. Then, on his way down the narrow drive leading to the garage, Maitland paused and rubbed his forehead as he stared bewildered before him.

The garage building straight ahead, with its bright green doors, was moving over to the right—soundlessly. The fence alongside it was moving, too! This time there was no mistake about it. The garage shifted at least two feet and came to a halt. At the same time the gravel drive bent suddenly, at a spot immediately in front of Maitland, so that he had to take a distinct, sharp corner to continue towards the garage doors.

Uncertain, he went forward slowly, turning sharply to the right even though he knew it was an idiotic thing to do. How foolish it was he discovered when he felt himself stumbling over the edge of the drive on to the flower bed at the side—yet apparently he was still on the gravel pathway. Abruptly he realized that he was faced with the impossible. He seemed to be treading on something he could see only two feet away from him, yet he couldn't feel the thing his eyes told him he was treading on. Then, even as he wrestled silently with the riddle, the garage and the drive moved back without a sound into their accustomed position—and Maitland stared open-mouthed, conscious of the fact that he was actually standing in the soil of the flower bed two feet away from the drive.

Delusions? Incipient insanity? He considered both possibilities with a cold, professional detachment, but neither seemed to fit. This was something new, vitally different—and as yet beyond explanation. He stepped back gingerly on to the drive, found it solid enough, and went on to open the garage doors. To his relief, everything remained apparently normal as he backed the car out. He left it with the engine ticking over as he closed the doors. Then he clambered back into the driving seat and swerved out on to the road.

To the home of his patient was some twenty miles journey along valley roads, between lofty hills and through quaint old villages. He drove swiftly, but not so swiftly that he could not admire the beauty of the countryside as he went. The Sun now was high above the hills, blazing down with gathering heat, picturing itself in a myriad microscopic reflections from the dew-soaked grass and flowers bordering the road. As he drove on, Maitland forgot his strange visual aberration–until he was cruelly reminded of it.

He had climbed out of the depths of the valley where his home lay. To his right were towering hills with scrubby fields nestling at their bases; to his left was a smooth panorama stretching for fifteen miles across pastureland, tarns, and lush valley sides. Such was the aspect when the narrow road he was traversing bent suddenly, directly ahead of him–not normally, but as he approached it. Simultaneously, the grass bank at the side of the road shifted to accommodate the bend.

Maitland put on the brakes and came to a stop. He knew perfectly well that this road did not bend ahead of him: it went straight on towards Wilmington village. The only curve in it at all was a slight one about half a mile further on, where stood a lonely telephone box. If he went round this pseudo-curve now, he might run over the edge of the road and down the grass slope. No sense in risking that.

"Something's up!" he muttered, convinced at last that it was not his eyes nor his health that was at fault, but that something in the nature of a mirage–or a series of them–must have occurred in this locality; though what could have caused such a thing was beyond him. Finally, he got out of the car with the intention of studying this particular mirage more closely. But he took only three strides forward before he stopped, tottering dizzily in the middle of the road.

In that moment he was frightened, really scared, as he had never been before. For all of a sudden everything about him seemed to have gone completely crazy. The whole landscape as far as lie could see was shifting violently. The fifteen-miles stretch of country before him was sweeping sideways at diabolical speed–shearing off to the west as a towering wall of blackness appeared to race in from the east, moving everything before it!

Maitland just stood and stared, petrified. There was no sound as the amazing thing occurred; only the titanic shadow which raced towards him with the speed of a total eclipse. Within a few seconds it passed over him, and the bent road ahead was blotted from sight. He stood, now, drenched in darkness, feeling no other sensation but a supreme dread.

It was several seconds before he could recover himself sufficiently to move, and then he began to retrace his steps slowly and cautiously towards the car, hands outstretched gropingly before him. Not a thing was visible–except the Sun, shining high in a sky still strangely blue! Shining, yet failing to light anything...

Feeling his way forward, he came up against the bonnet of the car and clung to it gratefully. He couldn't see even the dimmest outline of the car itself.

He stood and gazed up at the Sun, thankful that it, at least, held to normalcy but this relief was soon denied. One moment it was there in the dark blue sky; the next, it had started to sink towards the western horizon with incredible speed. It dropped like a meteor, vanished in the all-enveloping blackness that formed the limits of the landscape, and was gone.

Now it was utterly dark. Dreadfully, horribly dark...

There was something wrong out there in the depths of space; something so incredibly strange that the scientists who tried to examine the mystery found their accumulated centuries of knowledge faltering. It had begun with the amazing antics of the stars neighboring on the Milky Way. Fixed apparently for eternities of time in their courses, arranged much as the ancients had seen them when they stared up at them uncomprehending, they had now completely changed position—and in some cases disappeared entirely. Sagittarius, Hercules, Antares, Cepheus—they were visibly shifting across the wastes of heaven, moving at such an unthinkable velocity that the minds of the watching astronomers reeled, used though they were to cosmic speeds. And the Milky Way itself was shifting, bearing towards the westernmost limb of the sky.

The amazing part of the phenomenon, apart from its very occurrence, was the suddenness with which it had developed. On the night of July 7th the world's observatories had noticed nothing unusual. But on the 8th, between the hours of midnight and dawn, these fantastic perambulations of the stars were only too evident. Though it just couldn't be, because it shattered every basic law of astronomy. Yet it was... And from the space which the stars had deserted gleamed new and unknown constellations, hosts of heaven that made complete chaos of the world's star-maps.

The astronomers immediately got in touch with one another and discussed the problem. All had to admit themselves baffled. But, hesitating to make the same admission to their respective governments, they agreed to make no announcement of their startling observations until they had been able to study the phenomenon further and consider the enigma in the light of additional data. Given time, they agreed, they might find something to account for it. And that is where they made their great mistake.

Earth, in her majestic million-miles-a-minute sweep through the universe, was moving irresistibly towards that part of the heavens whose aspects had changed so mysteriously. And, although at that time the fact could not be detected, the disturbance—the Fault—was also moving towards Earth at a similar speed. So the whole of Earth's peoples had been caught unaware by the Fault.

The human mind, psychologists tell us, can absorb the most violent of shocks and still function. But it was a long time before Maitland found he could think intelligently, without letting blind panic scatter his half-formed thoughts. As he struggled to banish his primitive fears he searched the blackness around him, still clinging to the car bonnet, his only link with reality.

Here on the ground the darkness was absolute, and he could not discern the slightest hint of anything. But up in the sky from which the Sun had streaked, minutes before, there were now myriads of stars! To Maitland, who had no precise astronomical knowledge, these stars looked normal enough; but an expert would have noticed at once that not many of them were familiar and that the few recognizable constellations were far away from their customary positions.

Night, when it should be 9 a.m.? A Sun that disappeared from the sky in a flash? This was a problem beyond all understanding. Yet Maitland knew the elementary fact that the sudden shifting of such a vast body as the Sun should cause cataclysmic disturbances, perhaps throw Earth right out of its orbit. And yet everything was quite steady, without even the suggestion of a tremor. This point resolved, he felt a little better. He was still alive, with his feet on solid ground. But he was submerged in the inexplicable–

He stopped suddenly, listening. There were sounds ahead of him. Uneasy feet shambling over the gravel of the road.

"Hullo there!" he called.

"Hullo!" It was a girl's voice that answered. It was shaken, yet somehow filled with unquenchable courage.

"I'm here." Maitland shouted. "Come towards my voice."

The halting steps advanced again, but nothing came out of the darkness. That was the queer thing. Though there were stars overhead, Earth lay in an abyss from which every spark of light had gone. Maitland groped with both hands as the footsteps came nearer.

"Thank heaven I've–found somebody," the girl faltered, close by his ear. "I was just wondering what to do. What's–what's happened?"

"You're asking me!" he laughed. "I'm as bewildered–and probably as scared–as you. I–er–I'm Dr. Maitland, of Windermere," he said as the girl's outstretched hand gripped his arm.

"I'm Irene Carr." They clasped hands in the darkness. "This is the last day of my holiday–Last Day, indeed! I was on a hike to Rydal Water when–it–happened. The–the Sun's gone out, hasn't it? That's what it must mean! I know scientists have said something like this would happen one day."

"Yes, but not like this!" Maitland protested. "That must be a slow process, over millions of years. This is something different–and quite sudden! We had no warning..."

They were silent, oppressed by the unfathomable. Maitland found himself collected enough, now, to wonder with intense curiosity what the girl looked like. He was intrigued by her voice: it was slow and mellow with a slight Midlands accent, and he knew instinctively that she was young and possibly attractive. If only he could see.

"I know!" he said suddenly, and felt in his pocket for his cigarette lighter. He flicked it, but the flint made no sparks. Then he gave a yelp as, in feeling round the wick, he burned his fingers in invisible flame.

"It is working, then?" Irene Carr whispered in wonder, when he explained what had happened. "Yet we can't see it... Do you suppose we've–gone blind?"

"With the stars visible up there?"

"I hadn't noticed–" She gave a little gasp of surprise. "Yes, there are stars–billions of them. But no Sun–"

"And yet..." Maitland drew a deep breath and considered. "And yet," he went on, awed, "I can feel the Sun's heat on the back of my neck. Just as though it's still there."

The girl was silent as she evidently checked up on his extraordinary finding. He didn't know whether to believe it himself until she said simply:

"You're right. There is heat. I can feel it, too, on the backs of my hands. Yet there's no Sun!"

It struck Maitland what an impossible conversation they were keeping up. At the back of his mind, too, was the remembrance of a man who lay on a bed in the dark some ten miles away.

"I wonder if I can drive the car?" he said abruptly. "Let's see what we can do. There is a car here, you know!" He thumped the bonnet with his fist.

"I'll take your word for it," the girl answered, still trying to sound calm.

Maitland took her arm and they moved cautiously together over the rough surface of the roadway, felt their way round to the car door and clambered inside. Here, with the roof of the car shutting out the stars above, the darkness was crushing; it wasn't even possible to see the outlines of the windows. But by stooping they could see part of the starry sky through the glass, and Maitland thought he caught a brief glimpse of the girl's head silhouetted against the stars, though the outline was blurred and unreal. He pressed the self-starter, and the engine throbbed immediately—a good, wholesome sound in a world that no longer made sense. Then he switched on the headlamp, but not the remotest suggestion of light appeared.

"No good." He switched off. "Can't drive in this."

They both sat in silence for a while, listening to each other's breathing.

"You know," the girl said presently, "it's funny. I've read stories where this sort of thing happens, and everything turns out all right. But when it happens to you, when everything you've known and trusted lets you down and leaves you blind and bewildered, you just don't know what to do. I suppose," she went on musingly, her voice steadier as she got to grips with the problem, "that there is an answer?"

"A scientist might have one," Maitland suggested. "I'm not a scientist; I'm a doctor."

"I'm a school teacher... But, look, we've both got a fair degree of intelligence. We can reason this thing out, can't we?"

Maitland didn't answer. Thoughts were hurrying through his mind. Memory was at work, piecing together the incredible events of the morning. The mirror reflection that trembled; the garage that shifted position; the landscape that had been swept sideways by an advancing wall of darkness...

"All right, Miss Carr. We –"

"I'd rather you called me Irene. After all, we're in this together."

"Irene it is, then—and mine's Bob. As you say, here we are, two people without any specialized knowledge, but familiar with rudimentary facts. You will be especially, as a teacher. Now, if the Sun had really plunged into the deeper universe as it appeared to do, the Earth and all neighboring planets would have been wiped out in the terrific gravitational change. But that hasn't happened. We are quite safe and undisturbed; the world still moves in its proper orbit. And a means that the Sun's dive into obscurity was a—a delusion."

"Yes," the girl said, pondering. "Yes, that's right."

"On top of that," he went on, "we can feel the heat of the Sun just as if it were still there. In fact, in this car it is getting uncomfortably warm, and only sunshine–or, rather, heat–can explain it. That shows that the Sun is still there, although we cannot see it. If it were something that had destroyed the Sun utterly, its light and heat would be gone and the Earth would grow cold as its stored warmth leaked out into space. That, again, is not happening. It is night, but as hot as any July day should be."

"And down here, on the Earth's surface," Irene supplemented, "no light whatever will function. And the Sun went out of sight after light failed down here."

They considered this aspect of the problem for a while in silence. Then Maitland spoke again, his voice vibrant with discovery.

"Doesn't that seem to suggest something which first involved the Earth, and the Sun afterwards? Supposing that idea is right: what can we deduce from it? We know that what will bend visible light will not bend heat. Remember the old college experiment? A prism of glass will bend light out of its normally straight path, but that same prism is opaque to heat, involving a totally different set of circumstances. To refract heat waves we would use a prism of rock salt, or something like that."

"Refraction," the girl repeated slowly. Her voice sharpened. "Refraction! Dr. Maitland–Bob–do you think that could be the answer? You know, like a spoon in a tumbler of water? It looks sharply bent, but really it's not. Or like a mirage, which makes things appear miles away from where they really are!"

"A mirage–on a colossal scale– Yes, I'd thought of something like that." Maitland began a meticulous searching of his mind, trying to remember all he had learned about light. "We know that we see objects because of the light emitted or reflected from them. Then, if by some fluke the light waves no longer traveled in straight lines, we would not see the object at which we looked."

"Right!" the girl agreed. "I know a few things about light, too. I've taught it in physics class. The first law of refraction is that the incident ray–the normal, straight one, that is–and the refracted ray both lie in one plane; and the second law is that a ray of light passing obliquely from a less dense to a more dense medium is bent towards the perpendicular at the point of incidence. Good heavens!" she went on rapidly. "It's beginning to make sense. Before this happened did it seem to you that things kept jumping out of place and back again?"

"No doubt of it," Maitland declared, rather overcome by her growing control of the situation.

"Then doesn't it suggest that the Earth has come into contact with something—some region of space–that is a denser medium than usual, and because of it all light waves are bent to one side? Something so enormous in extent that it involves the Sun and, maybe, the whole Solar System? So, light waves don't move straight any more, but heat waves remain unaffected."

A scientist might have been very proud—or very jealous—of Irene Carr at that moment. Without any special qualifications, reasoning out the problem solely from elementary principles derived from her school-teaching, she had arrived at the amazing solution. Refraction—a gigantic mirage! This was the theory that was being discussed at that very moment by scientists all over the world, by long distance telephone and radio. Light alone was affected: that was the cardinal point. Every other kind of radiation was normal.

Something, somehow, was bending the light waves out of the straight line.

"But—but the stars!" Maitland exclaimed. "We can see them perfectly!"

They lowered the car windows and looked outside. The darkness was so intense that it made their eyes ache. It was a relief to gaze up to where the sky was still dusted with the multi-millions of stars that had sprung into being at the start of the mystery. Maitland and the girl were quiet for a long time, two puny mortals grappling with an infinite problem in a lightless world. Then Irene spoke again.

"Where," she asked, "is the Milky Way? My astronomy isn't so good, but I do know that smudgy band like curdled milk. And it just isn't there anymore."

She was right. That swirling galaxy from which the Earth itself had been born was not visible. Neither, if it came to that, were Sirius, Procyon, Pollux or Betelgeuse, though neither she nor Maitland knew enough to be aware of it. And the Pole Star, famous since time began—

"No Pole Star!" Maitland said, astounded.

Impressed by this new discovery, they clambered out of the car and stood holding on to it as though it were their last material support in a world doomed to everlasting dark. Soft wind, warm and summery, stirred the invisible grass at the side of the road.

"Do you suppose," Irene said, stumbling round to where Maitland was standing, "that the thing which is warping light waves is causing us to see stars which ordinarily we wouldn't see? That mirage again?"

"You mean stars beyond our normal range of vision?"

"Yes. Why not? Space is a big place. There are countless trillions of stars we never see in the ordinary way. But if the light from them were bent enormously out of focus we would see them—are seeing them now. By the same token, at some distant point from Earth our Sun is probably visible—and the Milky Way. Maybe the inhabitants of an unknown world are wondering at this moment how the unknown sun and galaxy got into their sky and where their usual stars have gone!"

"Yes," Maitland whispered. "By heaven—yes! A huge light-wave warp, bending everything light-years out of its usual track. I don't know how you worked it out, but it's the only possible explanation. It just has to be right!"

"After all," she went on, more confidently, "refraction has no definite limits: a mirage can take place within a few feet of the observer or cover dozens of miles. In this case, light waves may be bent millions of miles out of—" She gave a little gasp as a new thought struck her. "Of course! Remember how the Sun appeared to streak towards the west, and then disappeared? That must have been when the thing came between us and the Sun. It wasn't the Sun itself that skidded sideways; it was his light -waves. He's still there!" She stared blindly upwards.

"At least," Maitland said uneasily, "we won't freeze! But this is all so impossible—a world where no light will operate. I wonder what's going on in the cities—out on the oceans—in the air? I never stopped to think about it until now."

Neither of them dared to voice the thoughts that were in both their minds. In any case, the rest of the world was far away, remote. Maitland reached out and caught the girl's arm.

"Let's sit on the grass bank. Too oppressive in the car..."

Holding on to each other, they scuffed their feet over the gravel to the side of the lane, groped for the grassy bank and settled down on it, staring into the black void. They gazed anew at the unfamiliar stars that gave no light down here, because once their light waves reached an object they had become so completely refracted that it was not visible at all. Every object on the surface of the Earth was affected in the same way. The area of refraction was so vast that any image-reflection veered right off the Earth itself into surrounding space. It was quiet, too. Only the wind out of the blackness, gentle, caressing, like a comforting hand in deepest sorrow. No birds, no sounds of country life. No friendly voices of other human beings...

"Suppose," Irene whispered, "it goes on—and on?"

It was the human being in her that was speaking now. Cold logic had given way before natural emotion—before fear.

"It will be the end, I suppose" Maitland said soberly. "The end of the world. Without the Sun, Man couldn't survive.

"But we've got the Sun," she insisted. "It's there—warming us. It's the absence of light that's the problem. If we could only get over that— We might, underground. Maybe this thing the Earth has run into won't act below the surface. We might live down there, like—like Morlocks."

"If it goes on," Maitland said slowly, "it'll mean the end of vegetation as we know it; the end of staple crops, of everything that relies on photosynthesis. A new species of fungoid plants might come into being—"

"And yet, on the surface, we'll still get sunburned, because the ultra-violet rays are unaffected."

The whole crazy paradox quenched their conversation then. Though neither of them would admit it, even to themselves, deep down inside of them they felt a grim fear. The inborn instinct of the primitive, handed down through unguessable ages, was not to be set aside without a struggle. Darkness was ever to be dreaded...

"It's odd, in the midst of this," Maitland said at length, "but I keep wondering what you look like."

The girl's laugh sounded soft and ghostly in the blackness. "If this ever goes, you'll see,' she murmured. "But you might be disappointed."

Maitland smiled bitterly to himself. If this goes—! She was fearing, even as he was, that it might never go. Earth had, perhaps, plunged forever into an area of refraction where all light was dead.

"Wish I knew the time," he growled, raising his wristwatch and staring into the blackness. Then an idea struck him. He felt for his penknife and, after a moment's fumbling prized open the watch and felt gently for the hands.

"Ten to twelve." He whistled. "Nearly noon. Who'd imagine it?"

"Where were you going when this happened?" the girl inquired.

"I was going to see a patient... Look, there's a telephone box about half a mile down the road. I think I ought to try and reach it and give his wife a ring. This might go on all day. Do you want to stay here or -"

"Not likely!"

She grasped his hand and he helped her to her feet. Linking arms, they began to walk unsteadily down the lane, feeling before them at every yard. It was hard going, and they could not immediately rid themselves of the impression that they had been suddenly blinded in a world that was normal for everyone but themselves. Instinctively they kept listening for onrushing cars, until gradually they realized how unnecessary it was. Everything was blotted out completely, just as they were. For once Nature had the complete upper hand of her erring, quarrelsome children.

"Half a mile," Irene said as they shuffled along. "That's a long way, in this. How will you know when we get there?"

"It's just in a slight bend of the road. We'll do our best, anyway. It's better than sitting still waiting and wondering how it's all going to end. Sooner or later we should get to Wilmington village. We'll need food— I haven't had my breakfast yet!"

"And I've nothing with me,", the girl sighed. "I was planning to eat at roadhouses on the way...Well, let's hope it will pass soon."

In truth, nobody knew when it would pass; not even the scientists who were engrossed in the phenomenon. In totally dark observatories the world over, they were still discussing it with each other across land and sea, exchanging reports and impressions. Caught unawares by the terrific speed with which the Fault had developed, they had had no time to estimate its area. It might be untold light-centuries in extent, in which case Earth would not swim clear of it for hundreds of years. If, on the other hand, it was a mere patch as cosmic distances are reckoned, it would soon be left behind.

On one thing they were all agreed: something in the ether—they freely admitted they did not know what—was altering the incident rays of light so tremendously that laws presumed immutable had been completely revoked. The something must be a medium that was transparent to heat yet highly refractive to light; perhaps a semi-gaseous envelope, non-poisonous, created in the first instance by the explosion of a long extinct sun. This theory was extended tentatively, and for the time being it had to suffice. To a race that does not yet know exactly what the ether is, there is no shame in not understanding the real nature of the Fault. It may be centuries before we shall know the truth...

"I think," Maitland said, "the phone box is just a few yards further on, to our left."

He and the girl had come to the slight bend in the road: they could sense it with their feet as they advanced. Carefully they edged their way along, groping in the dark as they went. For a while they encountered the wire fence at the side of the road. Then suddenly they blundered into hard glass and steel.

"It's it!" cried Irene.

Maitland tugged the door open, groped for the instrument and lifted the receiver. He was thankful that this district still did not use the dialing system. Wondering if he would get a reply, he put the receiver to his ear.

"Hello!" came a girl's voice, quite composed.

"Er–can you get me Wilmington Seven Nine?" Maitland asked.

"I'll try, sir. I suppose you can't tell me your number?"

"Impossible. I'm in total darkness. How is it where you are?"

"Well, they tell me it's blacker than midnight," the girl answered. "I wouldn't know, though. I'm blinded, and trained as a telephone operator. They've called me out on emergency duty... Wilmington Seven Nine. Just a moment–" Then: "Insert money, please!"

Maitland fumbled with coins. There was the friendly buzzing of the ringing tone as he waited in the darkness. He could hear Irene Carr breathing gently beside him as she stood wedged invisibly between door and frame.

"Hello!" came a thin voice in the receiver.

"That Mrs. Andrew?" he asked quickly. "Dr. Maitland speaking.

"Oh, thank God to hear another voice, doctor!" cried the woman, fervently. "What in heaven's name has happened to the world? Is–is it the Judgment Day at last?"

"I wouldn't know, Mrs. Andrews–but I agree it's pretty ghastly. I'd like to know how your husband is. I'm stranded some ten miles from your place–"

"You don't need to rush yourself, doctor." The voice was strangely calm, now. "Something's happened to my husband that I don't rightly understand. When everything went dark he just lay abed and said something about he knew God was everywhere. Then he said he'd never thought about God while life went by, day after day, like clockwork. But now everything's still and dark and quiet, he says he can feel God near him. That's the truth, doctor. And he's goin' to be all right, I'm sure of it! He's sleeping quite peaceful, now."

"That's fine," Maitland said. "I'll come and look at him the moment the darkness passes."

He put the telephone back, brushed Irene's shoulder as he grasped the door. She stepped out into the road, and they stood side by side in the stygian gloom.

"Everything all right?" she inquired.

He told her what Mrs. Andrews had said. "He seems to have made a remarkable recovery–at least for the present. I'll have to see him when I can."

"I think I can understand it," she mused. "Normally, when we're healthy and active, we're inclined to take a lot for granted, just as we took the smooth working of the universe for granted–until now. It's only at times like these, when everything goes out of gear that we have to stop and think about such things. And when we find ourselves out of our depth, unable to make sense of what has happened, there's nothing left to lean on but the Almighty."

Maitland remained silent, holding Irene's arm. Sensing her nearness, he found himself longing more than ever to see what kind of girl this was who had such a simple solution for everything that baffled him. He turned aside and, just for a moment, he fancied he could see her. There was the faintest suggestion of a rounded chin, a straight nose, dimly outlined against the blackness beyond. Yes, and a slender figure...

While he stared disbelievingly, the silhouette took on depth. He saw the glint of light creep into hair of copper brown; and then she came out of the abyss like a vision, staring back at him with wide blue eyes that began to narrow beneath the impact of returning sunshine. Around her the landscape came gradually into view, as though floodlights were being turned on, slowly -

"Great God!" he whispered, and jerked his gaze upward. Then they both fell back, hands over their faces, as the stars paled out of the sky before an advancing tide of ever-deepening gray. Gray which merged into white, into blue, Then, blinding in its intensity, the Sun rose suddenly from the west where it had disappeared, and came to a stop at the zenith.

It was high noon. The Earth had swept clear of the Fault.

BRIEF GODS

"Nothing really exists," declared Professor Engleman, with due academic profundity. "That, of course, may sound preposterous, but it is nevertheless a fact and I am sure that the members of this erudite gathering know exactly what I mean."

Yes, everybody knew what he meant, but it was becoming increasingly difficult to concentrate. For one thing, the great lecture hall where Engleman was holding forth was intolerably stuffy; for another there were all the attractions of a warm summer evening beckoning outside. Not far from the lecture hall lay the Great Park, in the grounds of which the hail itself stood. Through the open windows floated the sound of children's laughter, the clack of cricket balls, even the distant sonorous strains of an open-air brass band.

Professor Engleman had been asked to demonstrate to members of the scientific profession his latest discoveries concerning the electron. This suited Engleman—who never knew what the weather was like anyway—down to the ground. But it made it tough going for his hearers who were compelled to be present.

"Nothing really exists because everything is based on the electron, and the electron itself is only a probability," Engleman continued, without resorting to his notes. "No scientist can say positively, even today, that an electron exists as a unit of electricity: he can only infer that it does because all mathematical laws point to its presence. But we cannot see it, my friends! The very action of even trying to do so, in bringing light-waves upon it to discover it, is enough to deflect it out of sight. Hence, I say, all existence—which of necessity is based on electrons—is nothing more than a probability. As such it is a completely unstable state..."

"Hear, hear," murmured an elder savant dutifully, and peered through sleepy eyes at the little, sixty-year old doyen of electronics who was responsible for this boring recital of known facts.

"To prove my point—and, I hope, usher in a new theory concerning electronics—I have here a machine..." Engleman indicated it standing on a massive table to one side of the rostrum. The apparatus looked like a glorified telephone switchboard with two tubes on the summit.

"With it," Engleman continued, "it is possible to set up a disturbing electrical field which will so displace the electrons of matter as to cause their atomic constitution to form entirely new patterns. My equations tell me that, as a result of this, certain species of matter can cease to exist altogether, whilst others can assume new shapes. How far the influence of this disturber-field reaches I do not know. My study of it shows it seems to have no limit but spreads out in an ever-widening circle. Possibly, even, it may reach to the limits of the Universe and then start to contract inwards again. One thing is certain: the outward speed of the field is many times greater than that of light..."

A certain sense of uneasiness crept over the members. It was just possible that the old boy in his enthusiasm might dissipate the entire hall and its living inhabitants. His genius was such that the possibility of his having invented a failure was unthinkable. Then his next words brought relief.

"Fortunately, the control of the disturber-field is absolute. I can automatically set it to operate at ten feet or ten miles as the mood dictates. I have therefore set it tonight for a distance of exactly seven and a half miles–which, I am assured on the high authority of the Borough Surveyor, is the exact distance from this hall to St. Michael's statue."

There was a murmur of assent. St. Michael's statue stood in a great deal, deserted space on the edge of London. It had been erected by some obscure religious denomination as a silent exhortation to infidels to heed more closely the Voice of Reason.

"I propose," Engleman proceeded, "to see what happens to that statue when the disturber-field reaches it. I have only to press the switch on this machine and the job is done. We can then set off and see for ourselves what has happened to St. Michael."

To this the reaction was unanimously in favor since it meant a jaunt through the summer evening and an exodus of the stifling lecture hall.

"I hope," Engelman murmured, studying his apparatus, "that all is well with this equipment. I was compelled to entrust it to the tender mercies of the carriers in order to get it here, it being too large to fit into my private car. Mmm, yes, all seems to be in order."

He peered short-sightedly at the dials and controls, and saw nothing wrong. Not that there was–at least not visibly. There were, however, certain difference in the internal workings, brought about entirely by the ruthless manhandling of the carriers who had dumped the equipment with complete lack of regard for its extreme sensitivity.

"All I have to do," Engleman said, "is press this button here, which immediately starts the emanation of the disturber-wave..."

* * *

In the center of Great Park an old man of eighty-seven sat studying a pocket Bible. In spite of his age he was fairly well preserved. His back was still upright: he held the Book in hands which did not tremble. Seated as he was on the rustic seat built round the bole of a giant cedar tree, the mid-evening sunlight casting a halo through his silver hair, there was something immensely venerable about him. He seemed apart from everything, lost in his assiduous study of the Scriptures.

The gamboling children nearby took no notice of him, but once or twice a young woman, perhaps twenty-two, sprawled alone on the grass, cast a sly glance in his direction. She was pretty, shapely, and appeared to have everything a girl of her age should have. It was not possible for her to go round with a label proclaiming she had only three months to live because of the inexorable inroads of galloping consumption.

Whilst she cast covert glances at the old man, seeing in him something saintly, something perhaps which could drag her from the death sentence passed upon her, she too was also under observation, though she was not aware of it.

A few yards away from her a young man was sprawled against a tree, a wisp of grass between his teeth. He was good looking, but hard about the mouth and grim around the eyes. Back of his mind was the contemplation of murder—this very night. He meant to snuff out a young woman who had completely misled him as to her intentions. Once that was done... well, here was another young woman, alone, extremely pretty. Pity she coughed so much, but probably a few throat pastilles could cure that.

"Not bad," Martin Senior muttered to himself lazily. "Not bad at all. Give it a bit longer and then accidentally fall over her feet as you leave. Corny introduction but better than nothing!"

He knew exactly in his own mind what he intended doing. But, even as Professor Engleman was at that very moment pointing out, nobody can be sure of anything, because nothing really exists. There is only the probability that a thing exists...

And, divided by only a scant fifty yards from these three characters and the laughing, then squabbling, children, there lay the tennis courts. The evening was too hot for anybody but enthusiasts, and into this class fell Jerry Maxbury and Edna Drew. They had been slogging at one another for over an hour, and from the look on the girl's face she did not at all like the battering she was getting.

"All very well for you!" she shouted indignantly, as she lost game, set and match and threw down her racquet savagely. "You've got legs a mile long and a reach like a giraffe! How am I supposed to stand up to that?"

"You're not supposed to," Jerry grinned, vaulting the net and hurrying to her side. "Somebody's got to win, Ed, and it may as well be me!"

"Beast!" Edna looked at him under her eyes, her lips pouting. She was a dark girl of average looks, usually marred by an expression of sullen resignation. Jerry, on the other hand, was a Nordic blond, the kind a teenager might swoon for—only Jerry was not interested in teenagers: only in Edna.

"You don't have to take it so hard," he complained, tying his sweater about his neck and then retrieving her racquet for her. "That's the trouble with us, Ed: we never seem to agree, and yet we somehow stick together. Maybe we're getting all our quarrels over before we get married."

"If we ever do!" Edna retorted and strode away angrily in the direction of the Tennis Club pavilion. Jerry sighed as he watched her go, but the slim lines of her figure in the sleeveless tennis frock drew him after her. Nearby the Park clock struck nine-fifteen.

He caught up with her at the pavilion counter. In here was the "honor counter" whereby drinks, sweets and confectionery could be obtained, the payment to be placed in a special box. Whether the idea worked or not was nobody's concern: on the whole the club membership was straightforward enough.

"Now, look–" Jerry began, and then he could not say any more because the thing happened.

He and Edna were suddenly flat on their backs, their brains and senses stunned by an inconceivable impact. They were transiently dead and yet in full possession of their faculties. They just lay, fixedly watching a blinding whirl of lights outside the pavilion windows. There was a monstrous sucking noise like an elephant going down in a bog. This terminated in a violent explosion that made the pavilion windows rattle–then all was quiet again.

Jerry stirred slowly, gradually struggled to his feet. With a dazed look in his eyes he lifted Edna beside him. Fright had completely destroyed her earlier anger.

"What–what was it, do you suppose?" Her dark eyes were racing with questions.

"Hanged if I know. Earthquake or something. Or maybe the much vaunted X-bomb has dropped at last."

He went to the pavilion's open doorway and gazed outside; then he nearly fainted from shock. Simultaneously he felt Edna's convulsive grip on his arm.

"Lord!" she gasped. "Oh, Lord!"

For some reason the Great Park had entirely vanished! Instead the pavilion seemed to be perched on some kind of desert island, only instead of there being ocean beyond the very near horizon there were stars! Stars set in a sky of violent blue. Wherever Jerry and Edna looked there were the stars. Right behind the pavilion itself there was a sheer drop into–infinity itself! Stars were behind, above, below!

"We're dead–or dreaming!" Jerry whispered at last.

"But not alone, thank heaven. Look–there are others!"

Jerry saw them now. Not far away were two big trees, looking ridiculously lonely and adding to the "desert island" effect. Under one of them sat an old man with silver hair; under the other was a young man, now rising to his feet and looking about him. In the middle distance a pretty young woman lay sprawled on the grass, one hand holding down the hem of her skirt as a brief hot wind gushed past and was gone.

"Hey!" Jerry yelled. "Hey, you folks! What happened?"

The young man began to advance, hesitated, and instead turned to help the girl to her feet. Then they both moved to the old man as he struggled up from the rustic bench around the cedar tree. After a moment all three came slowly forward, the younger ones held back in their urgency by the old man's slow progress.

It struck Jerry as he watched them that everything was brightly lighted. The sun, of course. The sun? He glanced upwards again at the multitude of stars and realized the oddity of the situation. There was a sun up there, certainly, only it had a bluish instead of amber light. Also it was at the zenith, whereas it had been evening before this–whatever it was–had happened.

"What happened?" It was Edna's urgent voice as the "outside" trio came up the pavilion steps. "We didn't see. We were in here."

"I just don't know what did happen," Martin Senior answered. "I was just lying there, thinking of this and that–then everything seemed to abruptly fly apart and snap together again, quick as a flash. Then I found myself looking at stars."

"Same as me," the consumptive girl said, her gray eyes wide in amazement. "Where's the Park? The kids who were playing? In fact where is anything?"

"'And in the twinkling of an eye all shall be changed'," the old man murmured, shaking his white head slowly. "Y'know, I never thought I'd live to see that really happen. And if you don't mind I'll sit down. My legs aren't what they used to be."

"Sure," Jerry agreed promptly, settling him on the pavilion steps. "Make yourself comfortable, sir, whilst we work out what's happened."

The old man glanced up with tired amusement in his blue eyes. "You think you can? The optimism of youth!"

"Well, there has to be an explanation, of course." Jerry reflected for a moment. "Now, let me see–"

"We're on some kind of asteroid, I think,"" Martin Senior interrupted. "Or, more precisely, a segment of Earth has broken away from the parent body, and we happened to be on it. Where we are now, God knows."

"God always knows," the old man said, musing. "And a grand mess we'd all be in if He didn't."

"I find that sort of remark both irrelevant and unhelpful," Edna snapped. "This is a desperately serious situation. We're utterly marooned, and we don't know where!"

"Take it easy," Jerry growled. "Things are tough enough without you blowing your top!"

"Then suggest something!" Edna spread her slim bare arms and glared.

Silence. The men looked at one another and the two young women exchanged glances. Finally Jerry cleared his throat.

"Your idea of a segment of Earth flying away and taking us with it is too Arabian Nightish," he declared, looking frankly at Martin Senior. "I'm not a scientist, but I do know it could not happen. We're breathing air for one thing, and in a case like that we wouldn't be. The air would be sucked like–like skin from a banana."

"It wouldn't be if the change were instantaneous, involving no momentum. Just a switch from place to place."

"Eh?" Jerry stared blankly. "But that couldn't happen!"

"Fact remains, it did." Martin Senior looked at the starry sky. "Notice something? None of those stars form constellations that make sense. And also that sun isn't ours at all. It's bluer, younger, and hotter. We're in a totally unknown area of space!"

"Perhaps," the consumptive girl ventured, "the rest of the world is here just the same only we can't see it for some reason?"

Martin Senior shook his head. "That is belied by the slight gravity we now have. You must have noticed it – I feel feather light, and so must the rest of you."

At which Jerry gathered himself together and then jumped. He seemed to travel right to the edge of the near horizon before he landed.

"You're right!" he yelled back.

"Come back!" Edna screamed hysterically. "You'll fall off into–that emptiness there!"

Jerry came back in prodigious leaps. "No chance of it, Ed, any more than you could fall of the Earth itself."

Edna looked out into the starry silences, a desperately bewildered young woman. The same frightened, lonely look was in the eyes of the consumptive girl, too. The two younger men were trying to look self-assured but the mystification in their eyes could not be hidden. Only the old man seemed undisturbed, sitting as calmly as a weather-beaten old fisherman watching a sunset.

"This," he said, brooding, "gives us the chance to look at ourselves, to decide how much we really count in the scheme of things. It's a wonderful opportunity!"

Edna hugged her elbows and shivered. "Then it's an opportunity in which I'm not interested. Look, do you others find it cold? Wish to heaven my coat was here. I left it on the chair beside the tennis court."

Nobody said anything. The tennis court! It might be millions of light centuries away. Might even be in another space altogether. Here there was nothing but infinity, the violet sky, the silly gravitation, and a sun that had no right to be there.

"Come to think of it," Martin Senior said presently, "it is getting cold, or else we got steamed up with fright and are now cooling off. Let's get into the pavilion and try and knock some sense into things."

His hard, matter-of-fact logic was just what was wanted at that moment. Edna and the consumptive girl followed him into the pavilion and seated themselves. Jerry stayed long enough to give the old man a hand; then with the doors closed they settled and considered one another.

"First things first," Martin Senior said, his jaw very square and determined. "I'm Martin Senior, engineer's draughtsman."

"Lucille Grant," the consumptive girl said, and looked anxiously about her.

Each in turn Jerry and Edna introduced themselves and then the old man smiled and sighed.

"What's in a name anyhow?" he shrugged. "My name's Jonathan Stone, and I'm a retired publisher. I've reached the age when I've about done everything there is to do. Where I end my life doesn't signify, be it in this incredible place or in bed at home. I'm prepared to let the good Lord make the arrangements."

"At your age you can't see it as we see it," Edna insisted.

"Speak for yourself," Lucille put in. "I can see things exactly the same way as Mr. Stone. What does it matter anyway?"

Jonathan Stone looked at her fixedly. "Strange words from a girl your age. What are you? Twenty-five maybe?"

"Twenty-two, but I'll never be twenty-three. The doctors have told me that."

"Come to think of it," Martin Senior said dryly, "we'll none of us live for long if we don't find the way home–and I don't think we've the remotest chance of doing that."

"Talk, talk, talk!" Edna beat her fists fiercely on her knees. "I always thought men came up with something brilliant in a crisis–and you spend your time talking rubbish! What do we do?"

"We've nothing to go on," Jerry protested. "And stop being so difficult, Ed. Things are bad enough..."

"We can only assume certain facts," Martin Senior said, his tone coldly calculating. "Some scientific process, or else natural forces, has hurled us on a fragment of Earth into unknown space. The transition was instantaneous for two reasons. We were aware of it and didn't lose consciousness, and our air came with us. Further, it was smooth and untroubled because the pavilion and the two trees remain firm. They were not uprooted and flung into chaos. We heard a violent explosion after a sucking noise. That could have been our air racing outwards and the gap closing behind. We know also we have traveled an incomprehensible distance because our own sun had disappeared, and we have a different one. Right so far?"

Heads nodded silently–all except Jonathan Stone's. He was not even listening. Instead he was pondering his small pocket Bible.

"And the time now is..." Martin Senior considered his watch. "Er–nine-thirty. Fifteen minutes ago we were in the Great Park on Earth and everything was perfect. No amount of reasoning or logic or anything else can explain a vast trip through infinity in the space of what must have been seconds. We just don't know what has happened."

"Could - it reverse itself and take us back?" Jerry asked, pondering.

"No idea. You're as wise as I am. It would take an Einstein to work this one out."

"Can an ex-high school girl say something?" Edna enquired. "I once learned the fact that you cannot take anything away from the Universe's structure without putting something in is place. Therefore–"

"Matter into energy; energy into matter," Martin Senior confirmed calmly. "So?"

"Just this. We must have left something behind when we departed. I mean, a great chunk of Earth couldn't vanish abruptly without something taking its place."

"Possibly the interchange was absolute," Martin Senior mused. "By that I mean that we abruptly changed places with another part of the universe; therefore whatever was here is now where we were. Maybe it was empty space, maybe a star, maybe anything. If a star, then Earth by now will be a cinder."

Silence. Jerry turned and looked at the "honor counter" with the banked-up shelves behind it. He gave a sigh.

"Well, there's a certain amount of food and drink here which will keep us going for awhile. When it runs out that's the finish."

"To my mind..." Martin Senior got to his feet. "To my mind I think we should explore this desert island segment of ours more thoroughly."

"Okay," Jerry nodded. "I'll come with you–"

"No you won't!" Edna interrupted. "You're staying right by me, Jerry! I'm scared! Mr. Stone's too old to be of any help if anything happens and–"

"I'll go," Lucille said, with a touch of contempt, getting to her feet. "That is if you think a woman is capable of revealing any commonsense, Mr. Senior?"

Martin Senior only smiled sardonically and then opened the pavilion door, following Lucille out into the blaze of the alien sun. They descended the steps with queer, bouncing movements and then began to cross the grass together.

"I could laugh," Martin Senior exclaimed, after a moment. "I really could!"

"So could I, for another reason." Lucille gave him a quick look. "I've about three months to live and find myself here! I never thought I'd watch others die around me at the same time."

"You seem mighty sure that you're going to push up the daisies!"

"That's rather a fatuous remark here, isn't it? And of course I'm sure. No reason why the medics should lie to me."

"Not necessarily lie, but they're not infallible. Believe only in yourself and nobody else. That's my motto."

"I wish I could, but I'm not made that way." Lucille looked about her towards the very near horizon. Then: "And what was it was going to make you laugh?"

"Just the fact that I'd planned to murder a girl tonight! Now she's light centuries away and perfectly safe. A classic example of 'Man proposes...' I suppose."

"You? Commit a murder? I don't believe it!"

"Thanks for the compliment. And, Miss Grant, unless I am permitted to call you Lucille, we are now leaving the pavilion right behind us."

Lucille stopped and glanced rearward. Then she gave a start. The top of the pavilion roof was visible, but that was all. The rest of it was below the horizon.

"This is preposterous!" she exclaimed, startled.

"Not a bit. We just happen to have walked beyond the horizon point - as seen from the pavilion, that is. Notice the ground? The grass has finished and instead we have this stuff! Soil, but flat as though a roller had been over it."

"So it is!" Lucille looked at it intently. "Looks as if a giant knife had cut it off."

They began moving again, and behind them the pavilion slowly vanished from view. They were now traversing a twilit plain of perfectly smooth soil on which no living thing grew. Overhead were the stars, but no sun.

"This segment we're on is only quite small," Martin Senior said presently. "At the moment we're on its underside, which is why the sun's gone."

"Which means we're upside down compared to our position in the pavilion?"

"Of course, but we're not aware of it because gravity keeps us apparently upright. No doubt of one thing, this clean-cut segment points to colossal elemental forces. This piece of Earth wasn't just ripped out: it was sheared off!"

"Couldn't be!"

"It could, though I'm not scientist enough to imagine how. Did you ever see anything so absolutely flat?"

They gazed over the expanse to the near horizon. Not a hillock, not an undulation, anywhere. Overhead the strange, unknown stars and the everlasting black of space itself. Somewhere, faded as a forgotten memory, was the world from which they had come.

"We can assess this by degrees," Martin Senior said, thinking. "We're on a chunk of Earth approximately three miles long by—say, two wide. It makes no pretence of being circular: it's plainly and simply a chunk. The upper part is normal with grass, trees, the pavilion, and so on: the under part is sheared off where the mysterious forces went to work. Air we still have—but it can't last."

"Why not?" Lucille asked, that depthless wonder still in her eyes.

"For one thing the gravity is so weak it won't hold the air for long; for another space will suck it out gradually. Also, the best of the sun will do its share to dissipating it. How long we have I don't know." Martin Senior surveyed the stars. "They're very bright. Our atmosphere here is desperately thin—or maybe you'd noticed? That tightness about the chest?"

"My chest's always tight anyway so I wouldn't know—" Lucille broke off in a fit of coughing. When at last it had subsided she was surprised to find Martin Senior's arm about her shoulders.

"Better?" he asked, with a kind of rough kindness.

"Uh-uh: it comes in spasms. We'd better be getting back and tell the others, hadn't we?"

Martin Senior nodded, and they retraced their way. They found the others still in the pavilion, Edna being in the midst of rationing what food there was. She glanced up at the two entered.

"Well?"

Martin Senior shrugged. "Nothing very exciting—except proof of the fact that our island home was pitched here by scientific forces..." and he briefly added the details.

"Very helpful," Edna commented sourly, slapping down a pot of shrimp paste. "At least you both managed to cultivate a good sunburn, anyhow!"

"Edna, for heaven's sake!" Jerry gave her an entreating look.

"For heaven's sake what? I can speak my mind, can't I?"

"I have the feeling," Jonathan Stone remarked, his spare form reclining in the wicker chair by the sunlit window, "that Miss Drew is not at all happy in her present surroundings!"

"Are you?" Edna demanded.

"Quite–but then I have reached the age where I can be philosophical. Out here we're somehow right on the rim of Eternity, and I have the hope that before I die I might even look upon the face of my Creator."

Because of his age, Jonathan Stone's statement did not sound at all blasphemous: indeed, the serene expression on his rugged old face made it appear that he really believed his wish would be granted.

"To get to more practical things," Martin Senior said bluntly, "we've fallen into an orbit. I've been watching the stars, and they're changing position very slightly whereas the sun doesn't move in the least. That suggests that we're flying round this sun and keeping one face to it. Fortunate it happens to be this one or we'd be completely in the dark."

"We are–utterly!" Edna Drew's mouth was drooping peevishly. "It's cold, frightening, and desolate. If there were not you others here I'd go mad!"

"Put my sweater on..." Jerry handed it across.

"No thanks. I can look after myself. Serves me right for putting on this fool tennis frock without sleeves in it. But how was I to know this would happen?"

"We none of us knew," Jonathan Stone said. "'In the twinkling of an eye–'!"

"So you said before," Edna interrupted rudely. "Surely, Mr. Stone, at your age, you can contribute something more useful to our dilemma than mere Scriptures?"

"I am afraid not, Miss Drew. I am too old physically to do anything, and mentally I am more preoccupied with the Hereafter than the present."

"As to the coldness..." Martin Senior reached down a packet of cigarettes from the shelf. "That's caused by the air here being unpleasantly thin. It causes rapid radiation of bodily warmth and causes the surface skin to chill quickly. You won't catch cold, though, because that takes germs–and I doubt if they're very prevalent on this remote chunk of Earth; or even if they are the thin air won't encourage them."

Edna threw herself onto one of the counter stools and looked moodily in front of her. She ignored the cigarette packet Martin Senior held towards her: Lucille also declined as another violent attack of coughing brought her to the point of exhaustion.

"I think," Edna said curtly, when the spasm had finished, "that it might be healthier outside. Come on, Jerry!"

"Why?" He was squatting comfortably on the floor, smoking one of the cigarettes Martin Senior had offered him.

"Because I refuse to venture out alone."

Jerry sighed and scrambled to his feet. He paused as he went past Lucille. She was still gasping for breath and the paroxysms had brought tears to her wide gray eyes.

"Sorry, Lucille, for what Edna said," he murmured. "I don't think she meant it. Sort of prides herself on being outspoken."

"Of course," Lucille smiled. "If I could help myself coughing I would."

"For heaven's sake come on and stop muttering!" Edna complained–so Jerry hurried quickly to her side and then followed her to the open. The three left behind gazed after them.

"Not ideally suited, are they?" Martin Senior asked cynically.

"Few people are," Jonathan Stone sighed. "I think they'd get along all right if they could compose the antagonisms in their natures. Each has something the other cannot assimilate, and until they find out what it is they'll always be at loggerheads."

"About the sunburn we've got–" Lucille seemed to have been thinking, and she was now inspecting the undoubted chocolate brown on the backs of her normally pale hands. "Isn't that caused by ultra-violet radiation?"

"Normally, yes," Martin Senior confirmed. "This new sun we've got probably radiates ultra-violet the same as our own does, but here we get the dose extra strong because of the thin air. On the other hand, it may not be ultra violet at all."

"It must be to produce sunburn!" Lucille insisted.

"Not necessarily. Cosmic rays could produce the same effect, and much more rapidly. Indeed, considering the speed at which we have got bronzed I'm inclined to think cosmic rays are at the back of it."

"But they're dangerous!" Lucille exclaimed. "I've read about them! They burn flesh and blood and go right through everything except lead."

"True enough–in the naked state. We have some atmosphere to shield us–" Martin Senior broke off and then nodded towards the almost sleeping Jonathan Stone. "There's our proof! Mr. Stone is becoming sunburned, too, and he hasn't been outside the pavilion yet–except at the very start. That shows the cosmic radiations are passing through this pavilion, something which ultra-violet cannot do. Come to think of it, Jerry and Edna looked remarkably healthy, but I put it down to their having been playing tennis in the sun."

"That sounds an awful long way off now," Lucille whispered.

After a while Jerry and Edna returned. They were still looking at odds with each other–and the increase in their "sunburn" was most marked. Moodily they came into the pavilion and then closed the door.

"According to my watch it's half-past twelve," Jerry said. "Back home that would be long past bedtime and by all the rules I ought to feel sleepy. But I don't–and neither does Edna."

Martin Senior looked vaguely surprised. "Come to think of it, I don't either. How about you, Lucille?"

"A bit–but not as much as usual."

"The only one who seems to be running to schedule is Mr. Stone," Jerry commented, glancing at him. "Fast asleep!"

"Don't you believe it, boy!" The old man stirred and looked at him. "Because I have my eyes closed doesn't say I'm asleep. Matter of fact I don't feel tired. In fact quite the contrary. Surprising thing, but since we landed here I've felt immeasurably younger."

"The air perhaps," Edna said, but she did not sound too certain of herself. "It's a bit thin, but immensely exhilarating. I don't feel cold any more either."

There was silence for a moment. Though as yet none was prepared to admit it—except perhaps for Jonathan Stone—they were all conscious of alerted senses, of the slow dissolution of that stagnation of the mind that more or less pervades every human being through the action of impurities in blood. Thinking seemed no longer a conscious effort: the concentration flew from one topic to another with astonishing facility.

"Sunburn and sharpened wits, eh?" Martin Senior asked at length. "Only one answer to that—the inflow of cosmic radiation affecting us all."

Jonathan Stone chuckled half to himself. "Good for you, son! You have your answer—and I have mine."

"You mean you have a different solution?"

"I wouldn't say it's a solution, but at any rate it's a suggestion. Just here, in this unknown region of space, we may be much closer to the Ultimate than we were on Earth. And by the Ultimate I mean the Artisan of the Universe, the Creator of all that is—"

"He's off again," Edna sighed, sitting down. "Just as I thought we were going to pin something down."

The old man looked at her reprovingly. "Trouble with you youngsters is you don't pay half enough attention to spiritual values—"

"For myself," Martin Senior interrupted, with an immense calm, "I'm an incisive, calculating man with no interest in spiritual values. You could call me an atheist even, and be quite correct. Therefore I say that the presence of cosmic rays, which are everywhere in the Universe, is the main cause of the slow change which is coming upon us. It is not, I contend, because we are nearer to some hypothetical Creator."

"You have your view, and I have mine," Stone smiled. "The Bible tells us that the power of the Creator is everywhere—everywhere! So are cosmic radiations. Is it impossible to draw a connection between the two? No scientist will positively tell you whence cosmic rays emanate because he doesn't know the answer. That they are caused by the breakdown or build-up of energy in remote parts of space doesn't settle the issue. They have always been there: they always will be there—steady, unvarying, ubiquitous. They are material—"

"Therefore not spiritual," Martin Senior snapped.

"Not necessarily. We are mortal beings accustomed to interpret everything from its material basis. The power of a Creator might, to us, appear as cosmic radiation - destructive, deadly. To one with clearer vision they could represent the beneficent outflow of a Creator, and here at this remote point of space we may be nearer to that source of all-intellect, all-power, than ever before. Also, being segregated from our own kind with the disturbance of their myriads of conflicting thoughts, we are able to think and apprehend clearly for the first time in our lives. At least I am."

Silence. Lucille stared blankly, too astonished to make any comment. Edna was smiling cynically yet with a half doubt in her eyes. Martin Senior lighted a cigarette and sucked in a mouthful of fumes. Jerry looked about him and then rubbed the back of his neck.

"Frankly, I don't get it," he confessed.

The old man opened his pocket Bible and considered it. "You would, son, if you'd studied this a bit more often. No, no, I'm not censuring you. At your age I was just as carefree. You still have time to catch up."

Edna got to her feet with the decisiveness of disgust. She gave Jerry a glance. "About time we had something to eat, isn't it?"

Jerry hesitated. "I suppose so, but somehow I–I don't want it. I'm not hungry. That isn't the aftermath of shock either: it's just that I never felt less inclined for food in all my life."

Edna looked at the others. "What about you folks?"

Each one shook their heads, at which she moved to the nearby piled-up rations and began to make selections. Then after a while she paused and slowly shook her head. She turned, a puzzled light in her dark eyes.

"Whatever it is it's got me too. I've no appetite–nor am I thirsty either."

"Now you know how the Ancients managed to fast for weeks on end without harm," Jonathan Stone commented. "They had the trick of utilizing spiritual power for their sustenance–an art submerged with the materialistic centuries which followed."

"Which, interpreted, means that the cosmic rays are feeding us?" Martin Senior asked bluntly. "Just as they fed the Ancients?"

"Your interpretation is correct, Mr. Senior."

"It's crazy! Idiotic!" Martin Senior spat out his cigarette and then stamped on it. "Cosmic rays destroy: they don't feed!"

"None of us is destroyed, though," Lucille pointed out gently. "In fact we all look a good deal better than when we arrived here. How do you account for that?"

"They just can't be cosmic rays, that's all. Something else."

"You don't believe that," Jerry said deliberately. "Out here in these wastes nothing else but cosmic rays could affect us. We wouldn't be as affected as we are by ultra-violet, seventh-octave radiations, or any of those."

Edna came forward in surprise. "How in the world do you know all that? I never heard you make a scientific statement in your life before."

"I–I don't quite know. It sort of came to me."

"The whole thing is perfectly simple to analyze..." Jonathan Stone rose from the wicker chair–not awkwardly under the cramp of age, but with the litheness of a young man. "Cosmic radiation and Creative power are one and the same thing: that is my contention. Scientists aver that cosmic radiation, in the Beginning, acted as a catalyst on certain chemical substances, and so life began. Very well: they're entitled to their material conception of life's beginning. We are also told that the Creator brought life into being by His emanations and beneficence. The two things–cosmic rays material, and emanations spiritual–could be one and the same. Science proves cosmic rays to be destructive to life. But suppose everybody had been educated through the centuries to believe that they are beneficial to life? What then?"

"They would be," Lucille said quickly, her eyes bright. "Every single one of us believes a thing because we are compelled to from the cradle. Believe otherwise and–"

"You'd get whatever you believe," Stone assented, smiling at her. "The old quotation– 'There is nothing either good or bad but thinking makes it so' is a profound truth. Now, to get to our point. Here there are only five of us, utterly removed from the mass opinions of multimillions of our fellow human beings. Their thoughts no longer cloud our minds: we are so far away from them we are unaffected by them. So we receive cosmic rays–or spiritual radiations–or whatever you like to call them, as they really are. We have no preconceived opinions about them: there are no educational beliefs to be overcome. We accept them and they are beneficent."

Martin Senior smiled oddly. "We talk indeed from the heights of Olympus, Mr. Stone–yet withal I can detect the logic of your argument. I am one who relies on proof, and in this case the proof is that we are not hurt in any way by this all-inclusive radiation that is pouring down on us with every second. That is enough for me. There remains the problem of what happens next. To have perhaps solved the conditions existing here does not by any means tell us how we get home."

"Do we want to?" Jonathan Stone turned and looked through the pavilion window, the eternal sunlight again casting a halo around his white hair. "Don't you feel, here on this outermost rim of the Universe, that we are nearer our chosen destiny than we ever could be back on Earth? The freedom of thought, the well-being of the body: those attributes I would never trade for the old life back on Earth."

"Well-being of the body," Lucille repeated slowly, and then smiled wryly. "From where I'm sitting, Mr. Stone, that has a decidedly ironic ring. I'm a doomed woman–or didn't I mention it?"

"Because of incurable illness?" Stone turned to look at hers "That was back on Earth, child. Are you sure your viewpoint is still correct, or have cosmic rays destroyed the trouble which was undermining you?"

Lucille hesitated and then looked down at herself, clearly uncertain. Martin Senior looked at her also, an odd expression in his sharp eves.

"It's a long time since you coughed," he said.

"That's nothing. Sometimes I go for days on end without any trouble. Just the same..." Lucille hesitated, distance in her eyes. "Just the same, I do feel different somehow."

Edna moved restlessly. "Conversations always bore me," she confessed. "And since sleep and food both seem written off I think I'll go for another walk. I'm even inclined to believe that there may be something in what you say, Mr. Stone. I'd like to think it out."

"By all means."

Edna turned pensively towards the door, then Jerry's voice gave her pause.

"Just a moment, Ed! I thought you were afraid to go out alone?"

"I was. Somehow I'm not any more. Still, if you want to come with me by all means do so!"

Jerry did not hesitate. For the second time they had so mysteriously arrived in this alien region the two who could not understand each other—and yet felt impelled towards each other—wandered out under the brittle stars.

* * *

Jonathan Stone had hit the nail on the head—and not entirely by accident either. His great age, his years of study of the profundities of life and mind, had in some subtle way groomed him for this moment, wherein he was positioned as a kind of revelator. He knew, with everything that was in him, that his theory of the dual nature of cosmic rays was right. It must be right for cosmic rays are everywhere. There is no place where they are not. Of the power of a Creator the same thing can be stated. Such a parallel could not possibly be coincidence.

And with every moment, every second, these invisible radiations were beating down from their unknown source, bereft of their deadly qualities because there were no influencing minds present to produce a material effect contrary to the normal one. So five people lost in the Universe, through the unintentional meddling of an aged University professor, were swiftly changing—following the course normal to the absorption of cosmic rays, and were evolving. Swiftly! Incredibly!

Not only those in the pavilion were aware of it, but Edna and Jerry also. Indeed, for them, the effect was if anything much swifter because there was no slight deflection of radiations from the pavilion roof.

"I have often wondered," Jerry said seriously, when he and Edna had come to the last grass knoll separating them from the "soil plain" on the fragment's other side, "what it must feel like to have godlike power. Now I know."

Edna had no bitter response to make this time. She accepted his words as absolute fact because she felt exactly as he did. In silence they both stood on the slight rise of grassy ground looking upwards towards the stars.

"Whatever it is that is the source of cosmic rays, be it material or spiritual, it's definitely up there—or out there," Jerry said slowly. "Can't you feel that? Far more so than the last time we came out here?"

Edna was silent for a moment, erect, her head thrown back as she stared aloft.

"I more than feel it, Jerry, I see it. Something—out there—incredibly bright and yet so infinitely gentle—"

Jerry did not answer. He could not sense exactly what Edna meant. Manlike, he could not even hope to realize that at that moment Edna was undergoing a complete transformation. As a woman, hard-surfaced though she had been, she had the innate qualities of conception, which Jerry could never possess. Yet even he glimpsed something for a moment. It seemed like a shaft of pearly radiance, evanescent, unthinkably lovely, projected straight out of the void down towards this hurtling, forgotten little fragment of Earth. For a moment even it looked as though both he and Edna were washed in cold fire... Then it was gone, but it had left behind the breath of genius.

"Somehow–somehow, Ed–" Jerry stumbled over his words. "Somehow I know now why we've never agreed. Our physical make-ups have been opposed. We've had mathematical strains in each of us that have cancelled each other out, making absolute unison impossible."

"Yes," Edna assented simply. "That's the answer. But now it doesn't exist because in that moment the mathematical strains straightened. The complexities which separated us, and yet attracted, have been resolved."

They looked at each other, god and goddess without realizing it. Mentally they had grown to immeasurable stature, had almost reached the stage of absolute evolution as far as their minds were concerned. Their bodies had responded in that they were young, lithe, bronzed, of superlative physique.

"It has been worth coming here if only to resolve those differences," Jerry smiled. "We'll never misunderstand one another again. Suppose we get back and tell the others?"

Before long they had returned to the pavilion, to discover about Stone, Martin Senior, and Lucille a certain radiant assurance that spoke for itself.

"We felt we should tell you what happened to us out there!" Jerry exclaimed eagerly. "We saw something, and somehow felt it too – then afterwards our misunderstandings vanished. We know just where we went wrong."

"I think," Stone replied quietly, "that we all of us know now where we went wrong. For myself I am completely satisfied in that I have achieved my life's ambition. For just one precious moment I was able to gaze upon the face of the Ultimate. It satisfied me that all I ever believed was correct."

"Then you saw what we saw?" Edna asked quickly. "A kind of radiant shaft of light from above–?"

"I saw much more than that." Jonathan Stone replied gravely.

"We saw something like a ray of light." Lucille put in. "I mean Martin and I–but it meant a great deal more to Mr. Stone. He's capable of seeing much further thin that."

"And did anything happen to you because of what you saw?" Edna asked quickly–at which Martin Senior nodded slowly.

"There was a strange shifting of viewpoint. Somehow everything mental became abruptly crystal clear–like looking into oneself, and the effect hasn't gone off either. I saw, for the briefest instant, how futile a thing murder is."

"Murder?" Jerry repeated, astonished.

"That startles you, eh? Well, let me tell you that up to that moment of conversion I had murder in my heart. I brought it with me from Earth. Just before we were whisked away I had planned, quite cunningly I thought, the murder of a young woman who was once a friend of mine. Frustration and a nurtured desire for vengeance had made of me a bitter, hard-lipped man. Now all that has evaporated. Not only do I clearly see the senselessness of murder, but I even turn from it with revulsion. One might put it all down to a purifying effect, I suppose?"

"Or to swift evolution," Edna mused, "Where formerly I had no scientific knowledge whatever I now have it in excelsis. I can even contemplate the infinite calculus and see the answer without the least effort. That can only be explained by a swift and profound mental advancement–and advancement is evolution."

"That's it!" Jerry snapped his fingers. "Each one of us has evolved to a point which humanity, under normal circumstances, would probably only reach in millions of years. Cosmic rays have done it–and are still doing it. As our minds have advanced and improved so have our bodies because the physical always obeys the mental. In one stroke, in a few hours of Earth-time, we have telescoped millions of years of advancement."

"And may yet go further," Lucille said quietly. "For me there has not come so much mental change as physical release from the disease which was killing me. I have nobody present who can positively say that I am cured: I just know that I am."

"If you know it," Stone said, "it doesn't matter what anybody else thinks. You are your own mistress, Lucille, as long as you retain an individuality."

The silence weighed heavy for a while. The assimilation of the fact that each one of them had become a genius, and that this state of rarefied intellectual eminence was still developing, was slow indeed. Earth-born habits and inhibitions were not that easy to cast aside. Each had been born of a human being and they had yet to outgrow the tenacious roots of heredity.

"How far do you suppose we can develop before reaching maximum?" Jerry asked abruptly–and as usual he directed the question to the venerable Jonathan Stone.

"Maximum," Stone answered, "is purely an arbitrary term set by human beings to denote a period beyond which they cannot predict anything certain. I would say that development is unbounded, infinite, free and–"

It was mid-evening. In the distance a brass band was playing on the barmy air. Children were laughing and gamboling some distance away. Jerry, instead of getting the complete answer to his question, found himself near the pavilion counter. Edna was standing close beside him. They looked at each other in profound bewilderment–and then around them. The rationed foods they had set out had vanished: they were back on their shelves. There was no sign of Jonathan Stone, Lucille, or Martin Senior.

"What's–happened?" Jerry demanded, his eyes blank. "Or did I dream something?"

"It was no dream," Edna reassured him, and those few words convinced him that he was not going insane. "Look at our sunburn! Just as it was when we were..."

Baffled, they raced to the pavilion doorway. Everything was perfectly normal. Ahead of them lay a stretch of grassy earth, with two trees–just as they had been in that alien space. Under one of them, on a rustic seat, sat an elderly white-haired man looking at a small Bible. Near him a shapely girl with golden-brown skin lay coiled on the grass. Further away still a young man sat against the second tree and looked about him. Beyond this immediate area children tumbled, giggled, and turned head-over-heels.

"I don't get it," Jerry whispered, his hand on Edna's arm. "Look at the clock over there!"

Edna looked, and started. It was just after 9.15—only the merest fraction, and even that time could have been occupied in moving to the doorway and contemplating the scenery.

"My watch also says nine-fifteen," Jerry whispered. "Last time I looked at it, it was heading for three o'clock!"

"Those children were just outside the slice which went elsewhere," Edna said, almost irrelevantly.

"It didn't happen!" Jerry insisted stubbornly. "It couldn't! Nothing's different and no time has elapsed. We had bad dreams - or good ones. Damned if I know which."

"Could you feel as you do towards me, and could I feel as I do towards you, merely on the strength of a dream?" Edna asked quietly. "That's something very real, Jerry, and very lovely. We no longer have the towering genius, but the character change in each of us remains."

"It seems so..." Jerry's admission was made with a frown of complete bewilderment, then his grip on Edna's arm tightened a little as Jonathan Stone, Lucille, and Martin Senior all began to move at the same instant. They glanced towards each other, rose from their various positions, and converged into a trio.

"That proves it did happen!" Jerry insisted. "Before the incident in alien space they didn't even know each other: now they meet like old friends."

The three came forward. In the eyes of Martin Senior and Lucille there was utter bafflement, but Jonathan Stone seemed to be smiling. And the vigorous uprightness which had come to him Elsewhere was still there. So, too, with the young man and woman the evidences were proclaimed by the bronze of their skin and the easy grace of their movements.

"Apparently," Jonathan Stone said, pocketing his Bible, "we are back!"

"But it happened!" Lucille insisted. "I'm absolutely sure that it happened! I know it did because I feel so well, so happy, so sure of myself and the future."

"And I know it happened because I no longer have murder in my heart," Martin Senior added. "But when did it happen? See that clock over there? It's still only a few minutes after nine-fifteen! According to that we never went at all."

"We went—and we came back," Jonathan Stone said, shrugging. "Whilst we were there we lost nearly all our human failings and weaknesses, and I had my unforgettable experience of seeing the Ultimate face to face. But, though the physical changes remain the genius of speeding evolution has gone like mist."

"Why?" Edna insisted.

"Because we are again surrounded by multi-millions of conflicting minds all unconsciously influencing our efforts to think straight. That means the evaporation of that brief genius, but it does not mean a step backwards to the former mental and physical state. Those conditions were destroyed forever and the correct adjustment made, not so much by the cosmic rays themselves as by the touch of the Artisan of the Universe himself."

"Yes, but—" Edna moved restlessly. "Mr. Stone, it still does not explain why it happened! We did so much, have brought back such incredible changes, and yet no time elapsed!"

"Time," Stone smiled, "is only a unit of measurement used by human beings to bring order into what would otherwise appear as chaos. In any case that experience was not Earthly, or even mundane, so how could Time as we know it be applied to it? Time is not absolute, you know. There is a flaw in it. Where, for instance, is the moment between present and future? You may say the next second is in the future, but the instant you say it, it is in the present, and before you realize it, it is in the past! What is in the tiny, infinitesimal gap between? No matter to what inconceivably small unit you reduce Time-instants, you can never find the bridge between this instant and the next. Maybe we did bridge it for a moment."

"There must have been a reason," Jerry insisted; then suddenly raising his voice he called over to him the children who were rioting nearby. They came immediately—dusty, happy, hot-faced girls and boys, their clothes in a condition that would probably give their mothers a fit when they arrived home.

"You kids been here for the last half-hour?" Jerry asked.

"Bin here all evening!"

"Time we went home, too!" One of the girls looked startled. "It's twenty-past nine!"

"Whilst you were playing about did you see anything queer happen?" Jerry insisted.

"Queer, mister? How'd y'mean? Queer?"

"Well, for instance, was there an earthquake or some sort? A loud explosion? Did this pavilion here vanish?"

The blank stares were enough; then a boy with freckles and a sawn-off nose made a rude face.

"You've bin out in the sun too long, mister! Come on, gang: time we got 'ome..."

"Satisfied?" Jonathan Stone asked dryly, and Jerry shook his head.

"I'll never be that. I'll go through the rest of my life wondering what caused our experience to happen."

"So will all of us probably." Martin Senior shrugged. "For myself I'm prepared to accept it for what it was—just one of those things."

"For which," Lucille muttered, "we should be unspeakably grateful. As to the reason for it: evidently there isn't one."

* * *

But of course she was wrong in this. The reason was nakedly plain, but such is the inscrutability of things Professor Engleman had not the least idea of having precipitated anything unusual. He stood now beside the switch of his disturber-field machine and contemplated it. Then he shook his head slowly.

"I have the feeling, ladies and gentlemen, that it might not be altogether safe to operate this machine this evening," he said. "I have just switched on and off–a matter of a split second–and I distinctly noticed a curious stress in the air, a kind of warping of forces. Now that should not be, particularly as I might miss our intended target of St. Michael's statue. It is possible the instrument has been thrown out of alignment in its removal to this hall."

"Surely you can risk it?" one of the scientists asked, quite disappointed.

"Risk it? Great heavens, no! You do not realize the power of this instrument, my dear sir. Not power, as such, but the power to cause a shift in the probability of matter itself! Unless I am absolutely sure of my target I dare not set the machine at work. You see, the field of disturbance set up, unless absolutely exact, might cause the electron-probabilities of any number of people or objects to suddenly yield to the probability that they are somewhere else. The whole thing is utterly unpredictable. In a single instant any part of the universe might change places with another part– such is the Law of Probability."

"Supposing," another scientist asked, "such a thing did really happen. Would the transposition be absolute? Permanent?"

"No, not necessarily," Engleman replied, after some thought. "Everything in the Universe has its proper place, and remains there unless interfered with by an outside source. My disturber-field is such an outside source. As long as it operated it would transpose a part of the Universe, but the moment the disturbance was cut off the normal process would instantly return, just as an elastic snaps back to its original length when tension ceases."

"During which time immense damage might be done!" another scientist protested.

"Damage?" Engleman raised his eyebrows. "Why no, my friend. The disturber-field operates in what I call hyper-Time, which is a complex way of saying it operates between the normal instants of Time. Since it is apart from the normal order of the Universe it cannot operate within the normal Time-span. Yes," Engleman sighed, "very unpredictable, and I am sorry not to be able to give you a demonstration. Indeed, perhaps I should work out the details much more carefully before I make any experiments. I'm glad I had the presence of mind to switch off my machine a second after I switched on. Had I continued, anything might have happened. As it is, all is well. At a later date I will call you all together again to witness something of real interest..."

Which brought the meeting to a close and left Engleman perfectly satisfied that, so far, he had not transgressed any laws of Nature. Five people at that moment walking thoughtfully from the Great Park could have told him a very different story.

ALICE, WHERE ART THOU?

This is the strange story of Alice Denham, whom I should have married ten years ago but did not. At the time, as some of the older amongst you will remember, there was quite a stir when Alice disappeared. I was even very close to being accused of her murder, along with Dr Earl Page. The only reason we escaped was because no trace could be found of Alice's body—and according to law, no body—no accusation. Instead the case of Alice became relegated to one of those 'peculiar' stories, such as footprints mysteriously ceasing to advance through unbroken snow.

I did not give the real facts concerning Alice ten years ago because I knew I would never be believed, nor Dr Page either. The thing was—and still is—so incredible. And yet it happened.

Suppose we go back to the beginning? My name is Rodney Fletcher. Ten years ago I had just started business on my own as a stockbroker and had every prospect of a successful business career. Today I am comparatively well-to-do, but still unmarried. There can never be anybody to take the place of Alice, so far as I am concerned.

It was just after I had set up in business that I first met Alice. She was a slim, elfin-type of girl with a wealth of blonde hair, smoke-gray eyes, and a tremendous amount of enthusiasm. She first came sailing into my orbit when I advertised for a secretary-receptionist. I had little hesitation over engaging her and in the space of a year she had become the supervisor of my ever-increasing clerical staff.

Inevitably I was drawn to her, and she to me. We exchanged confidences, we dined together. Our friendship deepened into romance; then one warm spring evening at twilight, as we were strolling through the city to keep a theater date together, we decided to become engaged.

At the time of this decision, which did not come as a surprise to either of us, we were just passing the brilliantly lighted window of a famous city jeweler's. I think it was the sight of a certain ring that prompted the abrupt decision to become engaged.

That certain ring! If only to God we'd never seen it! If only we had taken another street... but of what avail now to try to turn back the clock? There the ring was—compelling, seeming even to beckon us to look at it. We even forgot for the moment that we had decided to become engaged. Fixedly we looked at that ring. We wondered about it. We exchanged glances of awe.

The ring had been cunningly placed in the center of the resplendent window so that it automatically attracted the eye. Around it were grouped trays of diamond rings, together with pendants of sapphires, rubies, opals, and all the stock in trade of a high-class jeweler. The shop was still open and within, when at last we managed to drag our eyes from the ring, we could see a glimpse of an elderly man silently writing something in a ledger.

"Did you ever see anything like it, Rod?"

Alice's gentle, fascinated voice brought my attention back to the ring. The circlet holding the stone was normal enough and made of platinum, but the stone itself was as large as a small pea and radiated colors in a fashion neither of us had ever seen before. From the countless facets there flooded a blazing emerald green one moment, or ruby-red the next. We had only to move position by a fraction of an inch and the color changed again. Once even it seemed to me that there were faint glimpses of colors not within the normal spectrum, colors which one sensed rather than saw. Yet how am I to describe a color that has no normal parallel? By and large, the stone looked as though it were a composite of all precious gems rolled into one. Quite definitely, neither of us had ever seen anything like it.

And we had just become engaged. Was there anything illogical in the fact that we finally turned into the shop and asked to see the masterpiece at close quarters?

"Ah, yes—the Sunstone," the jeweler said, smiling, and put aside his ledger. "Quite a remarkable gem..."

He opened the barred cage-work at the back of the window and with exquisite care lifted the ring, complete on its plush display case. Still very gently he set it down on the glass-topped counter before us. And all Alice and I could do was stare at it, just as though it possessed some incredible hypnotic quality.

It had no such powers of course; it was simply that the unearthly, blazing luster held the eye with a magnetism all their own.

"A wonderful, wonderful stone," came the jeweler's voice, and at that I forced myself to look at him. He was an intellectual-looking man of late middle-age, with thick white hair curling at his temples.

"Where did it come from?" I asked. "I don't think I ever saw anything like it!"

"To the best of my knowledge, sir, and I have checked very carefully, it is the only specimen of its kind in the world. It was found originally in South America, became a sacred gem to a race now long forgotten, and eventually fell into the hands of an explorer. After that it traveled considerably, leaving quite a history everywhere it went."

"A history?" Alice questioned. "What sort of history, apart from its natural beauty?'

"A history which I find very hard to credit, madam," the jeweler smiled. "Or perhaps that is because I am too mature to be gullible. It does appear, though, that every owner of this ring up to now has vanished."

"Oh?" Alice looked surprised. "Vanished? To where?"

"That is what is so strange. Nobody seems to know. The ring has remained, but the various owners have disappeared—nor have they ever been traced...Of course," the jeweler continued, perhaps realizing he was jeopardizing his chance of a sale, "it may all be a lot of nonsense–and probably is. Just superstitious gossip, such as often does attach to a gem of unusual qualities. However, through various trade processes it finally came into my possession, and I am glad to say that in the two months I have possessed it I have not disappeared!"

Somehow it was a relief to laugh. And the ring still blazed up at us from its deep amethyst plush case... After a moment Alice withdrew her glove and reached a pale, slender hand tentatively forward.

"May I?" she questioned, and the jeweler quietly pushed the case towards her.

"By all means, madam. I have never yet seen how it looks on the finger of a woman."

With my help Alice slid the ring experimentally on the third finger of her right hand. Then she held her hand forward and turned it back and forth so the ring caught the lights. And the effect was breathtaking. It looked exactly as though sheer emerald and ruby fire were burning her finger away.

"Exquisite! Exquisite!" This seemed to be the only word she could whisper.

"But on the wrong finger," I smiled.

"So–an engagement?" the jeweler asked. "I do congratulate you. I am sure no other woman will ever possess so exquisite an engagement ring, madam."

Alice looked a little embarrassed, gently eased the ring from her finger, and put it back in the case. The jeweler waited, apparently sensing by some business instinct that he had made a sale even though the ring was back where it had started.

"It must be frightfully expensive," Alice said, and at that I imagine I looked indignant. Certainly I felt it.

"Who cares about that? I don't want the woman I love to wear any sort of trash... What is the figure?" I turned to the jeweler.

"As rings go it is not expensive, sir. Besides, its odd history, be it true or false, forbids a high figure... The price is ten thousand pounds."

I suppose that should have been a shock, but it was not. I mentally decided that should the need arise–which I considered highly unlikely–I would be more than able to get my money back by selling the ring. One always has to pay to be unique, so I made out my check there and then and handed it over. My business card was sufficient guarantee to the jeweler that I was a man of standing–and so we departed. Alice and I, she with the ring now on the third finger of her left hand and her smile one of ecstatic satisfaction.

"I shall never forget this evening as long as I live," she murmured, as we went on our way to the theater. "Engaged, and the possessor of the most wonderful ring in the world–all in one fell swoop."

"Nothing but the best for the best," I told her.

So we kept our theater date, but throughout the performance our attention kept wandering to that blaze of glory on Alice's slim hand. For that matter we were not the only ones looking at it. In our position in the orchestra stall we were close enough for the foremost members of the play to see us with some distinctness. I could not help but notice the fascinated stare of the young heroine as her eye caught that shimmering grandeur below. So fascinated was she that she nearly forgot her lines!

Yes, as Alice had said, that evening was a wonderful, memorable one. As for the strange story that went with the ring, we neither of us gave it another thought. We were both supremely happy, and before I departed from Alice towards midnight we had arranged to be married within a month. There seemed to be no point in a long engagement since we both knew exactly what we intended doing... From this day forward she would cease to be a member of my stock broking firm and make her arrangements for the great day.

On the following morning I was at the office as usual, too many business matters on my mind to give much thought to the aptly named 'Sunstone'. I was reminded of it, however, when towards evening Alice rang me up.

"Hello, darling!" I exclaimed, delighted to hear her voice again. "Everything fine?"

"No, Rod, not quite. That's why I'm ringing you. I'm - I'm a bit worried."

"What about? Nothing that can't be straightened out, surely?"

"Well, I –" The hesitation in her gentle voice puzzled me more than somewhat. "I wonder if you could spare the time to come over? There's something happened that's—that's not quite as it should be."

"Spare the time!" I echoed. "Nothing could keep me away. I'll come immediately."

Which I did. And I was inwardly shocked to find Alice's small, elfin-like face looking very pale and pinched. She seemed to have lost a great deal of her normal pink-and-white color. As I stood looking at her I was seized with the curious conviction that she appeared far more frail and small than ever before. Never a big woman at anytime, she seemed definitely to have lost proportions overnight! Ridiculous, of course! Probably the light, or something.

"What is it?" I asked her quietly.

She sank down on the divan and did not speak for a moment—then with a little touch of the dramatic she held out her left hand and shook it. Immediately the amazing ring on her third finger fell to the floor and lay blazing on the carpet. I stood there and just stared for a moment or two.

"How did you do that?" I demanded abruptly. "You just shook it off! That isn't possible, Alice. Last night, in the jeweler's, it only just fitted you."

"I know, Rod. It seems to have expanded, or something."

Alice gave me a queer look. Stooping, I picked the ring from the carpet and tested it on the end of my little finger. I had done the same thing the previous evening before giving it to her. The ring had not expanded in the least! A curious thought began to snake through my brain.

Catching at her slim hand I stared at it. I could have sworn it was far more slender and whiter than ever before.

"Alice!" I looked at her intently. "Alice, what's wrong?"

She shook her head. "How should I know? I seem to have lost weight and size overnight! I've been wearing this ring ever since you put it on my finger and—well, you've seen for yourself how slackly it fits." She gave a shrug and looked at me with hollow eyes.

"Oh, what's the use of trying to disguise it, Rod? My clothes don't fit as well as they did yesterday. I've lost size in many ways. Even this belt about my dress is a notch further in than usual!"

Still I gazed at her, totally unable to figure the business out. I said, "It's impossible!" without realizing that I had said it.

To this Alice made no comment; then coming to a sudden decision I took Alice's arm and had her stand over by the wall.

"Flatten yourself against it," I ordered. "I'm going to check up. What height is recorded on your Civil Registration Card?"

She nodded to the bureau. "Top shelf—left pigeon hole." In a moment or two I had the card out. Here, for once, the new law to register the dimensions, size, fingerprints, and so forth of every citizen was going to prove useful. It gave Alice's height at five feet two inches, and her weight as seven and a half stones.

"Kick off your shoes," I told her, returning to her side.

She obeyed and stood waiting. Then, with a book on top of her head and a tape measure in my hand I went to work. I made the measurement three times because I just could not believe what the measure said. She was now only five feet tall.

"Well?" she asked, as I stood thinking—and I made a quick evasion.

"Everything seems all right. What about your weight? Got a scale in the bathroom?"

She nodded and we went in to check up. Here, I had no chance to be evasive for she could see the face of the scale as well as I could. She was exactly one stone lighter in weight.

Her smoke-gray eyes were scared as she looked at me. "Rod, what does it mean? Why have I altered like this? Is my height any different? For heaven's sake be frank with me!"

I put an arm about her shoulders. "Matter of fact you're two inches shorter."

"But why on earth should I be? What's caused it?"

"I—don't—know." I was having a hard struggle to conceal my inward alarm. "Something to do with the ring, perhaps. I don't think there's anything to worry about," I added quickly. "After all, people do lose weight sometimes very quickly, particularly after severe emotional strain. Maybe our getting engaged was more of a tax on your nerves than you thought."

"That would not make me lose two inches of height, would it?"

By this time we had returned to the lounge and Alice had put her shoes on again before I had thought of an answer.

"At night, Alice, a human frame is less in height than it is in the morning because the gristle in the backbone compresses under the pull of gravity."

"Rod, you're a very bad liar." Alice looked at me gravely. "You're not fooling me one little bit, you know, even though I appreciate your trying to spare my feelings. The fact remains that I am less in size in every way and I've got to know why!"

I picked up the ring from where I had placed it on the occasional table. I turned it over slowly. To both of us it was no longer a thing of beauty but something to be feared and hated. Finally I wrapped it in my handkerchief and thrust it in my pocket.

"Frankly," I confessed, "this whole business is much too deep for me!"

"And for me! I keep thinking of the story the jeweler told us—about all the previous owners having disappeared. He didn't say in what manner they had disappeared, and it's sort of left me wondering... if..."

"Forget that poppycock!" I said brusquely. "Just a lot of rubbish. Won't do you any good to brood over such stuff. Tell you what we can do. I know a Professor Earl Page, and he's a pretty good physicist. Member of the same club as I am. Just a chance this business may be scientific and that he can explain it away. Grab your hat and coat and we'll go and see. My car's outside."

As we drove through the busy streets I reflected on the usefulness of knowing Earl Page, PhD. Though not an outstanding figure in the scientific world, he certainly knew his job when it came to scientific analysis. Indeed, his choice lay so obviously in the exploration of little known things that his fame was thereby obscured. Not that he cared. A man with half a million for his private income can be obscure in comfort...

Page looked decidedly surprised when the manservant showed Alice and me into the well-appointed library. He was by the window, under the reading lamp, the light etching out his sharp features and neatly trimmed black torpedo-beard and moustache. One could easily have mistaken him for a Frenchman.

Getting to his feet he came over to us—a small, concise man with a perpetual slight smile that revealed the white of his teeth through his beard.

"Hello, Rod! Quite a little while since I've seen you."

"Been busy," I said, and promptly introduced Alice. This done, and the handshakes over, Page stood with his hands plunged in the pockets of his velvet smoking jacket whilst I gave him the story in detail. At the end of it he made no comment for a moment or two; then he looked at us with his small, keen blue eyes.

"Quite a remarkable story! Without any apparent explanation beyond the acquisition of a strange gem, you Miss Denham, start to lose weight and height, eh? Unique! Most unique! Let me have a look at it, Rod."

I handed over the handkerchief containing the ring, and then added: "Better take care how you deal with it!"

"I can assure you that I shan't take any chances. Come along with me, both of you."

He led the way from his library to the small laboratory at the end of the hall. Floodlights came up automatically as the door opened. Removing the ring from the handkerchief with insulated forceps, Page put it under the electron microscope and peered intently. He spent nearly five minutes doing this, adjusting the instrument and murmuring under his breath. But the perpetual smile was still there when he glanced up.

"I assume," he asked, "that you are under the impression that the rays from this stone are simply prismatic light rays, like those of the diamond?"

"Well, aren't they?" I asked, surprised.

He shook his head, coming slowly forward. "No. This gem is the most amazing thing upon which I have ever set eyes... Most stones rely on their light-wave dissemination for their beauty—such as the diamond, ruby, sapphire, and so forth. On the other hand, stones of the opal class are absorptive of light. Here, however, is a gem of rare properties in that it radiates not only light waves but ether waves!"

Alice and I gazed, uncomprehending. Page continued:

"I hardly need to tell you, do I, that the air and space itself abound in different radiations such as heat, cosmic rays, radio waves, and so forth? So far we know of no mineral structure that will split up and radiate any of these radiations. Our limit is with stones which re-radiate light-waves with rare beauty. But here is a stone, apparently with natural facets, which re-radiates cosmic waves, and perhaps dozens of other radiations of which we know very little. It splits them up prismatically, hence the unholy luster and the suggestion that here and there are colors we've never yet encountered. The dominant blue is, I think, caused by the breaking-up of ultra-violet; and the red is derived from infra-red."

"But what has all this to do with Alice?" I demanded.

"I don't quite know—yet." But I fancied from his expression that he did.

"Most certainly she had better not wear that ring again. I shall try to get a better light on its history from the jeweler from whom you bought it. The point is, that a stone like this able to re-radiate various waves may be utilizing some that are harmful to a human being. If the ring is no longer worn the trouble should cease..."

As he had been talking Page had led us back into the library. "Now," he continued seriously, "you can rest assured that I'll find out all I can about it. The implications of this ring may be far-reaching. Now you have ceased to wear it, Miss Denham, I think you ought to be perfectly all right."

"Well, that's something," Alice admitted. "But what about the stone in weight and two inches in height which have gone into nowhere? Will they return?"

"Candidly, I just don't know!"

Alice gave a rueful smile. "Even at five feet two I always felt pretty small. Now I feel positively microscopic!"

"Petite, and as sweet as ever," I smiled, my arm about her shoulders.

"If there should be any further developments, come and see me immediately," Page advised. "In fact, perhaps both of you had better drop in tomorrow evening and I'll be able to tell you how I've progressed."

On that note we left matters. Alice said little as I drove her home, but I could tell that she was still very much alarmed. Nor was I much better myself. There had been something in Earl Page's manner, which to me—knowing him extremely well—had implied that he knew most of the truth but had not dared to tell it...

And the next day my alarm was sharpened considerably when immediately after breakfast, before I had set off for town, Alice rang me. Her voice was shaking with nervousness.

"Rod, I'm frightened! This business is still going on even though I haven't worn the ring! I've lost dimensions again in the night—I had some terrible dream, too. I seemed to be flying through space, or something —"

"I'll come right away," I interrupted. "Keep a grip on yourself, sweetheart. I'll soon be with you."

I only stayed long enough to leave directions at the office, then I was on my way again to Alice's flat as fast as the car would go and this time, as she opened the door to me, I could behold the diminution clearly.

Alice's clothes were hanging baggily on her lessened figure. She was doll-like, fragile, and pitifully frightened. From her gaunt, weary face it was plain what sort of a night she had been through. The moment she saw me she caught hold of my arm and hung on to it as though afraid to let go.

"All right," I murmured, embracing her gently. "Take it easy, darling. We'll get this mess cleared up somehow. Let's go and see Page right away."

When we arrived at Page's home he was in dressing gown and slippers, finishing his breakfast. His expression immediately became grim as his eyes traveled to Alice.

"Sit down, both of you..." He called for extra coffee and then proceeded slowly. 'I called on the jeweler last evening but apparently he could not add anything to what you had already told me. I then browsed through the library and read up all I could find concerning gems—but without result. The 'Sunstone' is not even mentioned. So I had to fall back on an analysis of my own."

The extra coffee was brought and Page resumed. "I spent most of last night making tests. As I at first thought, the gem does transmit radiations of all kinds. If a low-powered radio beam is directed at it, it reflects it again as a mirror does light. Absolutely uncanny! However, from the gem there is radiating a wavelength of such exceptional smallness that I cannot place it even with instruments—unless I accept the most unbelievable proposition ever heard of!"

"And what's that?" I asked bluntly.

"That the wavelength is being generated from somewhere inconceivably small and invisible to us. The wavelength also has a power that has a surprising effect on flesh-and-blood organisms. A white mouse which I put beside the ring for the night has decreased in size!"

Alice and I looked at each other anxiously. The coffee cups we were holding in our hands remained ignored.

"Strangely enough," Page continued, "the effect continues even when the ring is removed. That seems to show that once the effect—whatever it is—is absorbed into a living system it continues to exert its influence —"

"Then what happens to me?" Alice cried in horror. "At least tell me that! I've got to know!"

Page came forward and looked down at her seriously. "Believe me, Miss Denham, I wish I could give you the details, but for the moment I just don't know them. I'm fighting something I never even heard of before! I will be able to form a better prognosis when I have studied the final reactions of the mouse. In the meantime, if you can make arrangements to stay here, where I can keep you under observation, I may be able to do something for you. Think you can manage that?"

"Anything! Anything at all!"

"Good! I'll instruct my housekeeper to make the necessary arrangements. Be back here about noon with everything you require, then we'll go into the matter thoroughly."

He accompanied us as far as the hall, scribbled something on a card, and pushed it into my pocket whilst Alice's back was turned. Once I had left Alice at her flat with the promise to return to her at noon after a call at the office, I read what had been written on the card. It was not reassuring.

Return immediately before Miss Denham. Very important that I should see you.

So, with dire expectations of something dreadful, I went back immediately to Page's home–and he wasted no time in coming to the point now Alice was not present to hear the details.

"Rod, your fiancee is unwittingly fighting something of baleful power! Unless my guess is entirely wrong, that jewel is being operated upon by powers in the microcosm."

"Microcosm?" I repeated vaguely. "I'm a stockbroker, Earl, not a scientist."

"I'm sorry," he apologized. "I'm referring to the atomic world, which on an inconceivably small scale duplicates our known universe. It is quite possible that there might be highly intelligent beings in this microcosm, existing upon an electron. An electron cannot really be likened to a planet, of course, except for the purposes of analogy. However, since an electron is basically an electric charge, the only assumption we can draw is that the denizens of such an electron-world must themselves be electrical. Possibly even electric charges possessing intelligence."

"Intelligent electricity? Dammit, man, that's stretching things a bit, isn't it?"

He smiled wistfully. "Is it? We are intelligent electricity, too, remember! Maybe that startles you?"

It certainly did! Yet when I came to think of it I could see he was right. Everything material, including human and animal organisms, is based on electric forces. So after a while his idea did not seem so extraordinary after all.

"And you believe these electrical inhabitants of an electron world may be operating through the Sunstone?"

"I think so, yes. The action of the wavelength makes me think that, but the purpose of it I just do not understand! It is not remotely possible that Miss Denham was deliberately singled out. I think the whole thing was pure chance, and that she happened to be the recipient of these minute wavelengths."

"And not only Alice," I exclaimed, startled. "All the, other owners of the ring disappeared, too!"

"That," Page said, "is what is so disquieting."

A thought suddenly struck me. "What of the countless others who must have handled the gem? Even the jeweler himself for that matter! Nothing happened—least not to him."

"As to that, they didn't have it continuously in contact with their flesh for over twelve hours. There was no effect on the mouse either until twelve hours had passed. I had the ring fastened tightly against its body, by the way. You will recall that only the owners of the ring have vanished - that is those who must have worn it. We do not hear anything untoward about those who transferred it from place to place."

"Of all the damnable, horrific gems to be let loose in the world!" I breathed. "It's more deadly than the most virulent poison! It's so—so utterly beautiful, yet so fiendishly diabolical!"

"Very true," Page sighed, thinking.

"What you are telling me, Earl, is that somebody of incredible scientific ingenuity, living on an electronic charge—or planet—deliberately sent that gem into our vastly greater universe and thereafter used it for the transmission of certain inexplicable wavelengths which cause shrinkage. Is that it?"

"That's it."

"I don't see how that is possible." I gave a frown. "This gem must be countless millions of times larger than the world from which they sent it! How do you reconcile that?"

"There's a simple parallel," he answered. "Our modern scientists, by a play of vibrations upon certain mineral substances, can change the mineral gradually into a totally different atomic structure. For instance, they can change carbon into hard diamonds, and that's only one example... These electronic men of science, unseen, somewhere in the microcosm, have obviously transmitted from their world a series of vibrations to the extreme limit of their universe, knowing full well that beyond it must lie the greater macrocosm in which spins our world -"

"Why our world?" I interrupted. "Are there not tens of millions of worlds to choose from?"

"Certainly, but ours—as far as we know at present—is the only one with human —I say human—life. Hence Earth was, I suggest, singled out. The concentrated force of those vibrations reacted on some part of our world, perhaps determined beforehand, to produce a combination of chemicals that formed into the Sunstone. That, I believe, is what happened..."

I must have looked very doubting, for Page added: "The fact that they can do it is proved because they can still send vibrations through it even now, no matter where it is moved. That shows conclusively that the radiations are chained by some magnetic power or other to the jewel wherever it may be. Mighty science, Rod! Science pressed to its ultimate power for a reason we do not as yet understand. But we shall! I wanted to tell you all this in private. Once Miss

Denham is with us again I may not have the opportunity and it would be nonsensical to alarm her unduly. By examination, tests, and research I may yet solve the mystery and save her."

"There are no two ways about it!" I cried. "The alternative to saving her is unthinkable!"

Page clapped me on the shoulder. "We'll see what we can do—and needless to say, not a word to her!"

And so I departed to pick Alice up from her flat. I still do not know how I managed to keep a reasonably cheerful face on things, considering what I had heard. I was a victim to the knowledge that overwhelming forces had suddenly sprung into being, and the whole damned issue of them seemed to be concentrated entirely on the woman I held most dear...

Naturally, I made arrangements so that I too could stay with Page and be beside Alice in case of urgent need. There was at least a cold yet reassuring efficiency about Page, which was wonderfully heartening to both Alice and me. Indeed, her understandable fears abated considerably under Page's calm watchfulness.

From noon onwards until early evening he was the perfect host, never once mentioning the matter closest to our minds—but in that time I noticed how skillfully he wormed his way into Alice's confidence, how he watched her constantly whilst not appearing to be doing so, how his adding-machine brain made a note of her every movement and reaction.

We dined at seven, talked for another hour, and then at Page's suggestion went to the laboratory. Immediately he went into action. With his quick, capable hands he set about arranging his instruments, asking for and receiving the fullest co-operation from Alice. Neither of us understood much of what he did, though we certainly watched in fascinated interest... He used X-ray screens and took several plates; he tied elastic bandages around Alice's arm, in the fashion of a blood-pressure test—the difference being that in this case he attached electrodes to the bandage and then stood watching pensively as needles jumped in a panel of dials. He made notes by the score and went to work with other machines that bristled with tubes, wires, insulator banks, and multiple switches.

His final experiment did not concern Alice at all but the frightened and very much shrunken white mouse, and lastly the Sunstone itself. That deadly gem still shone with its unholy and transcendently beautiful luster.

At last Page was finished. He stood with his hands plunged in the pockets of his velvet jacket, beard touching his chest as he pondered.

"The facts," he said finally, "are not reassuring! There is nothing to be gained by evasion."

"Nothing at all," Alice agreed quietly, a tremor in her voice. "What is it all about, Dr Page? Since I am the victim I am entitled to know. I don't want promises or put-offs. I simply want to know, where I stand."

"It is only because I think I might be able to save you that I am going to tell you what is happening," Page replied. "In the first place, Miss Denham, the electric content of your body is three times that of normal. You did not know that, did you?"

"I certainly didn't. Would it explain a slight feeling of cramp all over me?"

"A mild pins-and-needles effect? Yes, that would explain it. Because you had that gem in close contact with your body for over twelve hours certain wavelengths have operated through it–wavelengths generated from somewhere in what we call the microcosm..." Page went into an explanation very similar to the one he had given me, except that it was 'watered down' especially not to frighten Alice too much; then he continued:

"This radiation has altered the normal electrical content of your body to such an extent that there is a distinct magnetism. I cannot work out the exact intricacies involved, but it seems that this magnetism is causing a closing-up of the electronic orbits that make up the molecular units of your body. As they close, you shrink, and also evidently lose weight with a kind of radiating by-product. Is that clear?"

Alice nodded, even though she looked completely bewildered. "Then what makes it progress? Why didn't it cease once the ring was taken out of the way?"

"Because the effect was by then stabilized. The electric content had been supplied to cause the alteration and it simply goes on functioning. Therefore, we must set to work to find a counteractive radiation that will arrest the trouble, or at least produce a negative result on the extra electricity absorbed into your body. Somehow we will find it, Miss Denham. Don't worry! This whole business has been devised by a brilliant science for an obscure reason, but I've one or two ideas of my own yet to try out..."

Page stood for a moment or two, considering, then he said: "I believe you mentioned you had strange dreams last night?"

"I did, yes, and I cannot understand what they meant. It seemed to me as though I were falling endlessly through space. I could see the stars and great abysses of dark. Then there were huge, empty worlds..." Alice gave a wistful smile. "It made me feel just like a goddess looking down on the universe!"

"Mmmm. As a scientist, Miss Denham, it sounds to me more like a definite telepathic contact, between worlds. Telepathy takes no cognizance of distance and some kind of contact might be established between yourself and this unknown spot in the microcosm... From here on, Miss Denham, take careful note of your dreams. Write down every detail of them the moment you wake up, no matter how trivial those details may seem. Everything helps.... For the moment I think that is all we can do. Tonight I shall work out a plan of attack to neutralize the trouble. Do all you can to sleep well, and if you don't I'll fix a sedative for you."

It was more than evident to me that Page wanted to hurry both of us off to our rooms. I waited about my own room for nearly an hour after bidding Alice good night; then I returned downstairs to the laboratory. Sure enough Page was there, as I had expected, a long pipe smoldering between his bearded lips, his compact figure bent over the brightly lighted writing desk.

He merely glanced up and nodded to me, then went on working. Every now and again he got to his feet and set to work with electrical apparatus. There were satanic cracklings of energy, the air becoming tainted with the odor of ozone discharges. Once or twice he tried putting the diminutive mouse in a glass tube between anode and cathode and subjected it to a bombardment of unknown forces. The mouse appeared unharmed, but evidently the effect was not what Page desired for I saw he was becoming increasingly irritated.

"It's damnable!" he muttered at last, and threw down the pencil on his desk.

I looked at him morosely. "I could think of an even stronger word that that, Earl!"

"I'm talking about this microcosmic world, wherever it is, and the fiendish inhabitants thereon! They must possess scientific knowledge far greater than ours. Why, they're even using a form of electrical energy that I just don't understand! And that, from me, is some admission!"

It certainly was! Earl Page was one of the foremost electrical wizards of his time even if he did keep his genius to himself.

"Like groping in the dark!" Page banged his fist on the desk.

I looked at him again. "Look, Earl, do you mean by all this that Alice is–"

"I don't mean anything yet for certain." His voice was sharp with frustration. "I've tried to neutralize the mouse and you can see for yourself what's happened. The poor little devil still goes on shrinking! Look at it!"

I looked. Then I said mechanically, "There must be a way, somehow! You'll find it, Earl. I'm sure you will!"

"You mean you hope I will! So far I have had nothing but failure to offer and upstairs there is that poor girl relying on my addled brains to save her from –" Page checked himself. "We don't know what from. That's probably the worst part of the whole business."

"Suppose," I said deliberately, forcing myself to speak words that were utterly deadening to me, "no cure can be found and Alice just... fades away? How long will the process take?"

"No idea. If she reacts as the mouse has there is no predictable speed to the shrinkage. Sometimes it is slow, sometimes fast–but it's always there! It never stops."

There was a long silence between us. Page lighted his pipe and drew at it savagely, his brows down, his face a pool of darkness under the diagonal rays of the desk-lamp. I turned the whole horrific business over in my mind and finally arrived at what seemed to me a logical inference.

"You say it is some form of electrical energy which is causing the orbits of the electrons forming Alice's body to shrink? Well, can't you find the opposite wavelength–or whatever it is–and make them expand?"

"That's what I have been trying to do, but it's like trying to work out a sum without knowing the basic principle of mathematics. I keep telling you, man, this electrical energy is not of the same type as we're familiar with."

"I can't understand that at all, Earl. Surely electrical energy is the same throughout the universe? Positive and negative and–"

He interrupted me with a dry chuckle. "We once thought the electron radiated energy, and that this would make it describe a continually decreasing orbit until it would spiral down into the nucleus and cause the whole atom to vanish in a flash of radiation. We once thought that, I say, until Niels Bohr came along with his quantum theory and showed that an electron whilst rotating in its orbit does not in fact radiate any energy whatever! It only radiates energy when jumping from one orbit to another, and the energy thus radiated is a quantum... So you see, if one supposed form of radiant energy can be supplanted so easily by another, why cannot electricity as such be in far more forms than the one we know? Come to think of it, electrical energy in a microcosmic universe probably would be very different from ours. Different laws. Different balance... The whole thing's plain hell, Rod!"

From here on he took so little notice of me, seemed indeed rather distracted by my presence, I took myself off to my room again. But as I passed along the dim corridor past Alice's room I paused and listened. I could hear her talking—or rather mumbling—at intervals, obviously as she slept. I pressed closer to the door and tried to catch the words.

"... shall be found and taken away... So vast and barren and alone... The machines! The robots! The cities! So far away... So far away... So small and yet so mighty!"

Then silence for a long while and deep breathing. At length I swung and raced quickly back to the laboratory to tell Page.

"Well, we obviously can't wake her," he said briefly. "But we might hear plenty with this..." He picked up a wafer-flat microphone attached to a small portable tape recorder. Once we were upstairs again he pushed the microphone under Alice's bedroom door and then we both kept a silent vigil in the gloom, our faces faintly lighted by the green glow from the recorder's volume control. When presently the volume indicator began to jump on its green dial we both slipped on subsidiary headphones and listened to Alice's amplified voice as the recording was made.

"... the city covers the planet. The last man is dead but the robots live on... Even the robots must die unless they make a being of flesh-and-blood who will grow into an intelligent, reasoning creature and supply them with the life-force to make them anew..."

Long pause. The night wind sighed gently against the big window on the corridor. Down in the hall the big clock struck two.

"Looks as though we might be getting some idea of what really is the basis of all this," Page muttered, dragging at his extinguished pipe. "I don't like the sound of it, either! Robots needing a flesh-and-blood creature! It sounds—"

"She's talking again!" I interrupted.

"... robots follow out the commands of the flesh-and-blood master who is dead ... They must have human life— flesh-and-blood... The microcosm is empty of life. But there is life on Earth. A mighty world is Earth, huge beyond imagining. One living being from that world and life can be manufactured from it, unit by unit. Unit by unit..."

A jumbled mumbling and then: "Once I am small enough they will take me in an intra-atomic ship, bear me across the gulf to their own strange world. By then I shall be little more than an electrical charge, but the flesh-and-blood basis will still remain..."

The words drifted off. Page waited for what seemed an interminable time; then he silently withdrew the microphone, and switched off the instrument. With a silent movement of his head he indicated that I should follow him to the laboratory where we could talk in our normal voices.

"Looks to me as though we're really up against it!" he said bitterly. "Those vague statements were obviously begotten of a telepathic contact with the microcosm, such as I theorized at first."

"Evidently," I admitted worriedly.

"Seems clear enough what is wrong," Page continued after a moment. "A race of robots—or at least they evidently seem that way to poor Alice's distracted mind - on a microcosmic world cannot continue indefinitely without a reasoning flesh-and-blood creature—or creatures. Following out the orders of the last flesh-and-blood master they have got to find more living matter from which to manufacture the life-force that animates them. There is apparently no life anywhere in their realm, so they have turned to this Earth of ours—hence the creation of the Sunstone; hence the disappearance of the previous owners thereof; hence the remorseless shrinkage of Alice Denham."

"What happened to the previous owners of the Sunstone, do you suppose?" I asked. "Did these microcosmic scientists get them? If so, why aren't they satisfied? Why keep on trying to get more flesh-and-blood?"

"I don't know for sure," Page responded, "but I have thought of one rather horrifying possibility. Miss Denham spoke of a race of robots that needed life-force to animate them: she also spoke of there being no life in the microcosm. It could be that this race has denuded the microcosm of all life, and are now having to turn to Earth to replenish their supply. As to why they are continuing their activities, it may be because of the different time-ratio. A few hours in our universe must be centuries to them; they must be using up the energy of living beings as fast as that damnable ring can supply them!'

I was too horrified to make any comment to this. Alice had mentioned 'units'. That could mean... vivisection! After a moment my gaze wandered from Page's troubled face to where the Sunstone was lying beyond him. It still lay on the bench not far from the greatly shrunken white mouse. A thought struck me, though I had no idea whether it was logical or not.

"According to your theory, Earl, once the gem has been in contact with the flesh for over twelve hours it produces an electrical effect which is progressive, whether the stone continues in contact or not?"

" That's right—and it's obvious my theory is correct."

"Are you sure, though? Is it not perhaps possible that the stone radiates or transmits its queer energy over an enormous distance and thereby sort of keeps replenishing the mysterious energy which it has imparted to the 'subject'?"

"Most improbable, I'd say. Why, what have you in mind?"

"I was thinking that we might isolate the gem completely, surround it with a lead wall or something, to stop any radiation getting through. Would that work?"

"It might. Matter of fact I have a lead container that was used recently for radium needles. It might suit our purpose."

"Try it!" I urged. "Nothing is too fantastic at a time like this. We can soon see if it has any effect on the mouse."

So we went to work–or rather Page did. Handling that terrible jewel was a task I preferred to leave to him alone, so I stood watching as with his insulated forceps he transferred the stone to the interior of the lead container and then clamped down the lid.

"By all normal laws this should block all radiation," he said, thinking. "The trouble is that I still don't know what kind of a radiation it is–even if it is radiation at all! I believe it's a form of electrical energy–"

"Makes no difference," I interrupted. "That container will still block it, won't it?"

"Definitely!"

So we started to watch the mouse as it moved with mournful slowness about its cage. There was none of the bright-eyed scampering usually attached to such a rodent. Just listless movements, and the obvious government of fear. Presently, since there was nothing we could do for a while, we went into the house proper and had some refreshment. It succeeded in partly chasing away our tiredness; then we returned into the laboratory and studied the mouse intently. Quietly, Page picked up the nearby ruler, lifted the mouse from its cage and laid it alongside the inches scale.

His face grim, he dropped the rodent back in the cage. and closed the lid.

"Still shrinking," he said.

Those words were to me an actual physical shock: I had been so sure my theory was the right one. Yet, just as quickly a new thought came, and I wondered why I had not grasped it before.

"Earl! How's this for another idea? The world from which this infernal energy, or whatever it is, is emanating, may actually be within the stone itself!"

He gave a slight start. "Why, yes," he murmured softly. "I never thought of that. More than probable, in fact, which would explain how it is always kept in focus. Not only that world but its universe, and maybe a myriad other universes besides."

"Destroy the stone utterly by electricity and we destroy that electronic world," I said solemnly. "Stockbroker I may be, but I can grasp that much!"

He hesitated no more. Quickly taking the gem from the container–once again with insulated forceps–he put it in the matrix of the atomic equipment. It seemed mighty force to use upon so small an object–the smashing of the nut with the sledgehammer indeed! –but the purpose merited it. Switches closed. For nearly ten minutes energy built up–then Page released it by throwing the switches. The Sunstone vanished in unholy fire and cascades of electrical energy, and to both of us it was a somber thought that maybe thousands—millions—of universes in the microcosm had been destroyed in that instant.

"Now!" Page breathed, moving back to the rodent. "Let us see... I still think the energy once absorbed is irreversible and continuous. But we can hope..."

In an hour we knew the answer. The mouse was three inches less in size...!

The morning showed that Alice was visibly smaller. Breakfast was an almost silent affair, neither Page nor I saying what we had been doing in the night. He still seemed to think there was something he could try.

What I found particularly hard to endure was the dumb look of terror in Alice's eyes. I tried to reiterate assurances - but as the hours flew by and Page labored to master a science centuries ahead of him, my hopes began to sink into my boots. Evidently the energy was progressive, for it was still operating even though we had probably destroyed the original creators of it. This again was an awful thought. Alice had muttered something in her sleep about being picked up in an interatomic ship. That might now never be. Where in the devil's name would she go if we could not save her? If we could not. Egoist! The whole thing relied, as before, on Page.

Alice could see that we were fighting the impossible - and Page left no channel unexplored. He called in other scientists, and once they realized the astounding implications they threw all their combined genius into an effort to overcome the devilish power which was reducing the silent Alice before their fascinated eyes.

Hour by hour now, Alice was changing incredibly. She went to her room and I was the only one whom she would permit to see her. I gave her the news of the grim battle we were fighting, and still I tried to assure her that we would yet win the battle. Her only response was to smile faintly. She lay there in the bed, overcome now by a tremendous lethargy, which all the drugs sent up by Page failed to break. Yes, she lay there, like a waxen doll, and when I looked down on her I openly cursed that heinous stone we had seen in the jeweler's window.

I could not remember meals, or periods of rest, or anything. I was flying up and down stairs all the time. Until at length it was early evening and I realized that all the feverish activity of the day was over. The scientists had departed and Page sat in the laboratory, his dead pipe forgotten between his teeth.

Presently he looked up at me. "It's no good, Rod! We've got to tell her—even if she doesn't know already. We're beaten! The latest reports from the other workers show that there is no known way of fighting this mysterious electrical force which, once infused into a living organism, causes the electronic orbits to shrink, and shrink and shrink!"

I stirred slowly as I stood before his desk. "Somehow I had thought, even to the last, that you'd pull something out of the hat."

"I'm not a magician, Rod." He gave my arm a brief grip. "Sometimes there drifts into the orbit of science a power, an unknown factor, which is completely beyond analysis. This is one of those times." He got to his feet and put a hand to his forehead. "God, but I'm weary...! We'd better go and break the news as gently as we can."

We went solemnly from the laboratory, through the hall, and up the stairs. When we had reached the corridor I caught hold of Page's arm.

"Earl—a moment. We can't tell Alice a terrible thing like this without giving her a way out. You've got dozens of potent, painless drugs down in that lab of yours. Can't you use one so that she..."

He hesitated. "That would be euthanasia," he said.

"I don't care!" I told him brutally. "Every court in the land would uphold a mercy killing in a case like this! I insist on it, Earl. I'll take the responsibility!"

He looked at me steadily, then without another word he went back down the corridor. Quietly I entered Alice's room and took a few steps forward, leaving the door open.

I stopped. There was a deadly quietness in the evening light. Outside the window the newly budding beech tree swayed in the evening breeze... I absorbed the merciless, overwhelming fact that the bed was empty! There were the tangled clothes, the sewn-in nightdress, which Alice had contrived to fit her diminishing proportions... And that was all.

At the sound of swift footsteps I turned and looked fixedly towards the doorway as Page came in, a phial in his hand. He looked at me, at the bed, and back to me.

"We shan't need that now," I said in a low voice.

Outside the window the beech tree swayed and was straight again...

JUDGMENT BELL

I had noticed the storm gathering for some time. During the afternoon while Enid Cleggy and I had picnicked amidst a carpet of green grass and buttercups, the heat had taken on a certain sullen, crushing load. It had become an effort to even move, so we had lain on our backs and gazed at the drowsy June sky, watching the slow but imperceptible gathering of deep smoky-blue clouds on the southern horizon.

Towards late afternoon quiet had fallen over the roiling landscape of this southern English countryside. Far away, cows stood with their backs to the hedges. This in itself was significant.

"Enid, we'd better be moving," I said a last, anxiously. "We have not the car, remember, and if we want to finish the day out in dry clothes we had better get moving for the 'bus. And that's three miles! Come on."

Enid nodded and helped me to pack up the picnic tackle into the wicker basket, then carrying it between us we hurried across the grass on the return journey to the 'bus stop.

Altogether though, despite this abrupt finish, it had been a grand day, one of the very few I was able to permit myself from a busy life in the city. Enid, too, had arranged it so that she could accompany me, for as the head saleswoman of a London dress salon she had little time to spare.

She was a practical sort of girl, good-looking in a sharp kind of way, with blonde hair and keen gray eyes. Never in so many actual words had we admitted to each other that we were in love. It was accepted for granted, as so often happens between busy people—but I was resolved it should not be long before I asked her to become my wife.

"It's raining!" she ejaculated suddenly, holding out her palm.

It was—big drops. The storm clouds had gathered now from blue to violet. Far away in the distance was a crumbling, rolling thud that marked the storm's overture: and now came a strange thing. During all this summer day I had been blissfully happy, yet with the first growl of distant thunder something happened to me.

An indescribable sensation of dread seized upon me, a sense of withering foreboding. I just could not understand it. After all, I had never been afraid of thunderstorms—not afraid of anything, indeed. Yet—

"What's the matter, Bob?" Enid asked the question in surprise.

I gave a start, forced a smile. "Eh? Oh—nothing. Just felt a bit strange, as though— Skip it," I growled. "Probably the electric tension before the storm breaks."

"Or those sardines," she reflected. "I had any doubts about them at the time– Say, we must hurry," she added in anxiety. "The rain's increasing and we're only wearing thin things."

We broke into a run as the rain came down harder. Soon it was hissing all round us, bubbling in the dry, sun-scorched grass, sending a miasma of steam floating up from the valley atop which rolled this undulating country. The further we went the more apparent it became to me that we could never reach the 'bus stop, much less home, without being drenched to the skin. Yet if we sheltered under one or other of the dotted trees we would be just asking for it.

I slid to a standstill in the muddy grass, rain beating on my bare head. Enid stopped too, her flimsy frock plastered to her slender form, and her hair a dripping mop.

"What about Kelby Abbey?" I suggested. "It's only half a mile away in the dip there. It's always open. We could shelter."

She hesitated; and I knew why. There is a legend about Kelby Abbev–but after all there are legends about all abbeys, more or less, especially one like Kelby, over five hundred years old.

"It'd be a sanctuary," I went on earnestly. "This looks like being the devil of a storm. We might be struck dead out here."

"All right," she agreed, but reluctantly. "Frankly, I've never felt too happy about churches since my uncle dropped dead in one twelve years ago."

It was no time to argue about this, so off we went as hard as we could go through slush and wet grass. As we went the first fiendish crack of thunder broke right over our heads simultaneously with the lightning. It was a terrific flash, drenching the storm-ridden land in bright blue.

Again with it came that sensation of unsupportable horror. It was a most terrible feeling, as though my soul had been momentarily plunged into a nethermost Pit of the Damned. I said nothing to Enid about it: she was alarmed enough already with the fury of the storm.

We ran like champion track sprinters along that last half mile, the picnic basket between us. The wind had risen by now and was bending and lashing the elms in a fury of gloom that had deepened into a near-twilight. Twice as we finished the course the lightning whip-lashed across the ebon sky and the thunder set the ground quaking; then through the haze of rain loomed the ponderous semi-ruined bulk of Kelby Abbey, with its ever-open door.

We floundered up the steps and into the quiet, somber interior. Peace dropped upon us immediately like a mantle. We paused a while, put the basket down, glanced back at the rain hissing down on the worn steps. We thanked God on that moment for Kelby Abbey with its doors ever open to the devout who might seek its hallowed precincts for a brief relief from the life material.

Enid gave a rather relieved smile.

"Well, we are out of that, anyway... Might be as good a chance as any to look at this place. I've seen it from the outside many a time, only I'm afraid I have not been interested enough–or religious enough–to look inside. Let's see, this is the modern part isn't it? This porch-way? And the rest is restored ancient abbey, with the real ruins at the far back. Hm-m, might as well start reforming. Coming?"

For some reason her words sounded cold and worldly in this mighty place. This was one thing I could never quite fathom about Enid Somewhere deep in her character there ran a streak of cold, frigid cynicism. It leapt to the surface every time she was confronted with something hallowed. Yet, knowing she had had to make her own way in the world, knowing she had all the sophistication a great modern city could instill into her, I had always ignored this brazen facet in her character. After all, I am no saint myself...

Turning, we gazed into the church itself down the nave. At the moment it was plunged into the twilight of the storm, but suddenly lightning came again and gave us a blue-lit impression of enormous stained glass windows, mighty stone pillars, carven saints, empty pews, end at the far end the choir-tiers and altar.

Enid gave a sudden little shiver. "Cold," she muttered. "All churches are cold, especially ancient ones like this. Besides, I'm wet..."

She wrung out the hems of her sleeves and skirt impatiently, shivered again as draught came hurtling through the open door. Finally, driven by curiosity, she went wandering along the nave into the dead emptiness of the church. I went after her, followed her past the mighty altar, through a passage and so into the cloisters, Here; though, one side open to the storm, we beat a hasty retreat. But not into the church. We opened an oak door and passed quickly into what we took to be a kind of ante-chamber.

It was some kind of crypt, however, or else a storehouse, since a crypt is usually below ground. Certainly it was old, thick walled, and dusty. Lightning played violently on the solitary mullioned window, lighting up a bare deal table, a hardwood chair, and shelf upon shelf packed with musty files and books.

"Looks like some kind of monk's reading room," I decided at length; then wandering forward I looked at the books on the shelves. With the lightning's help I made out some of the titles and found they were Latin. For the rest there seemed to be only Abbey files, no doubt packed with historical gems.

"Just what is the legend about this Abbey?" Enid asked at length, coming to my side and hugging herself to keep warm. "Isn't it something about a bell? I've heard of it but I don't just seem to recall... Probably gossip anyway!"

"The legend," I said, "is that a giant bell rings out just before a death is to take place in this church. Always the death occurs in this Abbey. Last time it rang out was about twelve years ago, I think."

Enid frowned. "But surely they ring the bells on Sundays?"

"The ordinary ones, yes; but this other bell of the legend is a solitary one in a belfry all by itself. Erected for some special reason, when this place was first built, there were originally four bells in this special belfry; then three were taken away and one was left. It was called, and still is, the Judgment Bell."

"Hm-m, you sound like a guide," Enid chided. Anyway, it sounds like a lot of bosh."

She turned, disdainful, ran her eyes over the files. It was as she looked at them and the lightning flashed again with savage brightness that the vast sense of evil domination swept me again. It was as though a nameless Presence–and that Presence unthinkably foul and Godless - were trying to overwhelm and crush me. Here, in the hallowed backwaters of the Abbey where even the thunder was muted by densely thick walls, the effect was infinitely greater than it had been outside.

An irresistible impulse led me to catch Enid's arm as she reached out towards the shelf. My grip was so tight she turned with a little cry.

"Bob–you're hurting me–!" Her voice was both pained and amazed.

I could feel that my face was a strained mask. With an effort I released her.

"Sorry," I muttered, as the sensation flowed away from me again. "Can't imagine what came over me– Sort of creepy feeling. Maybe it is this church, and the storm."

"The church more like it," she answered laconically. "Enough to give anybody the blues. For some reason these places never make me feel holy; only irritated and resentful. Wonder why things that are sacrosanct have to be depressing and shadowy?"

She meditated briefly on this, then returning to the shelf she took down a file. It was as though she did it with a hand other than her own. It was an unerring movement, so unerring indeed she even seemed surprised herself, for she stood looking in the dim light at the incredibly ancient dust-ridden thing in her hands.

"Now what on earth do I want this for?" she demanded. "I was going to look at those books on the lower shelf to pass the time away and instead I–" She shrugged. "We'll have a look anyway."

She flung the file on the bare wood table and dust flew in a cloud. At the same second a truly soul-racking crash of thunder broke over the Abbey, smashing its way along with the lightning that swamped us for a moment in blue fire. My head swam with the intensity of it. The hair on my scalp bristled for a second or two.

"Apparently coming right overhead," I muttered. "And so far as I know this Abbey is the only landmark for miles. A perfect target. Maybe we'd better get out?"

Enid glanced at the window down which the rain was swilling in cascades.

"Not for me. I feel as though I might get pneumonia even as it is. I'm taking no more chances."

She turned back to the file and opened it. Dusty parchment pages flickered under her slender fingers. The ink, though faded, was still legible, most of it in old English writing style. I gazed over her shoulder, mastering an unformed desire to snatch the file from her and hurl it out into the storm. A silly idea, you say? Perhaps so, looked at impartially, but you can have no idea of the crushing forces at work upon me–and for all I knew then upon Enid too–in that stormbound church.

Why, for instance, had she decided to open that file at the exact page headed–

YE LEGENDE OF KELBYE ABBEY

"Well, how's that for luck?" she asked cynically. "We were wondering about that old wives' tale–and here it is as large as life. But Lord, what impossible writing–" She started to quote aloud, slowly..."–and so ye tale doth run that ye saintly monk Dranwold wert slain by the assassin's hand, who didst creep -"

Enid broke off and sighed, "Whew! Whoever wrote this sure wouldn't sell much to a modern magazine."

"For Heaven's sake, Enid, stop your damned blasphemous chatter!" I exploded. "Stop it, I say!"

She stared blankly at me. Those words had hurled themselves out of me; and the odd things was that as I said them that sense of gnawing horror noticeably receded as though the sharp words had cowed it–whatever it was.

"Just who," Enid asked bitterly, "do you think you're talking to?"

"You, of course! What right have you to make fun of the hallowed files of this place? Don't you realize what that file is? It records the death of a monk–a holy, saintly man–who was murdered by an assassin! That isn't a subject for levity."

I saw her lips quiver as she formed a cutting reply; then she relaxed and gave a little shrug.

"The storm's getting into you, Bob. Never the less, all blasphemy aside, this stuff is queer to our modern sense. It looks as–"

She stopped, her eyes frozen to that ancient page, I don't think I ever saw such a look on a. human face. It was horror beyond describing. Even another terrific flash of lightning failed to make her blink, so entranced was she.

"Enid, Enid, whatever is it?" I cried, clutching her. "In God's name, why do you stare like that?"

Her hand rose slowly to her mouth in horror. Then with a vast effort she seemed to get a grip on herself again. She pointed to the page, traced a single line at the bottom of the Legend:-

... and so shall ye Judgment Bell ring for each descendant of this assassin of Dranwold. This assassin whose name is Cleggye...

"Cleggy!" I gulped. "Spelt in the old English style. But–but that's your surname, Enid."

"Yes," she whispered. "Yes, it is."

She looked at me with blank gray eyes for a moment. Her face had dewed with emotion in those few paralyzing moments. Now, with a hand that visibly trembled, she shut the file, fell quivering against the table.

"I don't understand it," she panted, her breast rising and falling stormily. "I don't understand–I feel lost in here. Oppressed! Do you realize what this file says?" she screamed.

"I realize that by a coincidence in names the assassin of monk Dranwold had the same surname as you." I said. "But after all, Enid, that might easily happen. Cleggy is a common name."

"No, it isn't!" she countered flatly. "Clegg, yes–and Clegger too–are good old fashioned English root names. Not Cleggy. That's definitely unusual... It means," she finished, fighting to control herself, "that assassin Cleggye was probably an ancestor of mine."

"It's ridiculous–" I started to say; then I stopped. Was it so ridiculous, after all? I recalled my own strange emotions, that sense of abysmal fear that had kept assailing me. Above all, I remembered how she had reached for that file almost automatically and had opened it at the desired place immediately...

* * *

We stared at each other as the lightning blazed again.

"Suppose," Enid said slowly, at length, "this is true? That this murderer is an ancestor of mine? What does it make me?"

"Only what you are," I said, almost roughly. "A modem girl in a modern world. It isn't possible that something that happened centuries ago could affect you now..."

She hesitated, then turned back to the file again. She read slowly, nervously, transcribing into modern English as she went–

"... 'Monk Dranwold was at prayer before the altar. Assassin Cleggye stole in from the region of the transept and stabbed him in the back... And his death shall be eternally avenged: such was the dying curse of Dranwold...' And his death shall be eternally avenged," Enid repeated slowly.

"All my ancestors and relations, as far back as I can remember, have died mysteriously... Bob!" Her voice was sharp with sudden hysteria. "Bob, we're going to get out of here, and quickly. It was no mere chance that brought us here, I'm convinced–."

I was commencing to think the same thing. Was it possible, I wondered, that force of events–a force totally beyond our comprehension–had led us out on the picnic, had trapped us in the storm, and thence directed us–at any rate Enid–to this Abbey? Was it possible that there was a spirit of vast evil abroad in this storm, striving to reach the girl, a descendant of a Godless assassin? Was that sense of insupportable evil I had sensed somehow produced through her, the modem equivalent of Cleggye? I gave a little shudder.

"Yes, we'll go," I said abruptly. "Things are happening in this place which are beyond our ken. Come on!"

We hurried back through the rain-drenched cloisters into the ghostly recesses of the church, went along past the silent pews to the porchway where our picnic basket still lay. Here, outside the main door, we paused.

The storm seemed to have centered with a demoniac fury directly over this ancient pile. Rain was pouring in through the open door in hissing sheets;

lightning flashed and crackled in the deluge; the tear and rip of the thunderbolts shook the Abbey to its very foundations.

"We dare not go out in this," I whispered. "We just dare not. We'd be struck dead before we'd gone a dozen yards."

"I don't understand this storm," Enid whispered. "It's as though the very elements have gone mad over this spot. It doesn't seem to move on as all storms should– Bob, I'm frightened." She caught my arm tightly, and I felt her hand trembling.

"Take it easy," I said, though I was not feeling any too heroic myself. "It's just a violent summer storm, that's all– Pass off in a while. Then we'll get moving again. Still be plenty of time," I added, glancing at my watch. "It's only six o'clock as yet."

"Six o'clock," she echoed hollowly; "and as dark as midnight."

She wandered back again into the church fretfully, stared down the nave. Then as the lightning blazed across it she gave a terrific scream, so intense and horror-stricken I twirled with a thumping heart.

"What on earth -?" I demanded, catching up with her.

"I - I saw him!" she chattered. "I saw him - there before the altar. Oh, my God–I saw him!"

"Saw who?" I demanded, staring down the lightning-illuminated expanse and beholding nothing unusual.

"Dranwold! The monk. Kneeling at the altar–"

She was so prostrated with fright she could hardly stand up. I caught hold of her, held her tightly to me. She kept her eves from looking into the church. I continued to hold her, her face pressed against my shoulder. Yet as I looked down the nave and each flash of chain-lightning filled the place I could see nothing unusual, certainly nothing to suggest a kneeling figure.

"There's nothing there," I said gently; "nothing at all. It was your imagination - - shadows cast by the lightning, I expect. Your nerves are all shot to pieces by the storm and the legend, that's all..."

Slowly she forced herself to look again, then just as quickly jerked her head away.

"He is there–kneeling," she insisted. "In hood and cassock! Don't ask me to look again. I dare not–"

This time I did not deny her assertion. There was something very real, very terrible, which she could see and vet I could not. Involuntarily my mind went back to the filed legend. Hereditary influence? The assassin Cleggye operating through her?

Then there came back that sinking sense of overwhelming evil, so much so that I shrank from before it. It was as much as I could do to keep a grip on Enid. I wanted to hurl her away from me in loathing as though she were the cause of my sensations.

"It's gone now," she said presently, straightening up. "Yes–it's gone." She stared wide-eyed down the nave at the distant lightning-bright altar. "Perhaps... perhaps it was only a shadow."

The way she said it convinced me she did not believe it. She knew she had seen something, and it left her badly shaken.

"Perhaps we'd better get back to our crypt," I said.

She nodded assent so we stole back through the flashing, rumbling gloom, across the stretch of rain-lashed cloister, and so back into our sanctuary. Now we beheld the most incredible thing.

The file, which had been left open on the table at the legend, had gone. Automatically our eves switched to the shelf. It was back in place among the other files.

"The figure I saw—the monk - he must have done it," Enid said hoarsely. "Only he could have done it."

"Good Heavens, Enid, do you realize what you are saying?" I cried. "You are suggesting a supernatural power returned the file to the shelf."

"Yes—I am!" she declared fiercely. "Oh, I know that ghosts are absurd; that phantoms can't happen— That's all right in the city; but here there is something different, a vast and malignant power abroad in this very storm. Trying to reach me. I know it is. Bob, I know it is. You've got to help me."

"But what against?" I shouted. "How can any man attempt to fight the impalpable?"

"You must help me to be strong," she implored desperately; and it was horrible for me to see how completely all the worldly sophistication had been torn away from her.

"This storm is not a natural one: I can sense that now. In it is the age-long struggle between good and evil forces, the battle of spirits long dead to mortal eyes, still centered over this Abbey. The battle of Dranwold the monk with my remote ancestor Cleggye. I know that is the truth. Don't ask me how I know— Perhaps it is instinct, hereditary knowledge stirred by occult forces... But it is there."

Slowly, in the light of her statement, I began to understand my own emotions. If indeed long-dead enmity was being fought out in the furious clash of the storm, it was equally possible—as I had already vaguely realized—that the spirit of Cleggyc was alive again through Enid. And his evil power was doing everything possible to protect his own, to protect her. Therefore this force had tried to overwhelm me: it had prompted me to restrain her from reading that file so the truth about Cleggye would never be known. That was it. An unholy reincarnation in which the very elements themselves had a part.

"It is the eternal cry of vengeance." Enid said in a hollow voice. Echoing down the centuries. And I am the pawn..."

She relaxed then against the hard table, somewhat calmer now she had solved the psychic implications of her plight. We stood in silence for a long time, our fares patterned by the unceasing rage of lightning as we gazed at each other.

"Perhaps," I said, making an effort, "if we ran out and took a chance we might get away from this storm? It only seems to be concentrated around here—"

"We cannot get away," she replied, shaking her head dully. "Surely you have realized it by now? Psychic compulsion, nothing more or less, brought us here. The same compulsion caused us to picnic near the Abbey—the same evil forces brought about a storm: we came here. And now..."

I forced myself out of this quagmire of inexplicable things. I took hold of Enid and shook her violently.

"Enid, do you realize what you are saying?" I shouted, over the roaring of the thunder. "Do you realize to what ridiculous dimensions we have allowed our imaginations to wander? To a summer storm we have applied occult explanations: to a shadow we find—you find anyway—a monk who has been dead for centuries...

"We're a modern man and a modern woman, sheltering in an Abbey. The mere coincidence of a name cannot— shall not! —bring about the total defeat of our sanity. It's - it's just an attack of nerves."

"No, Bob." Her face was ashy gray. "No; it is truth. There is too much in it for it to be just coincidence—"

Suddenly she stopped, the words stricken from her lips. For the briefest moment the roaring of the thunder had died and there was a sepulchral, crushing calm. It flayed our tautened nerves like a whip— Then out of this vast unnatural hush came a sound—the deep, solemn clanging of a bell from somewhere over our heads. It tolled once—twice - three times, filling the very echoes with its quivering pure-cast strokes.

"Judgment Bell," I hardly realized I said the words.

"No! No! No!" Enid screamed. "I can't stand it, I can't—"

She flung herself to the crypt doorway as yet another stroke clanged through the gloomy silences. Then thunder rolled again; but the bell kept on chiming, relentlessly, implacably, though, so far as we knew, there was no human hand to toll it.

"Enid!" I shouted huskily: then I darted after her fleeing figure. She seemed to have gone demented with fright. Once she had gotten into the church again she went blundering along up the aisle between the pews, obviously making for the porch and outer door.

"Enid!" I yelled again, but she took no notice of me.

Then I drew up short as she suddenly halted midway up the church and threw up her hands as though to shut out some monstrous obscene vision. She wheeled, clearly visible to me in the lightning; she came racing back towards the altar as though Lucifer himself were behind her.

"Monk Dranwold!" she shrieked. "Behind me. Seizing me— No! No!"

The echoes were brimming with her shouts and cries—the cries of the damned indeed. I was paralyzed with horror at the dreadful enactment going on, this pursuit of a helpless girl by something I could not even see.

Stumbling, gasping, I saw her at last on her knees before the altar

"Mercy!" she gasped helplessly. "In God's name—mercy—"

Abruptly, I found myself and jumped forward, determined to seize her by force and get her out of this damnable hole; but at that very moment there came a flash of lightning such as I had never known.

A blinding purple fork stabbed clean through the mighty stained window at one side of the altar, splintering it instantly. For the briefest moment I saw Enid crouched in frozen terror on the very spot where centuries before Dranwold had been slain at prayer– Then that terrible sizzling bolt struck clean upon Enid.

The awful shock to my nerves sent me reeling helplessly, my ears stunned by the most unholy din Thunder, the clamor of the Judgment Bell, the noise of splitting stone and Enid's dying shriek were all woven together.

Sickened, half-blinded by the flash, I went reeling forward, caught her body up in my arms. It was a. terrible sight upon which I gazed. One half of her body was charred to the bone!

"Enid!" I screamed. "Enid–"

The absurdity of shouting to this poor, dead, blackened corpse blasted in upon me. I lowered her again gently, sprang up with my fists clenched. What inhuman devilry was going on in here?

"Fiend!" I shrieked. "Fiend! Wherever you are come out and face me. Come out, I say–"

Silence - utter silence. The clanging of the giant bell had ceased now: even the thunder seemed to have died away miraculously. The blinding flashes of lightning were beginning to lose their power; through the smashed window I saw a clearing streak in the violet of the storm clouds.

"Trickery." I spat the word out. "Filthy trickery. Some escaped lunatic is in this place; he slew Enid–"

I think, from the things I said, that I was half crazy with fear and grief. I remember I went tearing around looking for a way to the belfry, and at last I found it–ancient stone steps. I hurtled up them three at a time, swung open the unbolted door and stepped inside. It was empty, ropes swinging in the fresh wind blowing through open windows.

What was I thinking, of, anyway? The Judgment Bell had a separate belfry. Of course! I wheeled and went to the only other door at this high point of the Abbey. It was locked. I slammed on it with bruised and bleeding fists.

"Devil of devils, come out!" I thundered. "Come out! You shall not escape me–!"

I thumped and kicked and yelled until my heart felt as though It would burst from exertion and hysteria. Gulping, I fell back against the wall, my head whirling. Then I stiffened as I caught the sound of footsteps on the stone staircase. I waited, my fingers outspread like claws...

The footsteps came nearer–slow and deliberate. They stopped suddenly– Yet it was no other-world visitor upon which I gazed, no demoniac being or a monk in hood and shroud, but a man in soft hat and dripping mackintosh. He came towards me slowly, and I saw he had a very pale, drawn face.

"My dear man, whatever are you doing here?" he asked in wonder. Then his face saddened a little. "But I think I can guess. That poor girl below, by the altar— She was struck by lightning?"

"Either that or there's some brutally clever trickery going on in this place," I grated back. "Who the devil are you, anyway?"

"I am David Bolton, Vicar of this Abbey," he answered quietly. "I heard the clanging of the Judgment Bell. But then"—he gave a little shrug—' 'I expected it when I saw the storm had come again."

"Again?" I echoed, startled. "It has been—before?"

"Yes; twelve years ago." His voice was very quiet, "That time a man died in very similar circumstances to that girl below. The Abbey was struck by lightning while he and a party of friends were sheltering. He was the victim of electric shock. His name... was Roland Cleggy."

I stared at the Vicar with gaping mouth. I was remembering that Enid had said her Uncle had dropped dead in a church twelve years before. At that time she would have been too young to knew the full circumstances and—.

"This girl," the Vicar said. "She too was named Cleggy?"

I nodded stupidly.

"So," he muttered, "it will always be, until every descendant of the accursed Cleggye is destroyed. Five have died in this very Abbey, through the centuries. Others will die here, too—forced here by occult power—unless that girl was the last of the line. We cannot deal with things like this, my friend—they are the powers of Darkness. The Monk Dranwold, as he died, placed an everlasting curse of retribution upon his assassin and successors. Always the curse has stricken down. There is always the Storm— a terrible Storm - in which the soul of Cleggy and the curse of Dranwold are still at grips; but always a Cleggy is vanquished..."

He laid a gentle hand on my arm.

"From records of past deaths I can imagine just what must have happened. You were directed by unseen powers to the crypt wherein lie the Abbey files. There the girl saw the Legend. Later, perhaps, she would imagine she saw the ghost of Dranwold himself praying at the altar. When at last she was stricken down where Dranwold himself died the powers of darkness abated; the Storm began to recede. The Judgment Bell ceased its tolling..."

"It isn't true, any of it!" I cried suddenly.

"It is true," he stated quietly. "Implacably true, but in a setting you or I can never understand this side of Eternity."

"Human agency rang that damned Judgment Bell," I shouted. "It was not one of the ordinary bells: it had a different sound— I say Enid Cleggy was murdered, that perhaps the lightning was—was a flash of magnesium or something. I demand to see inside this Judgment Bell belfry. It's the last hiding place and the door is locked!"

He smiled gravely. "The power that put the file back on its shelf also rang this bell," he said.

"How did you know about the file?" I flashed at him.

"I know because it has always happened the same way. However, you shall have your wish granted. Just a moment.'

He went downstairs and obtained a massive key, came back and, twisted it in the door lock. The door swung open. But this–the last and only hiding place - was empty.

"To the world," said the Vicar, "Miss Cleggy died by lightning: but we know that vengeance struck her down. I mention this point so you will know what to say at the inquest. You see, nobody would believe this."

In those seconds I realized how right he was, realized what he had meant by saying the same power had put the file back on the shelf.

For there was no bell.

I turned stupidly, framed words. "No–bell?"

"There has never been a bell," the Vicar said. "Where it really rings, or who rings it– No man knows."

9 781587 153266